HIDDEN AGENDA

A DAN ROY THRILLER
DAN ROY SERIES, BOOK 1

Including the novella HELLFIRE

Mick Bose

HELLFIRE

A DAN ROY NOVELLA

Mick Bose

For ABx2 and MA

USS BASTION
ARABIAN SEA
FIFTY NAUTICAL MILES NORTH OF SOMALIA
PRESENT DAY

Dan Roy, ex-Sergeant of Squadron A, Special Forces Operational Detachment-D or Delta Force, jerked awake as his head hit something hard.

Instantly, he was awake. Out of reflex his right hand slid under his pillow, and his fingers curled around the grained butt of his trusted Sig P226. In a flash, his elbow was ramrod straight, the gun pointing out. His arm moved around, scanning.

A few human beings have full awareness when their eyes open from deep slumber. Dan was one of them. It was one of the reasons why he was chosen to do the job he did.

Even then, awareness consisted of sights, sounds, and the signals the brain received and processed in microseconds. The reality might not sink in, but just like a ball player who connects at the mere hint of a speeding shape, Dan recognized an alien atmosphere almost by instinct.

He did not know where he was, but he knew he was somewhere different to the night before. And that could be dangerous. Lethal. The risk could be right in front of him, and he had survived this long by neutralizing those risks.

He felt bright light on his eyes, and cold steel against his forehead. A bunk bed. His body moved again, forwards, then back. A rolling motion. He smelled clean cotton sheets. The sense of olfaction is the oldest one. It reminded him of another life. As a child in Bethesda, West Virginia, rolling around in his comfy bed at home.

He lowered the gun and squinted. Sunlight poured in through the round hole of the cabin window. He rubbed his eyes. The cord-like muscles on his neck rippled as he flexed his neck. He yawned and swung his legs out of the bunk.

He was in a ship's cabin. He could see that much. Dan rested his massive shoulders by putting his elbows on his knees. His large, paw-like hands, the skin on them gnarled and thick from holding an assortment of light and heavy weapons, drooped towards the floor. He stared in the same direction.

Last night's memory started to come back to him. He had been flown from Djibouti in the Horn of Africa to a town on the coast of Somalia. A place called Bosaso. Not far from the tip of the Horn, and overlooking the Gulf of Aden. The channel of international pirates.

In Bosaso, he had neutralized the chief bomb maker of the local chapter of Al-Shabaab. It had been a long-range shot from nine hundred meters away. The extraction had been tricky, as the boat waiting for him had come under sustained fire from a pirate dhow loyal to the terrorists.

Once the 0.50-caliber Browning machine gun on the boat had started chattering, the dhow had ceased to be an issue.

And here he was. Nudging off the coast of Somalia, in the Arabian Sea, just one hundred nautical miles away from the Gulf of Aden. Aboard the latest edition of an American aircraft carrier. All eight billion dollars' worth of it.

Dan stood up. He felt slightly nauseous. The roll in the cabin, mild as it was, did not help. He went out the door and walked down the narrow hallway, stopping to say hello to a blue-uniformed US Navy serviceman. In the bathroom, he splashed water on his face and looked in the mirror. A square-jawed, brown-eyed face looked back at him. Not handsome. Not ugly. But one that had won admirers from the opposite sex. He rubbed water in his hair.

At thirty-four, he did not feel old. Served with Delta for last five years, then tapped on the shoulder to join a new outfit. An outfit so secret that even his own Delta brethren did not know about it. And those that did were sworn to secrecy.

Intercept. An organization with an executive arm that went straight to the highest echelons of power in Capitol Hill. An organization that was used when all else had failed, and a mission needed to be accomplished with the minimum of fuss.

That meant not getting caught. If he did get caught, then being captured and questioned was not an option. Silence was forever guaranteed. If that guarantee was not kept by Intercept operatives, then it would be enforced.

Dan looked away from the mirror. He didn't like looking at himself when that question bubbled up to the surface of his mind.

Why?

Why did he leave the Army to join Intercept? To undertake the most dangerous missions of his life, separated from his brethren?

He missed the banter of Army life. The comradery. But he did not miss the bureaucracy of the Army. The endless infighting. The often deplorable way that soldiers were treated.

In his new role, he was given a problem, and he had to eliminate it. No questions asked, no answers given. He had to admit it. The thrill of the fight was the reason why he had become a warfighter. With Intercept, he was able to take that life to a new level.

It was an answer he found strange. Of why he felt so calm with the enemy's head in the cross hairs of his rifle sight. Why he relished CQB, close quarters battle, to the extent that he did. Especially with his kukri knife, the curved, 16-inch blade beloved of the Gurkha warrior.

Dan shook his head once and toweled his face dry. Introspection was not always useful, and often frustrating. He was who he was.

A warrior. Most days, that was enough.

Dan walked back to his small cabin. He had to search for it, inside the labyrinthine deck levels of the massive ship, it was easy to get lost.

He found new cams on the bed. They were dusty yellow, not much different from the ones they had before. He struggled into them, as usual. At six feet, he clocked in at two hundred and twenty pounds. The width of his shoulders and chest accounted for that.

There was a chirp from the desk next to the wardrobe. Dan stepped to it, and saw a small cellphone with a green light flashing on it. He picked it up and answered.

"Who's this?"

"My name is Tom Slater, Dan. I work for Intercept." He did not recognize the voice. Another faceless official. He didn't care. The person obviously knew who he was. Dan waited for the person to speak.

"Briefing in ten minutes, CO's office," Slater said.

The Commanding Officer was Gary "Gaz" Peterson, US Navy Strike Force Six. There was a good chance the CO would not be there, and the room had been taken over by Intercept for the briefing. Intercept had enough clout to do that, but Dan surmised the US Navy would be happier with their own Special Ops guys, the DEVGRU and Navy SEALs.

Once again, he could not help wondering why he was there.

CHAPTER 1

The two men descended into the depths of the massive floating citadel. Tom Slater led the way. He looked middle-aged, and tired. Another CIA agent pulled in from his day job to provide intel on a clandestine mission, Dan thought.

The steel door of the CO's office was shut, and Tom rapped on it. An officer opened the door, nodded to them and stepped aside. Dan saw the bank of monitors against one wall, and the three big screens on the other.

On two of the monitors he could see a grainy image of a mud-walled compound. The monitor next to it had a map of Southeast Asia. One of the three large screens on the wall held a live image of a man in desert combat uniform. He was in his late-fifties, with pinched, sallow cheeks, sharp blue eyes and buzz cut silvery hair. Dan would have known Major John Guptill's face anywhere in the world.

He had been Dan's first mentor when Dan joined the Delta Force, from the 75th US Rangers Battalion. And he had been Dan's trainer when Dan had been the first one in his team to complete the last stage of Delta selection. That involved a forty-mile hike with full kit through the highest mountains of the Appalachian range. When Dan collapsed at the final station, he had asked Major Guptill for a drink. Guptill had eyed him coldly.

"Get it yourself," he said. "First operation begins in forty-eight hours." With that, he had turned and left his protégé on the floor, dying of thirst. Dan had to hike another two miles to get a jug of water from the nearest canteen.

An AV technician appeared and fitted the men with microphones, and showed them their seats in front of a camera. Guy Peterson stepped out of the shadows. He nodded stiffly at Dan, then stared at Guptill on the screen. The screen next to Guptill flickered to life. A clear image came on, of a shorter man in combat uniform, with salt-and-pepper hair.

Peterson appeared to know him. He turned to the screen and said, "Is it time to start the brief, Colonel McBride?"

Dan had heard of Lieutenant Colonel Jim "Fighter" McBride, one of the men who led the JSOC. It was the first time he was seeing the man.

"Hey, Gaz," McBride said in an even voice. "Hey, Guppy." Guptill nodded at them from the screen.

"You guys all set?" McBride asked the team. They all nodded and exchanged greetings. All knew one another from recent operations.

Then there was a silence. McBride cleared his throat and looked at Guy Peterson. So did Guptill.

"I am sorry, Gaz," McBride said quietly.

Peterson looked irritated. "What?" he demanded in a rough voice.

"This is for USSOCOM- and CIA-cleared personnel only."

"You are on-board my ship, Lieutenant. Have you forgotten that? I have a right to know."

McBride shook his head slightly. "I am sorry, Gaz. This comes from O'Toole in MacDill."

Dan sat up straighter. MacDill Air Force Base in Florida was the HQ of USSOCOM. O'Toole was the Command Sergeant Major and a National Security Advisor.

Dan stayed quiet. Gary Peterson stood up. He looked at Dan, then at his commanders on the screen. His eyes were scathing.

"I can promise you one thing, Lieutenant," Peterson said. "If my men or this ship is compromised in any way, then O'Toole will get a direct call from the President. Do you understand?"

McBride kept his face impassive. Dan knew from the man's reputation that he did not take threats casually. But he had a job to do. Not much space to do it in.

"I got that, Gaz," McBride said, keeping his eyes level with Peterson. The CO turned and stormed out of the room. His officer and the technician followed.

"We all alone?" Guptill asked from the screen.

"Yes," Dan said.

"Right," McBride took over. "We have a situation near a town in Afghanistan called Surobi. It's located along the Kabul-Jalalabad Highway, on the banks of the Kabul River. This is northern 'Stan, gentlemen." Many soldiers called Afghanistan by this nickname. McBride continued.

"Twenty klicks outside Surobi, in a village called Mumtaz, we have three CIA SOG men holed up with an Iranian national. This person is defecting to the West. They made it from Herat, up north near the Iranian border in the east, down to here, but then their luck ran out. An Afghan contingent was helping them. They came down by road. They were supposed to take the highway through into Pakistan, and travel to the nearest city in Pakistan, called Peshawar. There is a US Consulate office there. But they woke up one morning and found their compound surrounded by the Taliban."

Guptill said, "The compound is a former police station. It was taken over by Para 1 Company of the British Army. They held it till the CIA guys arrived, then they exfiltrated." Dan knew of the elite Parachute Regiment, which had three Companies.

"Why don't the Para 1 guys go back?" Dan asked.

"Operational reasons," Guptill said. "The enemy have launched a major offensive in the small towns around Surobi. Para 1 need to relieve two Infantry Regiments who have taken heavy casualties."

"You don't have any special forces in northern 'Stan already?"

"Yes, we do," McBride said. "But none with the experience you have of northern 'Stan. You have worked in tough situations up there. Remember the Delta push into Tora Bora? That's why you are here."

Dan did remember the mission into Tora Bora mountains, looking for bin Laden. Intel got it wrong that time. The terrorist had already fled. Dan and his unit had chased after them. Dan was part of Delta Squadron B then, and his actions had won him a Bronze Star.

Not being able to find bin Laden that time had weighed heavily on his mind. For him, it had been a failed mission. Now, his pulse quickened at McBride's words. Would he be able to make amends on this occasion?

McBride clicked some buttons on the desk in front of him, and pointed to the bank of monitors. The map of Southeast Asia focused on the Arabian

Sea and the Pakistan sea port of Karachi, then zoomed further up towards the border with Afghanistan. On the other screen, satellite images of the compound flashed up.

McBride said, "You will be dropped off at the Landing Zone ten klicks outside the compound under cover of night. Mission is to storm the compound, retrieve the CIA guys and the Iranian, then escape to the LZ. Exfil by Close Air Support from Bagram Air Base."

Dan pointed to the screen. "This is a large compound, sir. Seventy meters wide, going by the scale."

Guptill said, "You will have two CIA operatives in there, who are assets, I am told. Plus you have the Afghan National Police to help you."

Help is not what Dan would call it himself. His experience of the ANP had never been a positive one. But he kept his thoughts to himself.

"One thing, son," McBride said. Something in his voice made Dan look up at the screen. "It is mission critical to have the Iranian alive. For reasons I cannot go into. Roger that?"

Dan nodded in silence.

Guptill said, "Pack your bags. Your ride is waiting on deck."

CHAPTER 2

The flight desk was noisy even with his headphones on.

It was 1000 hours. The sun off the coast of Somalia was blinding.

Dan heard some shouts and looked up. Yellow-jacketed flight support staff were lined up in the distance along the runway. They wore red helmets and face wrap goggles. Dan could hear the F/A-18E Super Hornet jet gearing up for take-off, the swarm of men around it and the buzz of the engine getting louder by the minute.

The F/A-18E was one of four strike fighter squadrons that made their sea home on-board the massive aircraft carrier. Each squadron had eleven planes, which made forty-four anti-air and land strike fighter jets the ship carried.

On top of that, it had five EA-18G "Growler" electronic fighter jets designed to jam enemy radio, radar and GPS, and three whole squadrons of MH-60, Sea Knight and Raptor helicopters.

Together with the transport planes, more than seventy aircraft made a nest in this giant, floating city. No less than 6,000 men and women worked round-the-clock to keep it functioning.

The F/A-18E boomed and ran down the runway. The ground shook beneath Dan's feet, rattling every bone in his body. Everyone on deck flinched as the jet's rear emissions hit them, even from a distance. The plane rose up in the sky, doing a salute around the ship. The yellow jackets cheered and waved at it. Then the jet zoomed off, becoming a speck on the endless horizon within seconds.

Dan felt the salty mist of the Arabian Sea on his face. His sixty-pound bag was on his shoulders already. The helmet was on his head, with the NVGs attached on top. The sides of the helmet were cut off to make room for his earphones. A mic hung over his lower lip. An M4 carbine was attached by the belt to his waist, the same belt he would use to clip himself to the safety lanyard on the plane. Strapped to the Kevlar vest on his chest he had his trusted Sig P226 handgun. Three flashbangs and three frags on the belt line.

On the back, in a black leather scabbard, his trusted 16-inch kukri knife. Designed to chop limbs and tree branches with equal ease. Apart from the firearms, it was his weapon of choice.

Dan looked around at the mad rush of men. There was a rumbling sound behind him. Their transport had arrived. The C-2A twin jet Greyhound cargo aircraft was definitely the most pedestrian of all the aircraft the USS *Bastion* carried. As usual, flight support men gathered round the plane, getting it ready for flight.

Tom Slater, the intelligence guy, gave Dan a thumbs-up as he walked past. Dan barely acknowledged him. He worked alone. He did not have time for small talk, especially with someone who looked like they could faint at the sight of blood.

Slater got his ears close to Dan's, the only way to have a conversation on the flight deck.

"When we boarding?"

Dan held up five fingers, then moved away.

With their luggage, extra kit and ammo safely stashed on the C-2A, Dan strapped himself to the safety lanyard and sat back on the hard bench of the aircraft. They had a three-hour flight to the US Air Force Support Base in Muscat, capital of Oman. From there another flight would take them to Bagram Air Base near Kabul. Reflexively, Dan's fingers went to his radio for the comms check. Then he relaxed. They would not be operational till they got to Bagram. He closed his eyes.

Although getting back into north Afghanistan would give him a chance to lay old ghosts to rest, something about the mission bothered him. His eyes opened.

Someone had dropped the CIA guys and their asset into this mess. No way they could wake up the day after and see Taliban crawling around. They were expected.

In any case, he thought to himself, what the hell was an Iranian doing in Afghanistan with the CIA? Far from home, wasn't she?

The plane rumbled down the ship's runway. The ground crew waved at him, and he waved back.

*****

Mariam Panahi looked around the mud walls of her room, and the brittle wooden sticks that served as the grills for the square window.

The window was merely a hole in the wall, and it looked out into the moonlit compound. The air was dry and bright, what she had expected here. It was not far from her home town of Mashhad in Iran. She had been working in the Iranian town of Arak before that. There, too, the weather was now dry and cold.

The compound was large, and it formed a perimeter around the huts scattered at its edges. The Afghan policemen and the two white men had been kind to her so far. She had received the largest room in the enclave where they made their home. The compound was rectangular in shape. The mud walls were two meters thick and three meters high. A massive wooden door, three meters high, guarded the main entrance.

They had entered in the middle of the night, and she had not seen the village outside the gates. She had heard the gunfire the next day, and then the blast of the grenades as they had been lobbed into the compound. The older CIA guy in charge, Roderick Sparks, had told her to stay in her room. The fighting had not let up, and she knew at least two of the six Afghans traveling with them had died.

Her thoughts went back to the mad dash in the middle of the night from Mashhad to Islām Qala, the border town between Mashhad in Iran and Herat in Afghanistan.

At the guest house in Islām Qala, the heavily armed policemen had taken money from Roderick, the senior CIA agent.

Mariam had boarded one of the three Range Rovers with the two CIA men and the Afghans, and the convoy had left for Herat. She had always wanted to see Herat. It was an ancient town, part of the Silk Route, and known in the Middle Ages for its wine. All they did in Herat was change to another Range Rover. Then they drove through the night again. Her car was always the middle one of the convoy. Checkpost after checkpost followed. The leader of the Afghan policemen traveling with them was a man called Faisal Ahmed.

When they were stopped, Ahmed gave the checkpost guards money, and they were waved through.

As she stared at the compound, silvery in the moonlight, Mariam wondered idly if she would ever see Mashhad again. The clerics there had got on her nerves. Islam was not her religion. But, like all women in Iran, she had to wear a headscarf. It was a pain in the neck for her. At least here she did not have to worry about that. She got up to make for the door, and take a stroll while she had the chance.

The sudden explosion knocked her off her feet, and she fell backwards.

CHAPTER 3

Dan lifted his rucksack onto the trembling floor of the Chinook and got on it. The tailgate was down and the rotors where whining, gathering up speed. He switched on the comms system, located the channel and spoke into his mic.

"Desert One, this is Zero," Dan said.

Zero was his call sign for this mission. After a brief crackle of static, the pilot fed back to him.

"Receiving, Zero. Strap in, we are due to take off."

"Roger that, Desert One." Dan said.

The whining of the rotor blades gathered steam, then became a blur as the sound rose to deafening. With a jolt, the bird rose in the air vertically. Then it dipped its nose like it was nodding to someone and speeded up, gaining height rapidly.

As they approached the LZ, Dan heard the Chinook flight maintenance crew on his earphone.

"Alpha, this is Desert One. Requesting confirmation of green light. Repeat, requesting confirmation of green light."

The flight crew was seeking last-minute confirmation from the secret Intercept base in Jalalabad Air Base, which had live satellite connections to the Intercept HQ in Virginia. After a pause, a familiar voice crackled in Dan's earpiece. It was Major Guptill.

"You are a Go, Desert One. I repeat, you are a Go. Good luck. Over and out."

Dan could see a panoply of stars studded like diamonds in the black sky overhead. In the distance, he could see the faint outline of mountain ranges.

In just over half an hour they had arrived.

"5 minutes to LZ," the flight attendant's voice came over on the mic. Dan checked his lanyard and equipment. As the ground rushed up, a vision of his last fight in the Tora Bora mountains flashed before his eyes. Then it was gone.

The bird banked steeply down, then turned left and right. Dan and the flight support crew wobbled in their seats. The maneuvering was to confuse any enemy waiting with their RPGs (rocket-propelled grenades) or any type of surface-to-air missile. No one forgot the somber story of the SEAL team whose Chinook had been brought down by a Taliban RPG.

A crew member waited near the tailgate. In a blaze of dust and sound the Chinook got closer to the ground. Dan flipped on his NVGs. These new NVGs gave him excellent peripheral vision. Everything around was instantly bathed in a green glow. The tailgate swung open to reveal a blizzard of dust, seen as a brown haze through the NVGs.

"Go, go!" the pilot shouted into his mic.

Dan scrambled out and disappeared into the cloud of dust as it swirled up around him. Not much of a cover, but one of the flight crew doubled up as a gunner with the 50-cal machine gun on-board. That would silence any small arms within an eight hundred-meter range. Dan wiped the dust from his goggles and ran to the side of the Chinook. A technician was at the other end, doing the same thing as him. Together, they unstrapped the quad bike that was fixed to the side of the Chinook.

Dan checked the quad's ignition, and the small carrier load on two wheels that was attached to it. Then he heard the other sound.

TAKTAKTAKTAKTAK.

Staccato burst of rifle fire.

The pilot screamed in his mic. "Contact!"

Dan left the quad bike and dived for the floor. His M4 was out in firing position, and he was scanning for the source of fire through the target sight mounted on the rail. The telescoping butt was firm against his right shoulder. Blood was pounding in his ears, and his breath came in gasps. Two rounds pinged against the body of the Chinook, their ricochet whining against his ears.

DAMDAMDAMDAMDAM

Dan swore as rounds whined over his head. The sound had changed from small arms to heavy machine gun fire. This was the worst situation imaginable. They were out in the open and taking fire from a hidden enemy.

Dan ran round to the other side, bullets kicking the dust around him. Then he saw it. He said to the pilot, "Two o'clock! Two o'clock! Muzzle flash in the bushes."

Dan knew the two-man crew on-board would be getting the 50-cal ready, to lay down suppressive fire. But that wouldn't be much good if the Chinook got hit in the fuselage. He knew that's what the enemy bullets were searching for.

He also knew they were in a semi-arid desert valley, surrounded by hills. He needed to get out of there, that's why he had the quad bike. But now his main worry was the Chinook getting hit.

Even if the flight crew escaped, the last thing he wanted was a fireball that lit them up perfectly.

He located the source, and returned fire. The SOPMOD or Special Operations Peculiar Modification M4 carbine roared in his ear. The muzzle flash from his rifle blinded Dan as he was wearing his NVGs. It could not be avoided. Clips of 5.56mm NATO ordnance flew out of the breech as he squeezed the trigger.

"I'm gonna paint this fucker," Dan growled on the mic. "Then take him out with the UGL. Before they spread out."

Dan saw the infrared targeting beam from his rifle point to a clump of trees to their right. The beam was only visible in the NVGs.

Dan scrambled around the back of the Chinook and ran forward. Bullets whined around him, inches from his feet.

Thirty meters out he threw himself on the ground again. Through his night sight he could now see them. Four insurgents in the trees. He could see their dark keffiyehs rolled up on their heads, and the chain of ammunition crossed on their chest. Two of them were leaning over a machine gun on a tripod. From experience, he guessed the machine gun was a DShK or Dushka, a Russian artillery gun. It was a heavy gun, much heavier than the 50-cal. If they got hit by this they were finished.

He breathed out and focused. His right index finger caressed the trigger.

BOP.

One insurgent's head exploded into a red mist.

BOP.

Another down. That took care of the two over the DShK. Dan took aim and fired liberally now, as the other two insurgents had taken cover. The presence of the DShK machine gun bothered him. They needed transport to get this here. This was a planned event. Not good.

Not good at all.

Dan reached down the barrel of his rifle, and used the UGL, or Underslung Grenade Launcher. The tree clump exploded in an orange glow. Two more grenades followed.

"Evacuate, evacuate," Dan screamed ion his mic. "I am covering."

The radio buzzed in his ear. The pilot sounded scared. "Zero, are you sure? There could be more Tangos out there. I could stay."

Dan spoke fast, keeping his eyes on the burning trees. "Negative, Desert One. Right now, you are too big a target. The sooner you go, the better."

Dan switched to automatic mode and sprayed out a long burst of ordnance in the direction of the trees. There was no return fire.

The pilot said, "Roger that, Zero. See you soon, and take care."

"Amen to that, Desert One."

Dan looked behind him. In the green glow he could see the quad, powered up. He looked because he wanted to be sure of their position, because in a second everything would be invisible in a storm of dust.

The rotor wash from the Chinook pressed him down further as the big bird took off. The ground shook underneath him, and the dust storm felt like a blizzard. Within a minute the huge machine was airborne, and then rose swiftly up into the desert night sky.

Silence returned, save the crackle from the burning of the trees. It seemed as if he had got them all, Dan thought with satisfaction. But there would be more behind. He did not wait any longer. He ran to the quad, jumped on the seat, and pulled out into the cold night.

He had a GPS unit strapped to his wrist, showing him the map. He was twenty klicks out, and with the speed of the quad, and the bumpy terrain,

Dan knew he had a one-hour ride ahead of him.

If the Taliban had bought the DShK in a pick-up truck, there could be a convoy of vehicles behind it. They came with headlights switched off, hence the Chinook flight crew had not seen it from above. They must have been setting up while they landed. If the Chinook had gone down, the Taliban would take photos in the morning, and Al Jazeera would beam them around the world.

But they had not counted on Dan being on-board.

Now, they could be following him. Eager for revenge.

Be grateful for what you receive, Dan thought grimly as his bike speeded in the icy night air. He could feel the radio antenna bobbing up and down on his back, along with the Semtex breach explosive attached below it. His nose and lips below the NVG were freezing.

It was just the start of a long night.

CHAPTER 4

Dan glanced briefly at the GPS. He was still headed in the right direction – southwest. Surobi was fifteen klicks away.

Dan strained his ears, his senses on overdrive. The desert night was silent apart from the groan of the quad. Any minute now, he expected to hear something else. The rattle of gun fire, or the roar of engines.

For now, all he had was the whistle of cold night air. The road ahead narrowed between two hills and the ground got softer. It slowed the bikes down. Dan realized where he was. A dry riverbed. A wadi, in Pashto. Sparse vegetation grew around them. Dan slowed down and killed his engine.

A desolate silence flowed in around him. Dan got off his bike, and ran backwards. He checked the trolley, and took off its tarpaulin cover. It contained the heavier weapons.

Minimi was the name for the Light Machine Gun, primed for 7.62mm NATO ordnance. The gun, with its adjustable bipod, was strapped down on the floor of the trolley, along with two ILAWs or Anti-Tank Light Armor Weapons.

Ideally, Dan would like the Minimi to be set up on top of a Weapon-Mounted Installation Kit, or WMIK, as the machine gun-armed Range Rovers were known. Intel had told him there was a WMIK inside the compound.

Dan was considering what to do when his thoughts were interrupted by the chirp of radio in his ears.

"Zero, this is Alpha, do you copy?" Major Guptill's voice, from HQ in Jalalabad Air Base.

"Roger that, Alpha," Dan said.

"You better get a move on. The compound is under attack. I repeat, the compound is under attack."

*****

18

Mariam lay still for a while, wondering if she was injured. The sound of gunfire and screams filled the air, shattering the silence of the night. All her limbs were moving. She sat up, then raised herself quickly. She saw the flash of gunfire from her window, and another scream. She saw a figure fall from the compound wall, and land with a thud on the floor. Bullets streamed from one of the windows, and the body jerked around like a puppy on a string.

Mariam realized what was happening. The Taliban had launched an offensive. They were climbing over the walls. Fear turned her into cold ice. Including her, they were seven. Against how many? The door to her room opened suddenly. Mariam recoiled as a dark figure filled the doorway.

"It's me, Derek."

She sighed in relief. Derek Jones was the younger CIA agent. He reached forward, a black figure against a moonlit background, lit up sporadically by gunfire. Derek raised his voice.

"You fired a gun before?"

"No," Mariam said.

"Ok, look here." Derek stood beside her, pulled out a handgun and showed her how to use it.

"Anyone comes in that does not identify themselves, you fire at the chest. Not the head or legs, aim for the chest. Got that?"

Mariam held the gun in her hand, the warm butt snug against her palm. A Glock 22.

"Yes," she said. Derek took the Heckler & Koch 416 rifle off his back and started out the door again. He stopped and looked back at her. "And whatever you do, make sure you stay here."

A stream of gunfire swallowed up his words. Mariam watched as Derek slunk in the shadows, heading for one of the sangars, or raised wooden outposts on top of the compound wall. There was one in each corner, and one in the middle of the long walls. There was a sudden flash of yellow light, and an explosion rocked the compound. Mariam stumbled back inside her room. Her door had been flung open, and dust was pouring in, choking her.

*****

Five klicks out from the compound, Dan could hear the faint sound of explosions in the still night air. He speeded up. The sound of gunfire got louder as he approached. One klick out, Dan came to a stop. He had approached a small screen of trees. Behind it, Dan could see the dim outline of a single-story structure. It appeared deserted. He got out quickly, and used the night sight on his M4 to see. No movement around the structure, which looked like a concrete bunker. The sloping roof was broken in. In 'Stan, most of the buildings were made of mud. He had never seen a concrete structure like this before. He aimed further, and saw the clump of huts that signified the village of Mumtaz. The occasional flash of gunfire made the location even more obvious.

Directly in front of him, and further away, he could see the south wall of the compound. Through the night sight, he could see the wall had a sangar. But the sangar seemed empty. The fighting seemed to be concentrated at the north end. Dan could see why. That was where the village lay. Where the insurgents had most of their weapons.

The few huts to his left were like an outpost. But he could not be sure if they were occupied. If they were, then he could be in trouble. He had to cross almost seven hundred meters of open terrain, carrying the heavy weapons on his back. He wanted to hide the quad inside the bunker ahead of him. He could not get the quad inside, and leaving it by the wall meant it would fall into enemy hands.

The quad was also part of his route back to the LZ, if things went badly wrong, or if there weren't any WMIKs in the compound.

Dan settled down in the dust, and observed the concrete bunker for a while with his NVG. He saw a cat coming out, but nothing else. He rolled the quad bike down to the bunker. It was covered by weeds and bushes. The entrance had a small tree growing in front. He hacked away with his kukri and cleared some space.

He shone a light inside, finger on the trigger of his M4. An odd structure. Large windows at the rear, like they were made for sightseeing. On either side, concrete slabs like desks. Below them, he could see rusting old machines. They looked like old radios. Plants had grown between them.

He put the quad bike in one corner, and spent fifteen minutes covering it with branches and leaves.

Then he picked up the Minimi, and strapped it to his front. On his back went the ILAWs, twenty-five pounds each. He was now carrying almost eighty pounds in extra weight. It was going to slow him down. And it would make climbing up the ladder harder.

He adjusted his radio, and located the channel of the CIA team inside the compound. The buzz and static cleared, and he heard a humming sound.

CHAPTER 5

"Bravo, this is Zero, do you copy?" Dan repeated the message twice. Nothing but silence greeted his ears. He tried again after two minutes. Radio channels could be listened to easily. Anyone with a scanner and a set of microphones could hear what he was saying. It had always been a problem in 'Stan.

But the radio silence was a bigger problem for him now.

The CIA guys, with their asset, could be dead. In the fighting that was going on now. Dan had arrived too late.

His mission was over before it had started. But it also presented the possibility that he had to enter the compound and check for himself. Without it, he could never be sure. If the asset was alive, he had to bring her back.

Dan spoke again on the radio, and heard nothing but silence. He swore, then, with the weapons on his back, came out of the bunker.

Then he started to run on open ground. Directly ahead of him, he could see the walls of the compound. As the satellite images had shown, it was a large structure, about seventy-five meters wide.

Everything around him was bathed in a green hue. To the left of the compound he could make out several single-story mud huts. A few of them were on an elevation. Dan caught the sound of fire, and briefly saw a muzzle flash. It came again, and he knew with certainty he had found the source of the machine gun fire that was aimed at the compound.

The whine of the bullet caught him off guard.

More rounds followed and he threw himself to the ground. Breath left his chest as the heavy weapons pressed on his back. He heard a round go into something metallic above him and ping off. The round must have hit one of the ILAW covers.

Dan turned around. Another round whistled over his head, way above. Someone was shooting at him, but they had got lucky. Maybe they had seen something move in the dark. That was the danger with open ground.

Dan could set the bipod up, aim the Minimi and be blasting away in a couple of minutes. But that would give his position away. In this open terrain, he could be pinned down with heavy fire.

A few more rounds came his way. He used the ILAW as his shield and watched, staying motionless. He located it eventually. The clump of huts next to the compound. The ones he had noticed before setting off. As he had feared, they were guard outposts.

Now the scumbags had seen him. They could not see much more, as he was lying still now. They did not have NVGs, or IR night sights on their AK-47s. Dan put the seventeen-pound steel case that held the Light Machine Gun, Minimi, on his back, and slithered along the ground, leaving the heavy weapons out in the open. It was the best he could do for now. He could not take them and run. They would weigh him down. But neither could he leave the threat as it was.

Like every threat, it had to be neutralized. That was the way he operated.

Dan got up and ran, heading for the shape of a single-story building to the left of the main residential huts of the village. It was close to him. Less than a hundred meters. He ran tactically. Crouched for one minute. Run. Drop and assess. Repeat.

He had already clocked the building as empty. Unusually for a building out in the open in 'Stan, it seemed to be made of concrete. Like the bunker where he had stored his bike.

He could not detect any movement in his NVGs. But he could not take any chances. He unhooked a frag grenade from his belt. Twenty meters out, he went flat on the cold ground. He gave himself five seconds. The sound of more fire, directed to the spot he had just run from. He needed to get into this building, and see if he could use it as a lying-up point.

Getting in through the heavy main doors of the compound was out of the question – the heavy machine gun fire was aimed at it.

Five seconds gone.

Grenade in hand, Dan approached the building cautiously.

The square concrete structure seemed more like a bunker with windows that faced him, and the compound. The door was open. Dan's breath was a ragged whisper. If he was walking into an ambush, he would throw the frag, make sure he took them with him. Rifle pointed towards the dark door, and frag in the other, he nudged the door with his foot. Heavy metal door. It creaked open.

Dan flinched at the noise, and there was a sudden flurry of movement in the darkness beyond. He fired automatically, falling backwards as he did so. He landed with a thud, just in time to see a small, dark shape scurry out of the bunker and run away. A cat, or small dog. Dan did not relax. He got up and poked his rifle into the darkness. He lifted up his NVG, and flicked a switch on the M4 muzzle. A flashlight lit up the interior. He kept the beam pointed downwards. The smell of animal waste hit his nostrils. The floor was dusty with some leaves and weeds growing in the cracks. Next to the windows, to his right, there was a row of console desks. Old, rusting machines underneath them. Old TV screens and computers.

Dan only had a few seconds to process it. He ensured the room was empty, then crouched under one of the windows, and set off a volley of fire towards the huts. He guessed it might be the reception committee who had now caught up with them. It did not matter. He had to do something, and fast. Dan ran out of ammo, reclipped a new mag, and kept up the fire. As he had hoped, the insurgents fired back at him. Dan ducked as the heavy rounds knocked plaster off the walls. He unhooked the Minimi, and lay it on the ground.

He unchained the hundred-round ammo belt he was going to feed into the machine, and took up position on the window. The source of fire was at ten o'clock to him. In a minute, he had set up the bipod, had the butt against his shoulder, and let off a barrage of suppressive fire. The enemy firing stopped almost instantly, as the heavy rounds found their mark three hundred meters away with ease.

Dan emptied two-thirds of his ammo on the clump of huts that were firing at him. As soon as he took a break the return fire increased.

Dan scrambled away from the window, hearing the bullets whine above his head. He picked up his M4, and used the NVG's only visible infrared pointer to beam at the group of huts. There were about three of them, set apart from the main street.

He knew what they were trying to do. Their plan would be to keep up the fire, then send a patrol up around the back to the bunker to finish him off.

Dan would not let that happen.

He pushed the heavy metallic door open and stepped outside. There was still the chatter of guns aimed at the bunker, and further up front, at the compound. Dan went around the back and got his bearings.

To his left, three hundred meters away lay the beginnings of the village, and the mud huts. Dead straight lay the south wall of the compound. To his right, empty land with sparse tree cover. Where he had to leave the two ILAWs.

Dan stayed low, and ran towards the huts. The small huts were probably built as a sentry post before the main streets of the village began. The Taliban had obviously taken control of the village. Given the amount of fighting going on, he doubted any of the Afghan villagers still lived there.

Dan's feet slipped on something and he fell flat on his front. He shook his head, and put his palms on the ground to lift himself up. The ground was icy, and movement was not easy. He felt a hardness under his palms and took a closer look at the ground. It felt different. He brushed away some loose earth. He frowned, and used the butt of his rifle to dislodge more of the ground around him.

Black. Hard. Concrete. Dan skirted around quickly, keeping an eye ahead, kicking the ground around him. He was on a concrete road.

TAKTAKTAKTAK

He went to ground again as the bullets flew, but they went to his right, towards the bunker. Dan quickly calculated the arcs of fire. He was outside it, but a stray bullet was always possible. He would have to take that risk. Soon, the friends of the Taliban firing at them would join them, and probably bring another heavy weapon.

Dan ran fast. He circled behind the huts. The sporadic firing continued, clearly identifying the huts. Dan could now clearly see the main road that led into the village. A mud road, like in most Afghan villages. Huts were spread in a straight line on either side of the road. Dan had been in many villages like these. Normally, lights glowed from windows and smoke rose from the chimneys. But not these huts. They were dark and silent. The entire village was deserted. The moon broke free from the clouds above, bathing the scene in a silvery glow. It illuminated the large compound about four hundred meters in front. Dan looked away from the flash on his NVG with the natural light. He focused on the three huts ahead of him.

The central hut was the biggest, and seemed to be the source of fire. The two smaller huts on either side appeared deserted. Dan waited ten seconds. No movement from the two huts on either side, but plenty from the central hut. No animals in the backyard. He could make out the muzzle of a gun poking out the front window. Dan rose up. There was a rickety, waist-high fence, and he climbed over it easily. He watched his footstep.

Silent as a ghost, he approached the hut in the middle.

CHAPTER 6

Six feet away, he sank to the ground. He could hear whispered voices inside. They fired out the front window suddenly, a loud sound in the relative silence. The men in the hut fired again, a volley of shots that again went without reply.

Dan sidled up to the side of the hut. It was raised on a wooden platform, with three steps going up to it. Dan raised his head, rifle pointed up. With the NVG, he could see three men. Bent over their weapons at the window. Leaning against the mud wall, Dan pointed his rifle to the figure nearest to him.

Three in a row, like ducks. His first shot exploded the head, and the figure slumped to the ground. Before the figure had dropped, Dan had aimed and taken out the man next to him. But the third guy turned around. Fast.

Even as Dan squeezed the trigger, the man let off a flurry of rounds from his AK-47. Bullets splattered the door frame and Dan fell to the ground. The man kept up a wall of fire, bullets pumping out the doorway of the hut. Not good. These bullets made a big bang, which would alert his friends, if they were around. Dan checked himself, but he was unhurt. He stayed beneath the platform. The man stopped firing eventually, and Dan heard a sound. He was approaching the door. Silently, Dan unsheathed his kukri. He flattened himself against the mud wall.

Dan saw the snout of the AK-47 first, poking out the doorway. He grabbed it and pulled, pointing it upwards. Rounds flew harmlessly into the night sky. In the same movement, Dan dragged the Taliban into his body. The man was tall and strong. He wrestled for control of the rifle with one hand, and with the other clawed Dan's face. He was shouting gibberish in Pashto, probably trying to get some help. He did not shout for long.

The kukri sparkled in the moonlight as Dan lifted it high, then plunged the eleven-inch blade into the man's neck. It cut through the tight knots of the sternocleidomastoid neck muscles, and ripped out the trachea. Dan took the kukri out and thrust it in again, this time feeling the spine snap at the back. He put pressure and moved the long, curved knife sideways, and the head separated from the muscles, nerves and blood vessels of the neck. The head fell to the floor, and Dan let go of the limp body.

He spun around quickly, muzzle up, expecting more fire. There was none. Sporadic fire came from the front, where a gun battle still raged. But around him there was silence.

Dan looked down the village path. It went straight, then curved around the front of the compound. He could not see beyond that, but he knew the gunfire was coming from there. He thought quickly. He could go further into the village, but he could well be surrounded by the enemy. Each dark hut presented a threat. Besides, he had to assume the headless Taliban at his feet had fired enough rounds to attract attention already. Dan decided. He would have to pick up the weapons he had left and somehow get inside the compound.

Rifle up at his shoulder, Dan stepped out. He looked around him, jerking his weapon left and right. Once he had reached the bunker again, he used his radio.

"Bravo, this is Zero. Do you copy?"

He got silence again. Dan was getting a sinking feeling. If the compound was swarming with Taliban now, what happened to the CIA guys? He didn't like the answer. Death would be the easiest way out for them. As for the woman…Dan clenched his jaws. He would get into that compound, just to find out, if nothing else.

Suddenly his mic chirped. "Zero, this is Bravo One. Over and out."

Dan breathed a sigh of relief. "Loud and clear, Bravo One. I was starting to get worried."

The male voice said, "We need help here, Zero. How many of you are there?"

"Just me. But my mission is to evacuate you now."

"Negative, Zero. They have us surrounded. Getting out now would be suicidal."

Dan said, "The south wall is quiet. Throw down a hook ladder. ETA eight minutes."

"Roger that, Zero. Out."

Dan packed the Minimi up. He ran out into the open ground, ready to fling himself down at the first sound of gunfire.

None came. Dan put the two rocket launchers on his back, a total weight of fifty pounds. With his thirty-pound rucksack, weapons and ammo, he stood up effortlessly, and ran like a hare for the south wall.

The ladder was thrown down quickly when he arrived. A rope was sent down, too, and Dan tied the ILAWs and Minimi and sent them up. Then he climbed himself, as fast as he could.

There was a sangar at the top. Sangars were a common feature of compounds in 'Stan, and used to defend compounds. Before Dan went down the stairs, he stole a look around from the platform. It was a strange place to have a sangar. All he could see around him, with his NVGs, was dark and bleak countryside suffused in green. Anyone coming would be spotted miles out, and picked up easily. Opposite, almost seven hundred meters away, he could see the bunker where he had fired the Minimi from.

Roderick and Jones, the two CIA guys, were waiting for him at the bottom. They shook hands with Dan and introduced themselves. Dan put the weapons from his back down with a thud.

Roderick, the older guy, said, "Did HQ just send you? Seriously?"

Dan looked at him evenly. "I don't know which HQ you mean."

Roderick frowned. "Bagram HQ. Isn't that where you are from?"

"No. I am from Intercept."

Roderick's face cleared. "Ah. Heard of you guys." He looked at Dan curiously. "What are you, ex-Delta?"

Dan didn't like the questions. He had many of his own, but he was keeping them to himself. Why the hell couldn't this guy do the same?

He remained silent. Eventually, Roderick looked away.

Dan looked around him. It was chaotic. They were standing under the shade of a building. The courtyard was pock-marked with excoriations, and several of the buildings had their doors blasted in. The sound of gunfire increased even as they spoke.

"You been hit by mortars?" Dan asked.

Roderick shook his head. The tiredness was apparent on his face. "No, only grenades so far. But I figure it's coming."

Dan nodded. Exploding mortar shells in this closed compound would be a disaster.

"You got the woman?" Dan asked.

Roderick and Jones stood up straighter. "Yes, we do," Jones said shortly. Dan turned towards the younger man.

"Who is she?" Dan knew what answer he would get. But he had to ask it anyway.

"That information is classified. You know that," Roderick said.

"We need to exfil," Dan said.

"How?" Roderick asked.

"We go to an LZ about ten klicks from here. That should be enough distance. HQ will look at sat images and find a secluded spot."

"How do we get there?"

"Do you have a WMIK?"

"A what?"

"An armored car. A technical. Preferably with a central or rear-mounted gun."

Roderick nodded. "I think there is one here. We also have three armored Range Rovers."

Dan nodded. That should be ample transport, as long as they did not get ambushed.

"Talk about it tomorrow," Dan said. He pointed to the sangars. "Are they all occupied?"

Roderick shook his head. "No. One insurgent climbed over. We shot him down. We are down to four ANPs, and two of us. Six in total."

Dan asked, "Your call sign is Bravo One, what about Jones?"

"Bravo Two," Jones said.

"Ok. Show me the sangars looking at the village. That's where the fire is coming from, right?"

Jones led them across to the north wall that faced the main block of the village. "This used to be the police station. Before that, it was an operating base for the Russians."

"This is sangar 1." Dan turned to Jones who pointed out the sangars to them. They were standing in the middle of the compound. A small building, three by two meters stood in the center. A grenade must have hit it, as its roof was caved in. Sangars 1 and 2 took up the two corners of the north wall. Sangar 3 was on the side wall facing the village.

Dan said to Jones, "Take the Minimi and set up in Sangar 2. Don't start firing till I give the word. We need to locate the source." Jones looked at Roderick, who nodded. He jogged off without a word. Dan put his rucksack and both of the ILAWs down in a hut that Jones pointed out to him. Then with his M4, he strode out towards sangar 3. The stairs going up were wooden, and the sides were covered with hessian cloth to hide anyone going up and down.

"Hello," Dan called as he got to the top. He did not want to stay on the stairs for long. There was still a firefight going on. He could make out two figures on the floor of the sangar.

One of them turned around, and suddenly a round screamed in from outside and hit Dan.

CHAPTER 7

Dan was stooping low already, but he could not avoid the bullet. A roar erupted from his throat as he was flung back against the wooden slats of the sangar. He collapsed in a heap, on top of one of the men on the floor. They moved swiftly, pulling him to one side. One of them raised himself up on one knee and returned fire. Dan lay on the floor gasping. There was a pain on the right side of his chest. With an effort, he pulled his right arm out, and felt his body. On the bulletproof Kevlar suit he found a hot depression. An embedded round, still smoking. Dan grunted and reached underneath his Kevlar. It was dry. He felt further, his hands exploring all around his chest. No slick of blood. It was all dry. The pain in his chest remained, but he ignored it. He was still alive.

Gasping, he sat up against the sangar wall. The Kevlar had saved his life. He should not have waited on the steps. Dan tore the Kevlar vest off him and explored the rest of his body. No further wounds.

Both of the men in the sangar were now firing back.

"Hey!" Dan shouted. One of them looked back. He tapped his friend and they both turned to look at Dan. They were Afghanis, and one wore the blue uniform of the Afghan National Police. They looked Dan up and down, fear and curiosity mixed in their eyes.

"Do you know what you are firing at?" Dan asked.

The two men looked at each other. The one in the blue uniform answered. "Yes," he said.

"Show me." Dan nudged between them. "What's your name?"

"Ahmed."

Dan looked in the direction Ahmed was pointing. It was not easy to see in the dark, and the moon had scudded behind clouds. With his NVGs Dan could only see dark undulations of the mud huts. A few rounds suddenly splattered against the wood and the sandbags, and they ducked down low.

"Where was that from?" Dan asked.

"Same place," Ahmed said.

"No, it's not," Dan said. "If you fire without locating the source you waste ammo and also give away your location. They are sniping at us from multiple locations."

"So, what do we do?" Ahmed asked.

The main trajectory of the bullets, Dan knew, pointed to their two and three o'clock. He was about to say something but, right on cue, he heard the sound of more fire headed their way. Dan raised his head and took a quick peek.

"There's a hill facing us," he told Ahmed in an urgent voice. "To my eleven o'clock. It's on an elevation to us, so anyone up there can fire directly in."

"Yes," Ahmed nodded. Dan could not make out the young man's face properly, but his eyes shone in the dark. "It's called Butcher's Hill. The butchers slaughtered their sheep there. We have seen gunfire from there before."

Dan stole another glance. The hill rose at the back of the village. About seven hundred meters, but he could not be sure in the dark. It was too far away for the ILAWs, but a General-Purpose Machine Gun or Gimpy, as it was called, in sustained fire mode would be useful. He doubted they had such a weapon here, but it was worth asking. More rounds came in, pecking at the wood and sandbags, flying over their heads.

Dan waited for a lull in the fire. He told Ahmed, "Don't fire back. Wait for my signal. We have three sangars facing the village, and three arcs of fire. Let's use them."

Dan took a deep breath, then crawled out to the edge. He could see the stairs, covered by the hessian cloth. How had they seen him?

He took a deep breath, and ran down the stairs. He flinched as some more bullets hit the sandbags at the base of the sangar. Then he was below the wall of the compound, and on the ground.

He ran to sangar 2 at the far end of the north wall. Roderick was there with an ANP. Dan hunkered down beside them. It was a tight fit with all three of them.

"Where is it coming from?" Dan asked.

"Multiple places," Roderick said. "But mainly from the village center. There's a two-story house there." Dan tried to look, but they had to duck as bullets splattered against the wood decking.

"Shit," Roderick said, crouching. "They're coming on heavy tonight."

Dan shouted above the din of the rounds. "I'm going back to sangar 1. When I give the word, increase your fire. Understand?"

Roderick gave him a thumbs-up. Dan got up and flung himself down the stairs. He ran to the hut by the wall where he had stashed the weapons. He took one of the ILAWs out. He carried it back up to sangar 1. Ahmed and the other ANP were firing intermittently.

He pressed on his ear mic, calling Roderick.

Roderick answered straight away. The staccato beat of rounds interrupted the transmission but Dan could make out the words. "Still the same. Two-story building…center of village….my one o'clock."

Dan leaned out the back of the sangar and looked at the arcs of fire. He was at the corner, with Roderick opposite him. In the middle, Jones was in place. He did not want a blue on blue. Never, and certainly not with what he had planned.

Dan tapped Ahmed on the back. "Hold your fire," he said. The Afghan nodded, curiosity in his eyes.

"Bravo One," Dan instructed, "draw their fire. Both of you." He relayed the same message to Jones. The two CIA SOG men, along with the ANP, laid down heavy fire towards their right. Soon enough, rounds pinged back at them.

"Keep going!" Dan shouted. He bent over the ILAW and took it out of its case.

The rocket-launched missile was very effective at ranges of four or five hundred meters. It would go through a tank, and definitely blast the hell out of a house. Dan lifted his head briefly again, and this time he spotted the two-story house, whose upper floor was the source of fire. They were firing indiscriminately now. The sound of bullets and smell of cordite hung like a mist in the air. Dan could also see what he had suspected – the heavy ordnance came from that two-story house in the center, beyond the village square. Inside the square, and from either side, smaller fire from AK-74s came in, supporting the big gun.

Probably a DShK, RPK, or some other Russian heavy-artillery gun. Old but brutal. At eight hundred meters it would stop any infantry battalion dead in their tracks. That's why they had it placed further back, out of the range of small arms fire.

But they had not taken Dan's weapon into account.

Dan got the launcher out and prepared it. Then he put the twenty-pound rocket on his right shoulder. He would have to expose himself for this, but it was a risk worth taking. This guy needed to be silenced.

"Cover me," Dan said on his mic to Roderick and Jones. Then he tapped Ahmed on the back and nodded. If their sangar was quiet for too long, the Taliban would suspect something was amiss. Ahmed looked back, nodded, and got back to work.

Dan flipped his NVGs down, and taking a deep breath, clambered out onto the stairs where, a few minutes ago, he had been hit. There was a platform below it, adjacent to the sangar. The wooden base shook with the sound of gunfire.

Dan made sure the weapon was stable on his shoulder. He had earplugs on. He flipped up the night vision finder on the ILAW. He would have three to five seconds when he was down there. Out in the open. He knew where the target was: they kept firing. He would have to aim, fire, then dive back in. Hoping he did not get shot himself.

The firing continued, the cackle of machine gun exploding in the night. The bullets were smashing against the sangar above. Dan crouched and turned. He got out onto the wooden platform. Bent over, he looked into the night sight. Yellow traces of bullets, like LED lights, were pouring into the compound. He found the target quickly, and pressed the trigger.

BOOOM!

The rocket hissed loudly in his ear, almost deafening him, even with the earplugs on. He stumbled backwards. The missile thundered out and, in two seconds, the night sky was lit up in an orange-red fire glow. The double-story house was hit with a loud explosion, smack bang in the middle where the heavy gun was poking its barrel out. Dan heard Roderick cheering on his mic.

"Bullseye! Fuckin A, man!!"

Dan went out swiftly, and climbed back on the sangar. He was breathing fast. He wiped the sweat off his forehead. The two Afghans looked at him, wonder on their faces.

"What was that?" Ahmed asked.

"Anti-tank weapon," Dan said.

"Like an RPG?"

"Better." Dan said shortly.

"Who are you?" Ahmed asked.

"Helper," Dan said. He took a closer look at Ahmed. The man dropped his gaze and looked away.

The gunfire had stopped. The sudden silence was unnerving. Dan strained his ears, as he knew everyone else was. The moon broke free from the clouds again. Dan peeked above the sangar wall. Moonlight splashed above the domed huts of the villages. Some had flat roofs. The minaret of a mosque rose in the distance. Farther away, a black knot of mountains. To his right, moonlight made visible the destruction the ILAW had wrought. The building had been approximately five hundred meters away, and the entire top floor had been blown away by the missile.

Dan nodded at the Afghans, and made his way down the stairs. He was met by the CIA agents.

"Did you fire that weapon?" Jones asked. Dan nodded.

"Good work." There was a hint of respect in his voice.

Dan checked his watch. 0230 hours. Less than three hours till daylight. He suddenly realized how tired he was. And hungry.

"Time for an MRE?" Jones asked, reading Dan's thoughts. Dan nodded. Meals Ready-to-Eat would have to be all the food they had in this place. Dan turned to Roderick.

"Where do we sleep?"

Roderick pointed to a row of huts by the south wall. "The last one has been cleared for you. We keep a sentry duty, by the way. Two hours on and four hours off."

"Sure thing," Dan said. "Where do you guys sleep?"

Roderick said, "Next to you. The ANP sleep there." He jerked his thumb towards a group of huts by the north wall, directly opposite.

Dan headed out for his quarters. The wooden door was shut, and he opened it to find darkness inside. He shone his torch. Four beds were placed in four corners of the floor. They looked threadbare and uncomfortable, but to his exhausted body, they looked like a slice of Heaven. Groaning, he rested his body on one of them.

He took out one of the packets of MRE from his rucksack. He got the lamb stew and dumpling. He squeezed the contents down his throat. They all tasted the same. He chugged down some much-needed water from his can.

The CIA guys were in the hut next to him. He wondered where the woman was. She probably had the last hut, the one in the corner.

Dan decided to get some shut-eye before Roderick came to call him for sentry duty.

CHAPTER 8

It was dark inside the room. The night was cold outside, and Dan was wearing his life-saving Kevlar vest as he slept. Despite the door being shut, the cold night air seeped in. He listened to the snoring from the adjacent room. The rhythmic sound was like a gentle lullaby, and soon his eyelids dropped. He did not know how long he had slept for. But a sound awoke him.

A creaking sound.

It came from the doorway. Dan's hand curled around the butt of the Sig P226 at his belt. No safety catch. Round chambered. Point and shoot. Best thing about the P226. He lifted the gun, pointing it at the door.

The door creaked again.

Dan's finger caressed the trigger. He sat up in the bed without making a sound. One of the two door frames opened. A figure was silhouetted in the soft white moonlight. Dan gripped the butt tightly, but for some reason, his hands trembled. That was a first for him.

The figure was smaller than a man. It was slightly hunched as well. Dan swallowed hard as the dark figure came inside the room. Dan pointed the gun at the figure and stood up slowly.

"Who is it?"

"Dan, is that you?"

"Mother?" Dan lowered the gun. He stepped forward. Rita Roy's face was looking up at him in the darkness. She gripped his shoulders.

"Son, I had to come and see you. It's been so long. Didn't know if you were alive or dead."

Dan was bewildered. But this was real. No mistaking it. "Mom, what are you doing here?"

"I came to warn you."

Dan frowned. "About what?"

Dan heard a noise by the doorway and he looked up. He froze. Ahmed, the

ANP, was standing there, AK-47 in his hand. His eyes were burning with hate. They glowed like coals in the dark. He looked at Dan, then at Rita.

Before Dan could do anything, Ahmed had pointed the gun at Rita and fired. She crumpled to the floor.

"No!" Dan screamed. "No, no, no!"

Dan was sitting up in bed, sweat pouring down his face, and he was screaming. He heard guns being uncocked, and a flashlight suddenly stung his face, blinding him. The light left him and jerked around the room.

"What the hell?" It was Roderick, and he was standing at the open door. Out of instinct Dan turned his Sig on him.

"Whoa!" Roderick said, and pointed his weapon down. "What was that?"

"Nothing," Dan said sheepishly. "I reckon I had a dream. Sorry, just get back to bed."

Roderick gave Dan a look, then went off.

Dan did not sleep well. He tossed and turned in the rickety, creaking bed till he felt a hand shaking him awake.

"It's morning, pal." It was Jones. Dan saw a bright light coming in through the window. He was awake instantly. Jones looked tired. It was silent outside. 0630 hours. Dan got up, took his water bottle outside into the compound, and splashed water on his face.

He turned to head back to his hut and stopped in his tracks.

A woman was facing him. Six feet away, standing on the slightly raised mud verandah outside the huts. Her jet-black hair fell around her shoulders. Her skin was the color of milk, and her eyes were green. Her large eyes were expressive, with a curious twinkle in them. But they were also worried and watchful. She had a long, slender neck, a small nose and high cheekbones. Even in her bedraggled state, she looked beautiful. She was about his age, early thirties. She wore the same shapeless gown that women were made to wear in this part of the world. But it seemed tighter, and she wore it differently. Her figure was not shapeless.

Dan broke off eye contact, and walked back. Which happened to be towards her. When he was facing her, in front of the doors of his hut, he lowered his head and rolled his massive shoulders.

"I am Dan Roy. I was sent to help you get to safety." Dan did not know if the woman spoke English. He felt like an idiot after he opened his mouth. He should have just ignored her, and gone back inside. He did not owe her an explanation. But something about her held him there.

"I am Mariam Panahi," the woman said after a pause. "Thank you for coming." Her English was perfect, without any trace of an accent. Her voice was light. A faint trace of a smile appeared at the corner of her ruby-red lips, then vanished. She turned and went back inside the hut.

Dan stood there for a second. "Pleasure was all mine," he said. He spoke to empty air. The door was already shut.

Three ANPs were standing in one corner of the perimeter wall. Their weapons were out, with fingers on triggers. They gazed at Dan, sizing him up. Dan returned the favor. In his past contacts with the ANP, Dan had never been sure if he could trust them. What he had seen of the ANP so far was different. These guys seemed more agile, on the ball.

Another ANP strode out of the hut at the far end. Dan was close enough to make out Ahmed's features. He spoke sharply to the three ANPs and they brushed the dust off their hips and stood to attention. Ahmed looked at the guns and checked they were loaded. He turned around to see Dan.

"Hello," Ahmed said in English. "Good morning."

"Morning," Dan nodded. "Are you setting up for sentry duty?"

"Yes, as usual." Dan watched as Ahmed strode towards him. In the bright morning light, he could see the man's features clearly. He was much younger than Dan. He looked at Dan curiously.

"Which army do you work for?"

"I don't."

Dan stared at the man with a stony expression. It did not invite further comment, and Ahmed dropped his gaze after a few seconds.

Ahmed said, "You will help us exfiltrate."

"Maybe." Dan looked around but he could not see any Roderick or Jones. "Do you know if there is a WMI....I mean an armored car here?"

Ahmed smiled. "There is a WMIK here. Left by the previous platoon."

"You know what a WMIK is?"

"Yes. A weapon-mounted installation kit. I was trained by soldiers from the 1ˢᵗ Battalion, the Royal Welsh."

Dan did not reply. Ahmed said, "Would you like to see the WMIK?"

"Yes."

Dan walked with Ahmed to the long wall that faced the village. A row of mud huts, all with a domed roof and a flight of stairs going up their side, stood against the wall. Behind them, Ahmed pointed out the sand-colored open top, weapon-mounted, converted Range Rover. Dan noticed the GPMG, or Gimpy, that was still present. He checked the car over. It looked to be in reasonable condition. The fuel tank was still half-full.

Dan heard his name being called, and saw Roderick heading for him. The CIA man pointed to sangar 1.

"Seen something interesting up there. Care to have a look?"

"Yes," Dan said. "Thanks," he said to Ahmed.

CHAPTER 9

Dan crouched on the floor of the sangar with Roderick. He handed Dan a pair of binoculars. Dan looked out at the village in front of him. Typical rows of mud huts that seemed out of a biblical landscape. Yellow-gray, sandy, dusty streets. He had seen them a hundred times before in 'Stan – on foot patrol, on operations, and from a helicopter. But never had they been this empty. He was looking out at a derelict ghost village. Not one soul stirred in the quietness.

Dan heard a noise behind him, and looked around to see Ahmed squatting on the floor. With the three of them it was a tight fit.

"It might look empty," Ahmed said, "but they are out there. They dig tunnels to move from house to house. They use pulleys for their guns and ammo in the tunnels."

Roderick said, "And they wait till we get bored of watching. Then suddenly they attack. At high noon, when the sun is strongest. Or late at night, when we are tired."

Dan nodded. "You got their radio channels?"

Roderick said, "Ahmed has been using the Icom scanner to check the radio waves. Any news, Ahmed?"

Ahmed said, "We located one frequency. Their code for attacking seems to be *The harvest is gathered.* We heard that last night before you turned up." He indicated Dan.

"Good work, Ahmed," Roderick said.

Dan looked behind them at the rooftop of one of the huts at the north-west corner of the compound. He could see long antennas and a satellite radio dish pointing to the sky. He pointed. "That your comms tower?"

"Yes," said Roderick.

Dan scanned the area outside. He saw the building that he had decapitated with the ILAW that morning. It looked worse in daylight. But dotted around them, Dan could see double-story buildings, most of them level with the compound wall, and some higher. He pointed to those buildings.

"These are dangerous. They negate our height advantage." He swept around with the binoculars in the distance. He stopped when he saw the convoy of pickup trucks approaching. They were loaded with men. He could see their turbans, and some rifles poking up in the air.

Roderick said, "Have you seen them?"

Dan realized this is what Roderick had asked him to come up for. He counted five pickup trucks with men and ammunition. They were far, more than one klick away. He looked further, and saw a trail of dust rising in the air. More reinforcements were on their way.

"Shit," Dan said, lowering the binoculars. He asked Roderick, "Why all the interest?"

Roderick shrugged and avoided Dan's eyes. "Damned if I know."

Dan checked his watch. 0900 hours. He went down from the sangar, and walked towards his hut. The others were out already. They had their mics on. Jones chirped in his ear.

"Looks dead from sangar 1."

"Look again. A boatload of Tangos just arrived at the edge of town. Reckon there's going to be a big party soon."

Dan went into his hut and took his satellite phone out. He needed to speak to Guptill. There was too much going on here that he could not make sense of, and speaking to the CIA guys would not help. He was about to punch the number in when he saw something that made him stop.

The woman. Mariam.

She was poking her head out from one of the buildings in the north-west corner, where the ANPs lived. The building was made of concrete, and had blue and white stripes on it. Mariam looked around, then slipped out of the building. She stood by the doorway for five seconds, watching the compound. It was empty. All the men were up in the sangars. She could not see Dan as he was inside the hut. Mariam crossed the compound quickly, head bent low. Dan shrank back against the wall. He watched as Mariam went into her room and he heard the door shut.

His reverie did not last long. In the blink of an eye, all hell broke loose. There was a loud explosion, followed by shouts, and the sudden chatter of gunfire.

"RPG!" Several voices shouted at once. Dan ran out into the courtyard. He still had his radio on and called Roderick.

"Bravo One, do you copy?" Gunfire drowned his voice.

"Roger that." Roderick's voice was calm. Dan knew he was scanning around him from the sangar, looking for a possible source. An RPG would be fired from within two hundred meters, and smoke would be visible, especially through binoculars.

"What did it hit?"

"The wall to my right," Roderick said. "They were aiming for the sangar."

Dan clenched his jaws. A direct hit from an RPG would damage the sangar. Definitely wound anyone inside it. A second hit would be fatal.

Jones' excited voice from the north-west sangar, number 3, interrupted Dan. "Got him!"

"Where?" Dan asked.

"Smoke to the west, my nine o'clock."

Dan informed Roderick. The Minimi started blasting, rising stridently above the sound of small arms fire. Dan looked up. It was Roderick from sangar 1, letting rip at the position of the RPG. While commotion reigned, he caught sight of something that moved in the corner of his eye.

Mariam. She slunk across the perimeter wall, in the shadow of the huts. She went to the far end, by the ANP block, where she had been before. Dan saw her open the door, enter and shut it.

Dan made a mental note of the building she had gone into. Then he ran across and climbed into the sangar he had just vacated. Roderick and Ahmed were still in there. Both were hunched over, firing intensely. Rounds came at them thick and fast. Bullets splattered against the wood, pinged above their heads, thudded into sandbags.

The ear-splitting sound of heavy ordnance from the Minimi thundered again, making Dan cover his ears. Dan patted Rod on the back. He sprung around.

"Easy," Dan said.

"We got RPGs, too," Rod said.

"We need to move the GPMG you have mounted on the WMIK. I mean the armored car. We need the Gimpy up here, blasting away. Rusty has got the north. We need to hit the west of the village." Dan pointed. "And the bazaar area."

"Ok," said Roderick, "I'll get one of the ANP to help you."

After the prolonged burst from the Minimi, the guns were silent. They heard screams in the silence, coming from the village. Rod raised his head.

"100 meters ahead, one of the houses we fired on last night. We hit some of them."

Dan nodded, satisfied. "I need to have a talk with you. Can we do it now?"

Rod raised his eyebrows. He spoke to Ahmed briefly, then walked down with Dan. They walked to the CIA agents' hut. Dan shut the door.

"You need to level with me," Dan said.

Roderick wiped the sweat off his brows, and leaned the Heckler & Koch rifle against the wall. "Hey, you came here to help extract us. The rest is classified, I told you."

"The hell it is. Did you know about the ambush we landed in?"

The surprise on Roderick's face was genuine. "You were ambushed?"

Dan told him what happened when the Chinook had dropped him off.

"Jesus," Roderick said.

Dan said, "The way I see it, there are two options. There's a mole here, or in HQ."

"You suspect anyone?"

"I have some ideas. But nothing definite yet."

Roderick smiled. "Jones or me in any of your ideas?"

Dan ignored him. "Who is the woman?"

Roderick did not say anything. Dan said, "You either tell me, or I pick up the satphone and call HQ. Tell them there is a mole here. HQ can inform Langley right now."

"I cannot let you do that."

"Do you think you can stop me?"

CHAPTER 10

Roderick and Dan stared at each other for a few seconds. Roderick was the first to look away.

"She's Iranian."

"I know that."

"A nuclear scientist at the IR-40 heavy water plant in Arak."

"Defecting to the West?"

"Yes."

"The Taliban know," Dan said. He was not asking a question. Roderick did not say anything.

Dan said, "The Taliban know, and you can't figure out how. Informed by the same person who told them about us. You have had a mole right from the beginning."

"She knows a lot, Dan. This will be a game-changer. We have to take the chance, even if we have a mole."

"Maybe. But you are missing something here."

"What?"

"The Taliban let you get into this place. They followed you here, and then surrounded you. I don't think they have any intention of letting you leave."

Roderick was silent again. Dan said, "What's in those buildings next to the ANP quarter?"

"What building?"

"Don't play games with me, Rod. There is something here that the Taliban want. I'm not talking about the woman. What is it?"

Roderick said, "You are right. There's more to this. But right now, I've told you all I can."

"I have worked with you guys before."

"You should know, then."

"I know this is a suicide mission. There's seven of us fighting hundreds. We need a platoon-strength force here."

"What are you saying?"

"I am saying someone messed up pretty bad here. Either you were not expecting to land in this shithole, or…"

"Or what?"

Dan said quietly, "Or you are the mole."

Roderick narrowed his eyes. "You are barking up the wrong tree here, my friend."

"I hope so," Dan said.

He left Rod standing there, and walked out. He strode over to sangar 2 on the north wall. Jones and one of the ANP were watching the huts and alleyways.

"Gone very quiet," Jones murmured. "Why did they fire that one RPG?"

"Probably testing their range. They stopped because we got their position, and fired back," Dan said.

"So?"

"So they will come under cover of night."

"We have to be ready," Dan said.

"How many ILAWs we got left?" Jones asked.

"Only one now. But we can get the Gimpy out of the WMIK and bring it up to sangar 1. That sangar is best positioned for all arcs of fire."

"Shit," Jones said. He was looking through the scope on his M4.

"What?"

"Movement. 100 meters away. About ten Tangos."

Dan grabbed the binoculars. He focused them in the right direction. Sure enough, he saw about ten Taliban, wearing their distinctive headgear, covering their faces as well. The men slipped behind a house, and more appeared, before vanishing inside another house.

"They're getting into position," Dan said. He flicked the switch of his radio to get Roderick's channel.

"Bravo One, this is Zero."

"Roger that, Zero."

"Enemy seen on north-west village section. Be on high alert. Contact imminent."

"Roger, out."

Dan spoke to Rod again briefly and came down from the sangar. He was walking over to the WMIK when he saw Ahmed climb down from sangar 3 and join him.

"Agent Roderick told me to help you with the Gimpy."

Dan nodded. They crossed the compound together. They unhooked the Gimpy from its base and put it on the compound. Dan lifted the twenty-six-pound machine, while Ahmed helped him. Together, they carried the weapon up to sangar 1 and positioned it between the sandbags.

"You ever fired a machine gun before?" Dan asked Ahmed, wiping the sweat and dust off his face.

Ahmed looked awed as he gazed at the gun. "No."

Dan showed him. "You need to get some oil," he explained. "The machine needs it after a long firing spell to help it cool down. About four hundred rounds."

He held up the ammo chain. "Straighten this out. Any chinks in the chain could stop the gun, and that could be the difference between life and death."

Ahmed nodded vigorously, his face a mask of concentration.

Roderick was watching outside. He had turned around when they came up, but had not said a word since. He spoke now.

"Sangars 2 and 4 have also reported enemy movement. But none with guns. We are getting ready for a contact."

"Make sure all sangars have enough ammo and drinking water. We don't want to be running up and down these stairs, getting shot at by snipers."

Dan went down into the compound. He looked up at the satellite dishes. They were a big worry. If the enemy hit that, they would be out of contact with HQ. They had their own radios. But it was better to have a direct satellite link.

He watched across the courtyard as Mariam came out of her hut.

She looked around, and Dan pressed himself against the shadow of the stairs. She went inside the blue and white striped building at the northern end, and disappeared inside. Dan gave her five minutes, then followed.

The door had a padlock chain, but it was unlocked. He opened it and stepped inside. He let his eyes adjust to the sudden dark. Inside was cool, and silent. Dan blinked. The walls were of concrete, and the floor had a timber frame. Shafts of sunlight came in through the ceiling.

The room was empty. Completely. It did not have any windows, and no doors apart from the one he had just opened. Mariam had disappeared. Dan looked at the walls carefully. He went over and ran his hands along them. Smooth, no breaks.

Then he stared at the floor. He got down on his knees. Felt every inch of the floor with his hands. He found it at the far corner. A section of timber that looked like the rest of the floor. But this section moved. He pushed it, and it slid back to reveal a black space. A hole. Dan flashed his torchlight inside. Looked like a concrete slab.

Dan pushed the floor again, and another section slid back. He could see more of the concrete. But something else as well. Two hinges, and a heavy, round copper ring. A trapdoor, built on a concrete slab. He grabbed the ring and pulled. It was heavy, and made a rusty, groaning sound, but came up easily. He used his flashlight again. Concrete steps going down. He got his shoulders inside with some difficulty, and put his feet on the stairs. Then he shut the trapdoor over his head. Flashlight on, he could see below him. He was in a dark, cold, silent place. The stairs descended below him. The flashlight's beam got swallowed into a black hole.

Dan climbed down slowly. He counted the stairs as he went down in a straight line. No curves or rolls. The stairs were broad and flat, designed for big shoes like his. After one hundred and fifty stairs, he touched flat ground. Concrete again. He shone his light up. Steel beams criss-crossed the ceiling. He was in an underground bunker. He was in the atrium, and corridors branched off all around him. The corridors were narrow, and seemed to have shelves on them. Like a storage vault. The ceiling was tall enough for a man to stand.

"So, you found me at last," Mariam said from behind him.

CHAPTER 11

Mariam flicked a switch and lights came on. Dan squeezed his eyes shut and opened them. Bulbs hung on naked wires from the ceiling. Mariam came and stood in front of Dan. Her hair was tied back in a ponytail, throwing her features into sharper relief. Her large, green eyes flicked over Dan's face. Serious. Her elegant, thin neck was straight and her chin was raised. She looked slimmer and after a while Dan realized why. She had tied the silken black gown at the waist with a tie. The hem was raised, exposing her ankles.

They stared at each other for a moment without speaking.

"What's going on here?" Dan finally found his voice.

Mariam's expression did not change. "Whatever the CIA guys told you."

"Not much."

Mariam said, "They told you about me."

"Yes."

"What?"

"You are a nuclear scientist. You work in Akra."

"And?"

"You are leaving Iran. Going to America."

"Is that it?"

"That's all I know."

Dan pointed to the now lit corridors behind them. "What is this?"

"Come. I will show you."

Mariam led the way. As they walked into the first row, Dan looked up at the sign. It said something in Russian. Mariam spoke without turning around.

"That says *Ostorozhno*. It means danger in Russian."

Dan gazed at the floor-to-ceiling rows of black mortar shells, arranged by size. They took up both sides of the corridor, leaving them with a narrow space to walk in the middle. They walked for a minute and came onto a clearing. From this space, more corridors branched out. Like spokes radiating out from a hub. Mariam flicked another light switch, then pointed down another corridor.

"This way."

Dan craned his neck up to see rockets nested within their launch pads. They had sharply tapered noses, and went up in size. He stood close to a black rocket, more than two meters high, taller than him. He could not read the Cyrillic writing on the side, and the numbers did not mean anything to him.

"The CR-2," Mariam said, coming closer. "One of the first surface-to-air missiles that the Soviets made in the 1950s. Range and speed are both limited, and they are not nuclear warhead capable."

Dan looked at the other rockets lined up in the corridor. A flight of steps went down to another level. He took a deep breath, and followed Mariam as she went slowly down the stairs. When he came to the bottom of the stairs, the breath got stuck in his chest. His heart hammered against his ribs.

"Oh my God," he said.

"You recognize these?" Mariam asked.

She looked up at the long, tall missile that towered over them. Dan was gazing, too. He guessed the height was more than ten meters. About one meter thick. He saw the fixed broad fins on the base. Steps on the side for engineers to climb up. It was dark gray in color, and its nose narrowed to a cap of a white circle, then narrowed again to a sharp tip with an antenna.

Mariam said, "The *R-17 Zemlya* ballistic missile. Capable of conventional, including chemical, and nuclear warheads up to fifty kilotons. Maximum range of two hundred miles, and capable of a speed of Mach 5. A game-changer in the SAM field."

Dan blinked once. "A goddamn Scud missile."

"Yes, that is the name NATO gave them."

"They need command vehicles to launch them, and erector trucks to transport."

"Yes, and no. The early Scuds did require TEL or transport erector launch vehicles. These can be wheeled on rail tracks, and can be erected by cranes. But yes, they need a command and control station, which can be portable, in a truck."

"That is why there is a runway outside. Control towers. This is a missile silo."

Mariam sounded surprised. "You saw the runway?"

"I stumbled upon it while trying not to get shot. There are control rooms in there as well. Those concrete bunkers. Five hundred meters from the south wall."

"Yes."

Dan touched the Scud missile. Cold, metallic. He had seen wrecks of them in the second Gulf War. Saddam Hussein had been an enthusiastic collector. Russia had been a generous donor.

He felt unreal. He said, "What the hell are Scud missiles doing here?"

"More Scud missiles were fired in Afghanistan between 1989 and 1992 than in any other war. Including the Iran-Iraq War, which saw the greatest deployment of these ballistic missiles."

"Really?"

Mariam nodded. "After the Russians left in 1989, civil war broke out here. The Russians backed the Afghan government. Delivered more than five hundred Scuds to them, with advisors to help them launch them."

"Jesus."

"Afghanistan, in fact, has seen more missile launches than the Second World War. Most of the five hundred plus got fired. But when the advisors left, some missiles were left behind. That's what you have left here."

"How many are in here?"

"Twenty-five."

"How do you know about them?" Dan asked.

She replied after a pause. "My professor in Iran trained in Russia. He was approached to help."

"Approached by who?"

"That is classified."

Dan stared at her, then looked back at the missiles.

Dan said, "The Taliban are a Pakistani construct. They were formed out of Afghan refugees during the Russian war. The CIA helped fund them directly, and through the Pakistani Army. The Taliban movement grew out of madrassas in border towns between Pakistan and 'Stan."

"You know your history."

"That is why the Taliban are concentrated in the south of Afghanistan. Close to Pakistan. The north is ruled by the Northern Alliance, but the Taliban is still strong in pockets."

"What is your point?"

"I think the people who approached your Professor were agents of the ISI, the Inter-Services Intelligence Agency. The Pakistan Army's secret service. They heard rumors about this site from the Taliban. But they did not know the precise location. You did. Hence they let you in here."

Mariam folded her arms in a gesture that was both delicate and thoughtful. Her white hands showed against her black gown.

"How do you know any of this is true?"

"Because you agreed to help the CIA in tracking this place down. You don't want this to fall into Pakistan's hands."

"Why not?"

"They are Sunni, and Iranians are Shia."

"That's true. But I am Assyrian Christian."

"You are?"

"We are a substantial minority in Iran now. Many of us have fled from neighboring Iraq and Syria. Some of my cousins have been killed in Iraq." She looked down at the floor.

Dan said, "I am sorry. So your parents are Assyrian Christians from Iran?"

"Yes. From Shiraz, a city in the south."

"Iran took a huge battering from these Scud missiles during the Iran-Iraq War. You don't want that to happen again."

"Yes."

"But there is another reason why you are helping the CIA."

"What is that?"

"You are not Iranian."

Something changed in Mariam's eyes. A sudden lack of composure, then she corrected herself. A half-smile played on her lips.

"What am I, then?"

"You are American."

CHAPTER 12

Mariam stood very still, her eyes not leaving Dan's face. The mirth in her face slowly disappeared.

"What makes you say that?" she asked.

Dan said, "You cannot take the West Coast out of your voice. I am thinking Los Angeles, or somewhere in Orange County."

"Do you?"

"Yes. You thought I would not recognize your accent. But I am American, too. I am guessing you don't speak to Rod or Jones much, just to hide your accent."

"You guessed right," Mariam said softly.

"I thought so. Your parents immigrated to America. You were born there."

"Yes. But how could I be American, and also an Iranian nuclear scientist?"

"Everyone knows the CIA have assets inside Iran. The Persian-American community is based around LA. It's where the Shah's son lives, and thinks he leads a government in exile."

"You did not answer my question, Dan."

It was the first time she had said his name. She had given up hiding her accent, it was obvious now.

Dan said, "A number of ways. Did you go to college in the USA?"

"Yes."

"I'm thinking UCLA, Berkeley or Stanford. Maybe you came to Iran after that to work. Help the fledgling atomic industry. Then went back to do your PhD in USA. That's when you got recruited by the CIA. Or maybe as an undergrad. Less likely, as you did not have much direct Iran experience as an undergrad."

"Carry on."

"Something happened recently. In Arak, your cover was blown. Maybe one of your contacts got caught. The Republican Guards tortured the truth out of him. You had to escape. The land route was easier as no checks at the borders. You were doubly important to us. You know about the nuclear industry in Iran, and you knew about this missile silo, too."

Mariam regarded Dan thoughtfully. "How did you know?"

"Your accent. You carry a weapon. It's under the sleeve of your right arm. You exposed it briefly when you lifted your arm to point at the Scud."

Mariam peeled back the sleeve of her gown. The black Glock 22 was taped to her wrist.

She said, "You work for the CIA."

"No."

"Some other government agency."

Dan did not answer. She was right, but he could not admit it. He would *never* be able to admit it.

Silence. They stared at each other, eyes searching. Dan's eyes moved to her neck and below, then jerked back up quickly.

Mariam said, "You are very good. You should work in intelligence."

"I prefer dealing with the enemy directly."

Dan said, "Do the two agents know?"

"Roderick does. Derek does not. He's subordinate to Rod."

Dan nodded. No need to tell Jones what he did not need to know. Speaking of which, he had to get back upstairs. The outline of a plan was forming in his mind.

He pointed to the ceiling above the Scud missiles. "How are these raised to ground level?"

"The ceiling is bifolding. It separates into two. Opens out into the compound floor."

"Does the mechanism still work?"

"Not been tried, but I'm willing to bet it does. The cables are still connected. Electricity works here."

"Alright. I have to go back up. The enemy is coming for a big push tonight. You would be better off either in your hut, or down here."

"Thanks."

Dan walked backed to the first corridor he had entered. He squatted on his haunches and looked at the mortar shells. He left the heavier shells alone and focused on what looked like 82mm mortars. He found a number of base plates and launchers for the 82mm. Mariam had come up behind him.

"That's the 2B14 Podnos range," she said, reading off the side of the base plate.

"82mm, aren't they?" Dan asked.

"Yes."

Dan tried to lift the base plate. He could move it, but lifting it alone was difficult. One man could not take it up that flight of stairs. He would have to come back with help.

"What are you trying to do?" Mariam asked.

Dan picked up a mortar shell in each hand. "Trying to survive tonight," he said.

He jogged up the stairs. He went up to sangar 1 and got hold of Roderick. Jones came down from sangar 3 and they went down into the missile silo. Mariam was still there.

"I figured you would need to know where the lights are," she said.

"Good thinking," Dan said.

Roderick gaped at her. "You American?"

"Yes," Mariam said. The three men followed her into the corridor.

"Holy shit," Jones said. He walked around with wonder in his eyes. He disappeared down a corridor, and Dan heard him yelp. Jones poked his head in at the far end.

"You gotta come and see this."

Roderick rolled his eyes, and Dan followed. Jones was gazing at a hallway with row upon row of rockets. About one and a half meters tall. White in color, with black fins and black warheads.

Mariam said, "Katyusha rockets. First deployed in the Second World War, but these are the 1980s models."

"This place is like a museum," Jones said.

"You ain't seen the Scuds yet," Dan said.

"No way." Jones' eyes were big.

The tour ended in a half-hour. It took two of them to lift each one of the ninety-six-pound base plates and tubes up to the surface, and several more trips to get the mortars. Roderick and Jones were waiting for them in the room by the time they finished unloading. Dan did not want them out in the compound. He explained to Roderick why. The CIA veteran nodded and went to work.

*****

Dan climbed into sangar 3. Ahmed was keeping watch.

"I don't like it," he told Dan.

"They are organizing weapons for which they need a light source at night. Easier to set them up now," Dan said.

"How do you know?" Ahmed asked.

"Because that is what I would do."

Ahmed's handheld radio crackled. He spoke into it and listened.

"Agent Roderick wants me downstairs."

"I'll stay here and keep watch," Dan said. He took the position vacated by Ahmed.

He was looking at the bazaar, and a collection of one- and two-story buildings beyond it, including the one he had hit. About one hundred meters distant. About three hundred meters away the mud huts became less numerous, and there was a clump of trees.

Dan unhooked his M4 from his back. He used the weapon's image magnifier to focus on the screen of trees. Their base was obscure. He was in a straight line to the trees, and he looked harder. He swung his rifle around, searching. Then he saw it.

A row of three black, linear, tube-like nozzles sticking up at forty-five degrees. Attached to metal base plates. Similar to the mortar base plate they had just unloaded. Only these seemed larger. For 120mm mortar shells, he guessed.

Cursing, he took out the grid reference map from the shoulder pocket of his vest. He marked the rough coordinates on the map.

Dan aimed the Gimpy at the clump of trees dead ahead, four hundred meters away. He fired a long burst, feeling the machine shake in his hands, and watched the shots raise puffs of small dust in the distance. He kept firing for thirty seconds.

Then he watched with his weapon's scope again. He had hit all of them. The nozzles were on the floor, and he could see where the springs had burst from the base plates. He fired another round to be sure, then told Jones to keep an eye out from their ends for more base plates or rocket launchers. The RPGs they could not do anything about. Those things were portable, and it was just a matter of luck when and where they hit.

Dan spoke briefly to Jones again and went down from the sangar. He headed towards the communication room, from whose square roof the satellite dish and antenna sprouted. Ahmed was inside, listening intently in front of a radio receiver, headphones over his ears.

"Are you on their channel?" Dan asked.

Ahmed nodded. Dan took a seat opposite him.

He said, "Sangar 1 took a hit last night. We need more sandbags up there."

Ahmed glanced at Dan and nodded again. He took his headphones off.

"There is some chatter about mortar base plates."

Dan said, "I know. I just hit some of them. We need to keep an eye out for more. Are your men ready?"

"To be honest," Ahmed said, "their training is basic. They can fire an SA80 rifle and lob grenades, that's about it."

"That will do," Dan said. "Looks like we will be holed up here for another night, at least. Try your best to find out what they are planning."

Ahmed gave him a thumbs-up. "I will."

Dan went outside and spoke to his team. He went to Roderick's hut and spoke to the two CIA agents. Then he spent some time chatting to Guptill on the satellite phone. When he finished his conversation, it was time to wolf down an unappetizing MRE. Dan got up on the south wall sangar, designated as sangar 4. The ANP who had been on duty had gone for his lunch.

He poked his head above the wooden slats and piled up sandbags. Barren land stretching out for miles greeted his eyes.

Directly below him, underneath the sandbags, he could see the wall they had scaled the first night with their hook ladders. With his binoculars, Dan located the concrete bunker where he had taken refuge. To his extreme right lay the beginning of the village. Straight ahead, he could make out the dim, small shape of the other bunker where he had hidden his quad.

The Taliban were experts in guerrilla warfare. They knew their terrain. They would be easy pickings for a sniper out in this zone, bereft of any cover. Hence they never attacked from here. The tree cover was more than eight hundred meters away. Most of their weapons would be out of range. Their cover was the village. Dan searched the south side with his binoculars and rifle sight for a while longer, then started down the stairs.

He flinched as the loud sound of machine gun fire shattered the silence of the afternoon.

CHAPTER 13

"Contact!" It was Roderick's voice, sharp and excited. He said something else but it was drowned out by gunfire.

Roderick was back in sangar 1. Dan knew he could not go up to it while the firing was this heavy.

"Where is it coming from?" Dan asked on his radio.

"Damned if I know. But it's heavy!" Roderick yelled.

Dan ran up the steps to sangar 3. He had barely hit the wooden floor when rounds began to pop around him. They hit the sandbags with a dull *thwack*, and pinged off the wooden arches. Dan lifted his head momentarily and looked. More rounds greeted him. He tried to look for the source, but it was difficult. The firing was accurate. More than five guns had to be aimed at the sangar. Heavier for Roderick, Dan felt.

"I got a sighter," Jones said in his mic.

"Where?" Dan asked.

"Three-story house, behind the bazaar, dead straight to me, north-west."

"Roger that."

Dan knelt on the floor and got the Gimpy ready. He could not aim well with the rounds flying above him, and hitting the protection, but he could fire in the desired direction. He took a quick peek, and then checked his grid reference map, sweat pouring down his forehead.

BAMBAMBAMBAMBAM

The heavy gun shook in his hands. The magazine was full, and he squeezed the trigger remorselessly. He saw his rounds hitting the house, mud splattering off the walls. The incoming fire lessened, and he saw a weapon appear at a window on the first floor. The snout of an RPG was unmistakable.

"RPG! Take cover!" Dan shouted into his mic and fired straight at the weapon.

He snarled with glee as his bullets hit the mark. The weapon fell from the window, out of sight, and he realized he must have hit the insurgent holding the RPG.

The firing towards sangar 1 lessened, but Dan was now taking heavy fire. Sangar 3 shook with the reverberation of heavy ordnance. Dan tried to see the direction but the firing was too heavy. Dimly he heard something in his mic. He could not understand it, but he heard the Minimi on sangar 1 open up. It was joined by small arms fire, and he knew Jones was firing back.

Dan looked through a gap in the sandbags. Streaking flashes of light were flying out from sangar 1 towards the tree line. The tree line where he had hit the mortar plates. Dan took the Gimpy and fired at the trees. The sangar was filled with gun smoke, and the smell of dust, sweat and anxiety. Dan switched radio channels, his heart hammering against his ribs. It was 1400 hours. They did not have much time.

"Bravo One, this is Zero."

"Are you ok up there, Zero?" Roderick sounded concerned.

"Yes. Time to get set up."

"Roger that."

Dan fired for another minute with the Gimpy, joined by sangar 1. He stopped when he realized there was no return fire.

Slowly, the eerie, creepy silence returned. Only the dusty breeze rustled and moved in the air. An empty, cloudless blue sky stretched overhead. It seemed as if they were at the edges of the known human world.

Nothing moved or happened here. Apart from sudden and deadly gunfire.

*****

Roderick was in the communication room, standing next to Ahmed. The Afghan was hunched over the radio again, headphones on.

Dan said, "We need to start getting the mortars ready."

Ahmed looked up. Roderick said, "Do we have coordinates?"

"Not specific, but we can use the grid map. We have enough base plates to set up a barrage, so missing by a meter won't make any difference."

Dan asked Ahmed, "How many Taliban are out there now?"

Ahmed said, "More than a hundred and fifty. They have gathered from surrounding villages."

Dan said, "We need to get the rockets as well?"

Ahmed sounded surprised. "We have rockets, too?"

"A whole lot," Dan said. "There are masses of weapons stored underneath this compound. Tonight we have to launch a major assault. It's the only way we will survive."

Roderick said, "Ahmed, keep scanning their channels to make sure we know what their plans are."

"We wait till nightfall. The fireworks begin at 2100 hours," Dan said.

Dan headed down to the missile silo. Jones had climbed up the steps of a Scud missile and removed the warhead cover. Mariam was on the floor, directing him. Dan stood next to Mariam, looking up at the men.

"Any news?" he asked.

Mariam said, "Ten are loaded so far. Conventional nitrate-compound explosives. The rest are empty."

"What's the payload?"

"Five hundred pounds in each, approximately."

Dan whistled. "That's a lot. Should be interesting."

Dan went upstairs, crossed the compound and entered his hut in the south end. He jabbed numbers into his satellite phone and had a quick chat with Major Guptill. He listened, hung up, waited for ten minutes, then rang Guptill back. He listened again, his head bent.

He called Roderick, and went into the communication room, where Ahmed was on his own, glued to the radio. Dan went and sat in front of him, on the opposite side of the table.

"Any news?"

"No." Ahmed's eyebrows were furrowed in concentration. Dan saw Roderick enter the room from the back, shutting the door without a sound.

"Did you tell them about the rockets?" Dan asked conversationally.

Ahmed looked up, confused. "What?"

CHAPTER 14

"The rockets. You used a code word for them. Hailstones. You were just on the Taliban channel. Your exact message to them was: *Hailstones* will fall tonight, and a *Toofan* is coming. *Toofan* means storm in Farsi and Dari."

Ahmed's face had lost all color. He opened his mouth and licked dry lips. "I am a captain in the Afghan National Police. Why would I tell the Taliban our secrets?"

"Because you have been doing it all along. They knew you were coming here because you told them. You told them about us coming as well, hence we had a welcome party."

Ahmed took the headphones off his head. "This is ridiculous. Why would I do this when I know you can catch me easily?"

"You speak to them in Pashto and Dari. We don't understand that. But you forgot about Mariam. She overheard you one day when she was going down to the missile silo. Then I spoke to HQ, and they hooked onto the channels you were surfing. We know it's you, Ahmed."

Ahmed tried to stand up but he could not. Roderick's hands clamped down on his shoulders and pushed him down on the chair. Ahmed wriggled to get free, without success. Dan stood up and walked around the table.

"Shortly after I told you about sangar 1 needing protection, it was hit by heavy fire. You knew about their mortar base plates, because you told us about them. The Taliban would use a code word for mortars in their radio transmissions. How did you know the code word?"

Silence. Ahmed looked at Dan with baleful eyes. Dan watched them, and his jaws clenched.

It was only a dream. But you appeared in the doorway, when my dead mother, God bless her soul, had come to warn me.

It was only a dream, but you pulled the trigger.

My subconscious was trying to tell me something.

Aloud, Dan said, "You are the mole who has been in this operation from when Mariam escaped from Iran. Who do you work for?"

Ahmed stared at Dan, hatred burning in his eyes. "I don't know what you are talking about."

"What else have you told them, Ahmed?"

Silence again. Dan glanced at Roderick, who nodded.

Dan reached for his belt and with a flourish pulled out his kukri.

Ahmed's eyes widened at the sight of the hooked, eleven-inch, serrated blade. The five-inch handle was made of wood and black leather, making the entire knife sixteen inches in length.

With his other hand, Dan took out a Zippo lighter from his pants pocket. He flicked the cap off and lit the flame. Roderick pressed down on Ahmed's shoulders, grabbing him with a neck hold. He pulled Ahmed's hair back, thrusting his face forward.

Dan ignored them while he used the flame to make the tip of the kukri glow to a red-hot point. Then he squatted on his haunches, and got closer to Ahmed. The man struggled under Roderick's grip, and his breathing was fast and loose. He looked at Dan with wild eyes.

"I hate to do this, Ahmed," Dan said. "These are standard field interrogation techniques. You tell us what I asked you, and I promise, you die quickly. If you don't tell us, we have a long way to go. And you won't like what happens."

"Are you doing the eyelids first?" Roderick asked. Dan liked it. He was improvising.

"Yes," Dan said. "Becomes easier to take the eyes out. The heat from the knife will melt the eyeballs."

"Last time we did the fingers first. I got the hammer."

"We can do that after the eyes."

Roderick did his best to shrug while holding Ahmed down. "Whatever. Just hurry up."

"No," Ahmed whispered.

Dan pressed down on Ahmed with his knee, holding the chin steady with one hand.

Dan lifted the red tip of the kukri, and reached it just under Ahmed's eyebrows. Ahmed jerked and twisted, but Roderick pulled his hair back tightly. Dan paused. "Last chance, Ahmed. I know you told them about the rockets. What else?"

Ahmed spat something out in Pashto. Dan shrugged, and touched the tip of the knife to Ahmed's right upper eyelid. The flesh singed and burned, turning black.

Ahmed screamed, stomped his legs, and tried to slide down the chair. Dan removed the knife. The touch had been enough to scare the man out of his wits. Dan lifted his knee and stood up. He still had his hand on the man's chin, while Rusty pulled back on the hair.

"This is only the beginning, Ahmed," Dan whispered. "Shall I carry on?"

Blood poured down Ahmed's right eye, trickling onto his chin. He was gasping. "I told them…I told them about the woman."

"What else?"

"The rockets, the mortars, everything you told me."

"Have you told them what time we are launching the rockets?"

"You said 2100."

"How many did you say we had?"

"Hundreds. Thousands even. I told them the missile silo was here. It was all here."

"Good man."

Dan removed a pair of plastic handcuffs from his vest, while Roderick took out a black head mask. He pulled it over Ahmed's head and stood him up. Dan tied his hands.

They both looked up as Jones came in through the door.

"We got their weapons," Jones said. "They surrendered without a word." He was talking about the other ANP guards.

"Probably innocent," Dan said. "They might not have known what this guy was doing. But we can't take that chance."

Dan turned his radio on. "Let's go outside and set the base plates set up. Fixed on the coordinates from the grid map."

"Divide the Afghans up, and lock them in the hut," Dan said. "Keep Ahmed in the compound, out in the open where we can see him."

*****

At sunset, pink and golden light played on the shoulders of the far granite mountains. Dan kept watch from the south-facing sangar. The skies were soon shadowed in dark blue and indigo, and the mountains disappeared into folds of black.

1800 hours. Dan pressed on his mic. "Bravo One, this is Zero. Steel rain."

"Roger that, Zero. Wait out."

Dan checked with Jones in sangar 2. He was all set with the Minimi, and Dan had the Gimpy.

There was a sudden boom from the compound, followed by a loud whoosh as the first mortar flew out of the launcher. Dan heard the whoosh become fainter, then a whine as the shell flew through the air. A dull thud and a mild tremor followed as the shell hit its target six hundred meters away.

That was the signal.

Immediately, the loud staccato burst from the machine guns started. Roderick kept loading the mortar shells and firing. As an SOG operative, Roderick had received paramilitary training, and knew how to operate most field artillery guns.

Smoke and the smell of cordite filled the compound. The ground shook with the sound of explosions. Dan did not have any earplugs, but he had picked up two spent cases of the 5.56mm ordnance from one of the rifles. They worked perfectly as earplugs. While the bombardment went on around him, Dan turned his back on it. Taking out his night sight, and putting his NVGs on, he kept a lookout on the south side.

Up to five klicks out, the place was deserted. He scanned 180 degrees. The edge of the village on the right was still empty. He could not see any telltale flashes of light, nor any movement with the NVGs. That right side would be his trouble zone.

It was all part of a plan. They had at least one klick to get to the bunker where they had stashed the quad bikes. One klick of open ground. Best to do that while the mortars and guns were pumping away. Create a diversion.

Dan switched off his mic. It was time for radio silence. He ran down the stairs of the sangar. Roderick and Mariam were standing there, bags on their backs. Mariam had cut her gown off, exposing her legs from the knees down.

"Ready?" Dan asked. They both nodded silently. The hook ladder was flung over the wall. The night sky was lit up behind them with exploding mortar shells. Jones had now taken over. Dan ran back up the sangar, took out his M4 and scanned the ground, ready to fire for cover.

CHAPTER 15

Dan saw the dim outlines of the two figures drop down the last rung of the ladder, and flatten themselves on the ground. Everything was bathed in the green hue of his NVGs. The two figures got up and ran, bent at the waist. Roderick was grabbing Mariam's hand. Dan tracked to the right. The edge of the village. Still nothing.

The Taliban would come soon. Their return fire was now hitting hard, rattling the sangars. Heavy ordnance punctured the air thick with smoke, whining above their heads. Dan looked behind him. The sky was lit up like a bonfire night. Tracer rockets zigzagged up into the air, their lights dimming and falling just short of the compound with explosions that shook the thick perimeter wall.

Dan knew the Taliban would launch a counteroffensive, and it was happening now. They could not wait till the rockets were fired – if that happened, they were finished. They would take heavy casualties. No, they would try and stop it. As long as the Taliban knew they were holed up in the compound, they would try and get inside tonight. Kill them all, and take over the missile silo. Job done.

But not while Dan Roy was alive.

Dan turned the magnified night sight of his M4 to the village. He could see at least forty Taliban. Three streets away, by the bazaar. Fifty meters and closing.

Dan took one last look from the south wall. Mariam and Rod were close to the bunker. They would get on the quad now, and get to the LZ. He looked at his watch. Twenty minutes to ETA.

Dan came down, and ran across to sangar 3. Jones was still pumping the mortar shells.

Dan hoped his ears were ok. The compound walls were getting blasted with bullets. Dan had to do something about the forty fighters closing in.

Their plan would be to target the main gate, where the walls dipped. Hook ladders, and they would be looking to get inside, under cover of heavy fire.

This was it. A desperate do-or-die.

Up in the sangar, Dan kept his head low against the volley of incoming fire. He grabbed the Gimpy, and checked it. He used his NVGs to locate the large group he had seen coming forward. For a while he could not see much. They would be sticking to the shadows, creeping in.

The sound of the blasting mortars masked all sound. The sky was lit up with the sight of distant and near explosions. Then he saw a movement. Close by. Twenty meters away. He could make out the snout of an RPG. Pointed straight at his sangar. Dan did not hesitate.

He let rip with the Gimpy, the heavy ordnance catching the RPG holder full in the chest, sending him flying off the ground. At close quarters, the power of the Gimpy was formidable. Dan literally shredded the remaining fighters who had dared to show their faces. He moved the Gimpy in an arc, the rounds smashing in through the mud walls of the huts, dislocating doors from their hinges.

He stopped after a while. He ran down, and tapped Jones on the shoulder. "Your turn," Dan said. "Go."

Jones went to get his rucksack, and Dan scrambled up the south wall sangar.

He heard a sound down below. Jones was now climbing up the ladder. Dan kept his lookout.

No movement from the right. He looked into the mid-distance. A small, black shape was moving away, fast. That must be Rod and Mariam on the quad bike, he thought with satisfaction. Below him, he saw Jones reach the other side, and then sprint across the open ground.

Only one left. Himself. Dan picked up his satellite phone.

"Alpha, this is Zero. Requesting FAS. Repeat requesting FAS." Fast air support. Maybe an F15, maybe a Reaper drone. Armed with enough Hellfire missiles to take out a small town.

Guptill's calm voice came on the line. "Zero, this is Alpha. 15 minutes to FAS. Do you copy?"

Shit. Shit.

Sweat poured down Dan's face. 15 minutes was too long. The Chinook would arrive on time to pick them up. But Dan had to stay behind to keep them at bay. If they were chased to the LZ, another firefight with the Chinook in the middle was not a prospect he looked forward to.

They could all die.

And with the Taliban closing in, 15 minutes was a long time. Dan could keep blasting away with the Gimpy, but he could not cover every angle.

"Alpha, I need it quicker. PID of multiple Tangos closing in."

"Negative, Zero. 15 minutes to FAS. Wait out."

Guptill hung up.

The compound was suddenly quiet. Bullets still poured in from outside, and loud explosions came from outside the perimeter wall. Dan came down the stairs quickly.

When the bombs fell on the compound, and the Scuds ignited, Dan knew he had to be at least one klick away. Otherwise he would not survive.

Dan caught a flicker of movement in the north-west perimeter wall. A shape. It became a head and shoulders, lifting itself above the parapet. Dan turned, and fired from his M4. There was a scream, and the figure fell backwards. Another explosion thundered against the perimeter wall, breaking off chunks of mud that rained down on the compound.

They were coming in. He saw more heads raising themselves above the parapet. He fired again from his M4, moving in an arc. More screams, and the sound of more bodies falling over.

He had no time to get to the Gimpy on sangar 3. He needed a vantage point, right now. He scurried up the stairs of the south wall sangar.

Dan ignored and kept firing. He sneaked a look at his watch.

13 minutes left.

He suddenly remembered the ILAW he had left. In the hut where he slept. Close to the base of the sangar he was on. Dan let off a long burst from his M4. He ran out of ammo, ejected the mag, unhooked a new one from his chest strap, and slapped it in. The he went down the stairs like lightning. He was inside the room in a flash. He got the rocket, and put it on his back using the straps.

He came out, and saw a figure at the edge of the compound. The first Taliban to make it inside. Dan fired before the man had time to react. The rounds shredded his chest, and he fell backwards. Without looking any further, Dan climbed. He needed to get up inside the sangar.

He got up there, and let loose a barrage of indiscriminate fire at the heads that kept popping up now all over the north wall of the compound.

Dan knew his position was insecure. He was exposed, for one thing. More dangerously, it would take the enemy only a second to figure out where the fire was coming from. Right on cue, rounds flew at him. Popping against the sandbags, bursting them open. Dan dived for cover. He heard a sudden loud whine and looked up in alarm.

An RPG, heading straight for him.

Dan needed to reach the wall behind him, with the ladder still dangling. But there was no time. If this was a direct hit, he was dead. He ran to the rear of the sangar, ready to jump. He felt calm all of a sudden. This was it.

The way it was meant to happen. He had done his job.

The RPG streaked in with a hellish glare of orange-yellow and burst against the sangar.

CHAPTER 16

The grenade hit below the sandbags, on the long, wooden legs of the fortified position. The flames flew up into the sangar. Licks of hot fire burned his skin. Dust and smoke saturated the air around him. Dan felt the wooden floor shake, and then do a sudden lurch forward.

Dan fell backwards, the breath leaving his chest on the impact. He knew what was happening. The legs had given way. If the sangar crashed into the compound, and he was in it, the Taliban would be on him right away.

He would fight with his kukri. Till enough bullets had drilled holes in him. He was ready, but it also meant he would not be able to hold them for long.

He heard shouts and screams from the compound.

"Allah hu Akbar!"

Blindly, he groped for his M4. It was still fixed to his shoulder strap. He plugged two grenades into the UGL, and fired them into the compound. He sprayed bullets down as well, but then felt the sangar tipping further down, into the compound.

Dan ran to the back of the platform. He jumped on top of the sandbags outside, then used the wooden lip as a leverage to jump onto the perimeter wall. He was weighed down by the ILAW on his back, so he jumped as hard as he could.

He aimed for the hook ladder, praying it would take his weight. He landed on the wall, fingers scratching wildly for purchase. He slipped down. His hands clawed for the ladder desperately. His palms burned as he scraped the mud wall, falling down further. He stretched out a hand for the ladder, blind panic seizing him.

The fingers of his right hand closed around the rungs of the ladder. Then his left hand.

Behind him, the sangar was blazing with fire. With a loud groaning sound, it crashed down. Dan climbed. As fast as he could. He was over the wall, and climbing down to the other side when he heard the sounds. They had figured it out. They were climbing the ladder from the other side.

Dan jumped the last five feet. He rolled over and came up, pointing his weapon at the wall. A head appeared and Dan fired. A scream, a thud, and the head disappeared.

8 minutes left.

Dan turned and ran. His left leg held up suddenly, and he winced in pain. He looked down. The ankle was wet with warm liquid. Blood. He could still put pressure on it, but it was going to slow him.

He had to be one klick away when the Hellfire missiles hit. He was not going to make it. He heard the whine of bullets. They kicked up dust around his feet. Dan turned and returned fire.

One head dropped with a scream, but more appeared. Ladders were being set up on the wall. Dan knew what he had to do. He unhooked the ILAW, and put the weapon on the floor. Working quickly, he took the weapon out of its case and pointed it towards the wall. His earplugs had fallen off, and he did not have any spent shells to use. There was no time.

He knelt on one knee, ignoring the bullets that splattered dust around him. He aimed at the largest collection of shapes appearing over the wall, and squeezed the trigger.

There was an ear-splitting explosion as the missile left its launcher, streaking in a yellow haze towards the compound wall. A massive bang followed as the weapon tore through the wall of the compound, splitting the south wall in two. Sparks of white light flew in the air, as did the Taliban who had been caught in the blast. Screams filled the air, drowned out by the missile's furious noise.

Dan did not wait to see the result. He had stumbled forward from the force of the weapon, and his ears were deaf. All he could hear was a ringing sound. He turned and ran as fast as he could. He zigzagged, while maintaining a straight course, trying to present himself as as small a target as possible.

He switched on his radio as he ran. It chirped in his ear immediately. It was Roderick's voice.

"Zero, this is Bravo One, are you receiving?"

Dan gasped as he replied. "Receiving, over."

On the radio, Dan could hear a loud buzz, and Roderick having to shout over it. That would be the Chinook coming in. He felt a surge of hope. They would get out alive. He was not so sure about himself.

But he was a survivor. Dying was not an option.

"Where is Jones?" Dan panted.

"Just arrived…." Roderick said something else, but the sound was drowned out by the rotor waves of the big bird landing.

Dan ran as hard as his injured left leg would allow. He only had his rucksack on the back now, so he could run faster, in theory. In practice, he realized he was limping.

He looked at his watch.

5 minutes left.

He was now close to the bunker where he had left his quad. He heaved a sigh of relief. Twenty meters away.

Movement. From the side wall of the bunker three figures appeared. Dan could barely make them out: his NVGs had fallen off. He could see them crouching, getting ready to fire.

Dan fired the M4 from his right hip with one hand. With the other he unhooked a frag grenade. He lobbed the grenade as hard as he could, and dived for the ground, still firing from the M4. He heard screams as his bullets found their mark. As soon as he hit the ground, the grenade went off with an orange fireball, shrapnel flying everywhere. He was just out of range, but he still kept his head down. In five seconds, he was firing again, staying flat on the ground. He ran out of ammo. He hooked another mag, and slapped it in. It was his last one.

3 minutes left.

Dan got up and ran as hard as he could. The noise came from behind him. They were chasing him. Bullets kicked up dust around his feet. They had found him. Dan cursed, and turned around. He saw them clearly in the IR vision of his M4 night sight. Five figures approaching, firing straight at him. At moments like this, when he was almost out of ammo, and outnumbered, calm was more important than a hot head.

It had saved his life every time. Dan aimed, picking out the one closest. He dropped him with a double tap to the face, then focused on the others. They went down before their throats, ripped apart by the bullets, could even make a sound.

But Dan did hear a sound. Behind him. He turned quickly. One of the survivors of the grenade blast had lurched closer. Five meters away. Dan could make out the headgear, and the loose dishdasha on his body. The man had a handgun, and he was starting to lift it. Dan fired, and the rounds carved out a hole in the man's chest. He fell backwards.

Feverishly, Dan glanced at his wrist.

1 minute left.

He looked up at the night sky. The drone was getting into position, high above. Had to be a drone, for he had not heard a fighter jet. He got up and ran. He could hear more shouts behind him. The reinforcements had found their fallen comrades, and were now chasing after him. Dan jumped over the dead bodies near the bunker, and headed behind it.

30 seconds.

Dan used the bunker wall as cover, and fired at the ones who were approaching. They were out in the open. It wasn't even a contest. He fired three bursts, then decided to save his ammo. He still had two grenades left. He took out the pin, and lobbed one, flat and hard. It exploded on impact, taking out three more.

15 seconds.

Dan ran like a madman. The bunker was approximately 800 meters away from the compound, so he needed to get another 200 meters. He put his head down, and pumped his muscular legs faster than he ever had in his life.

He saw a wadi on his left and turned into it, his chest heaving with the effort of the sprint. Sweat blinded his eyes.

The slopes of the wadi obscured a direct view of the compound – a dark hump in the background, fading around the bend. Dan's feet scattered stones as he ran along the dry riverbank.

Five seconds.

Four

Three

Two

One…

The sky was illuminated like it was daylight. Fissure spread along the horizon, crackling like white lightning. A thunderclap sounded, but very close, like it was next to his ears. The ground swelled and heaved around him like it was an ocean.

Dan screamed as he flew in the air. He landed in a heap, covering his head with his hands. The ground was soft, being a wadi, but the small stones stung him sharply. Debris rained down on him. The ground shook and thundered, the aftershock trembling through the bowels of earth deep below them. Dust covered the air.

Then there was silence. An eerie, total, absolute silence. Like a blackness without any light.

The silence of death.

Dan shook his head. Dust flew off his hair, choking him. He coughed and spat. He looked up. In the distance, a giant cloud was lifting up into the sky, lit up from below. Sparks of blue lightning flashed at its base. It was an ethereal sight.

Dan tried to stand up. He winced as his left ankle touched the ground. He checked his ammo. Not good news. Only eight rounds left, and one grenade. He fiddled with the radio. Thankfully, he got a signal. His GPS was still working. He got his bearings quickly, and started moving.

He glanced behind as he ran. Expecting bullets any minute. His radio chirped.

"Zero, this is Night Sky, do you copy?" It was the Chinook pilot. Dan breathed out.

"Loud and clear. Are the others ok?" Dan asked.

"Yes. Grouped at the LZ." A pause as the pilot checked the time. "We've got five minutes to evacuation."

"On my way," Dan said. He could not afford to slow down. The deathly quiet around him persisted, but he did not let that fool him. There could be Tangos all around. They had spread out already, hence they had been waiting near the bunker.

Dan ran fast. He ignored the pain in his left leg. His senses were alive to the night around him, expecting gunfire any second.

His main worry was the Chinook being targeted again. This whole area was now awake, and Taliban would be crawling around. Chances are, they had seen the Chinook already.

CHAPTER 17

Dan crested the top of a small hill, his fingers gripping the rocky surface. Below him, in the valley, he could see the outline of the Chinook. Its engine was off, and the rotors were silent.

They were waiting for him. Dan did not like it that the engines were off. If there was a contact, then it would take some time for the bird to fire up. He scrambled down the hill as fast as he could.

Roderick was the first one he saw. He, Derek, and two of the flight crew had formed a perimeter around the Chinook. Dan shouted out his name and call sign, and they put their weapons down.

Dan said urgently, "Get the bird moving, now. Tangos are on their way."

One of the flight crew picked up his weapon and ran back. Dan followed with the others. His throat was parched dry, and he could not swallow. His left leg was hurting like mad. But he, and the others, were still alive.

The Chinook's massive tailgate was lowered, and he clambered on-board.

"You took your time," a female voice said. Dan peered into the darkness, and saw Mariam. There was relief mixed with admiration on her face. Dan stepped up to her. She stood up.

"Take off your boots, and let me look at your leg," she said. Before Dan could answer, a shot rang out. More rounds followed, aimed for them. Dan grabbed Mariam and went down. He looked up, and his blood froze.

Roderick was on the floor, lying motionless.

Dan shouted, "Lift the tailgate, now!"

He lifted his weapon, and fired out even as the tailgate rose up. But it was slow. More rounds kept pinging inside.

"I need ammo," Dan shouted. Jones heard him, and lobbed him a new M4 rifle. Dan grabbed it and fired. He pulled Roderick in. It was an abdomen wound. Blood poured out of it. Dan looked at the back and found the exit wound. It was to the side. Below the level of the spleen. Chances were that it had missed the major abdominal organs and arteries. He put pressure on the wound.

"Hang in there, Rod!" he shouted at his pale face. Rod moved his lips but no sound came.

Bullets were raining on the Chinook now. Mariam appeared beside him. She began to put a dressing on Roderick from the first aid box.

The rotors were moving. The engines of the mighty bird were loud, throbbing the inside of the carriage.

"Take the windows," Dan shouted at Jones. With one of the flight crew, they returned fire from each of the windows. The ground shook beneath their feet, and a blizzard of dust obscured their vision. But the firing continued.

With a huge lurch, the Chinook lifted off the ground. Within seconds it was airborne. Dan did not stop firing. He saw the convoy of cars that had appeared a hundred meters away. The bird lifted higher up, and soon the cars and enemy figures were smaller, like pins on the ground.

Dan threw his weapon down, and slumped backwards against the seat. He rolled over to Roderick. Mariam was still pressing on his wound. Dan checked: the blood seepage was less.

Jones handed Dan a flask of water. Gratefully, Dan downed it.

In half an hour, they had reached base. Roderick was carried out on a stretcher. Mariam met his eyes before she alighted. Dan looked at her and nodded. She smiled at him. Then she was led away by a uniformed private.

Dan staggered inside the base, and saw Guptill standing there. They walked into a room, where Dan sprawled in a chair.

"You did well," Guptill said.

Dan did not reply. Guptill said, "There's a new mission waiting for you."

Dan shook his head. It was always like this with Intercept. One mission faded into another. Like night into day. But right now, he needed to rest. Guptill knew that, too.

The older man said, "Have a sleep. Medics are waiting to look at you. Let me know tomorrow."

Dan said, "You knew about the compound, didn't you?"

Guptill paused. He opened his mouth to say something but then seemed to change his mind. He said, "Yes, we did. But we did not know for certain. The CIA guys could not confirm on radio."

"You could have given me a heads-up."

Guptill smiled. "I figured you would find out soon enough. I didn't want you to approach the mission any differently. That's why I kept it from you."

Guptill turned, and walked out the door.

Dan stood up. Every bone in his body ached. Tomorrow was another day. He would live to fight it, and whatever else came his way.

THE END

HIDDEN AGENDA

A DAN ROY THRILLER
DAN ROY SERIES, BOOK 1

Mick Bose

For Mersedeh, my secret, and special, agent

CHAPTER 1

Soho's narrow, crowded streets form the bustling heart of London city. Under its glaring neon lights, and inside its intimate, cozy pubs, gather the bohemians who give London its character.

The artists, the losers, the drug dealers. The nine-to-five single mothers who work in the lap dancing parlors in the evenings. The immigrants of Chinatown working for less than minimum wage in the glitter of Chinatown. The bankers stopping by for a drink, and perhaps a small bag of cocaine.

Dan Roy walked down the street into this melting pot. He kept his head low and tried to be inconspicuous, but being Dan Roy, that wasn't easy. He was a shade over six feet, two hundred and twenty pounds, with wide shoulders and biceps that strained the fabric of any shirt he wore. His brown hair was longer now, and it fell over his large, dark eyes. Eyes that were restless, but also expressive. They glinted like diamonds in the neon lights of London's underbelly.

In truth, Dan was scanning the crowd for signs of threat. He did not expect any danger, but looking for threats was part of Dan's DNA. He had spent years as a Black Ops specialist for the most secretive Black Ops organization of them all - Intercept. That experience had hard-wired anticipation of danger into his brain. He would and could kill without hesitation if the need arose. For self-protection, if nothing else.

But he did not want to.

The Army and Intercept had trained Dan to become a ruthless killer. It wasn't difficult, given that he was already a member of Squadron B, Delta Force, by the time Intercept came knocking on his door.

With Intercept, Dan had found his calling in life. He had been a warfighter already, but Black Ops took his skills to a different level. His kills became the stuff of legend.

But there was a price. His soul had no respite from constant war. The ravages of combat can be like claw marks on the mind. He had plenty of those.

He needed a break, like what he was enjoying now. He could not talk about what happened, but a clean break had made him sane again.

Dan saw the sign for the Duke of Edinburgh pub, and stepped inside. Soft, glowing lights and the warmth of human bodies standing close together enveloped him. He pushed his way to the noisy bar. The bar girl recognized him.

"Hey, Dan," the red-haired woman said. Their eyes met and her cheeks went red as Dan stared at her with his dark, intense eyes. Lucy Sparks was petite, no more than five feet six. Her figure was slender, but she was filled out in the right places. A figure that Dan liked. He stopped by the pub to chat to her, and often had his lunch there as well. Lucy was a student at Birkbeck College, doing a part-time PhD. She did her college in the mornings, and started work in the afternoon, staying till late at night.

"Hey, Lucy," Dan said. "How are things?" He had to raise his voice above the din.

"Busy," Lucy rolled her eyes. "How are you?"

"All the better for seeing you."

Lucy smiled, her cheeks touching crimson again. She did not disguise the fact that she had a thing for him. They flirted often, and Dan was on the verge of asking her out on a date.

"What can I get you?" Lucy asked.

"A pint of Camden Hells lager please." His mouth watered. When it came to craft beer, few places in the world topped London. Including Charlotte, NC, and that was saying something. He thanked Lucy, closed his eyes and took a long sip from the tall pint glass.

He looked around him carefully. The usual smattering of creative types, financial professionals, students and workers. He heard a cellphone buzz. It was nearby, but not his. Dan did not carry a cellphone. He did not want to be traced. He did not want to be called. He did not want to wake up and curl his fingers around the butt of his Sig Sauer P226 the second his eyes flew open.

He wanted to enjoy his drink in the company of strangers. This was the start of a trip for him. From London, he would fly to Morocco, and spend a week in Tangiers. From there he would fly to Mumbai, and taste the waters of the Arabian Sea with the hippies in Goa. Thailand beckoned after that. He had not planned any further. It was good not to have a plan, to go where his eyes would take him. He was looking forward to it.

Dan finished his drink, paid, winked at a blushing Lucy, and left. He would have two more drinks, catch a theater in the West End, then end up in a restaurant in Chinatown before going back to his small hotel on Charing Cross Road. A small en suite room cost a bomb, but the money he had made working for Intercept was more than adequate for his purposes.

Dan was close to Soho Square Gardens when he felt someone following him.

A shadow crossed the street ten yards behind. Dan stopped to buy a newspaper inside a kiosk. He looked but saw nothing apart from tourists. That alerted him further. A professional would not have fallen for that simple trick.

The gardens loomed in front of him. Dan went in, and the footsteps followed. Dan knew the park well. It was well maintained, with the help of London's high tax-paying public. He walked inside the gates quickly, then suddenly broke into a run.

He disappeared round the thick stump of a pine tree. He could hear the pounding feet now. Two men, running fast. Panicking that they had lost him.

Who? Why? Two questions he didn't have answers to. It didn't matter. Old reflexes took over.

Dan waited till the second man was about to pass him. In a blur of movement, he grabbed the man's midriff and pulled him under the tree. Dan slammed the man's head against an overhanging branch. He followed it up with a short arm jab to the right jaw. The blow sent the already dizzy man stumbling backwards. He sagged against the tree, unconscious.

Dan had dived for the ground in preparation for a bullet streaking towards him. The man's partner would have drawn his weapon. British cops did not carry guns, but Dan was willing to bet these guys were not British. He crawled behind the tree trunk and waited, his senses working overtime. It was quiet, the sounds of traffic now faded in the distance.

He didn't expect what he heard next. A voice he knew very well.

The voice said, "Dan, it's me. Come out and show yourself."

CHAPTER 2

Dan did not answer. After a beat, the voice spoke again.

"Don't be afraid, Dan. If I wanted you dead, there would be no need for this. I just want to talk."

The logic was irrefutable. The speaker was not one to make idle threats. Dan remembered his first mission as a Delta operative. This man had been his CO. Later on, his handler for Intercept. Major John Guptill. The man who had helped to sharpen his skills when he entered Delta and make him into a killing machine.

The only man Dan trusted implicitly. After all that had happened, his trust of intelligence agencies was broken. He would never trust any intelligence agency, big or small, ever again. They played games that had wrecked his life.

John Guptill had pulled him back when he had been staring at the dark abyss. The only one who had cared.

Guptill said, "We haven't got all night, Dan. Tell me, what's it gonna be?"

Dan stayed behind the tree and said, "Tell these guys to throw their weapons where I can see them."

Guptill gave out an order, and there was a sound of metal clattering on the floor. Dan saw a Colt M1911 and a Sig P226 handgun appear near him. They were close enough for him to reach. He saw a shadow appear. An average-sized man, slightly stooped and wearing a black overcoat. The figure spread its hands. It was John Guptill.

Dan stepped out. In the same movement, he picked up the Sig off the floor, and kicked the Colt to one side. He held the gun by his side.

Dan said, "You could have just tapped me on the shoulder."

"Where, inside a pub?"

"How long have you been following me for?"

Dan had spent the last month in London. He had traveled around Surrey and Berkshire, but not gone too far. He had got sloppy. He should have picked these guys up ages ago.

"The last two weeks," Guptill said.

"Why?"

"Shall we sit down?"

Guptill knew better than anyone else that Dan had left Intercept. He had done his final, exit interview. Promised his silence. A break of that promise was rewarded with death. He had also collected his last paycheck. He had not received all of it as yet: the money came to him in stages. Intercept wanted to be sure Dan did not divulge any critical information to the media or a foreign government before they paid him for the last time.

The question buzzed around his head. If Guptill knew this, then why was he here with two guys packing weapons?

His old CO seemed to read his mind. "First off, there was no other way to contact you. Your last known location was London, UK. These guys would not have harmed you. Their weapons are for my protection."

Dan looked at his mentor. Under the street lights, Guptill's silvery buzz cut appeared dull. But his blue eyes glinted.

Dan said, "You have an apartment in London, right? You come and go. Why do you need protection here?"

In answer Guptill reached a hand inside his jacket pocket. Anyone else did that movement, Dan would have stiffened. But this was the only man he trusted. Guptill sat down on the park bench close to the tree and pulled out a brown paper packet. He shone a flashlight on it. He took out a sheaf of photos and handed them over to Dan.

Dan looked up briefly. One of the men was helping his injured colleague up from the ground. They leaned against the tree trunk, keeping an eye on him. Dan looked away. He took the photos from Guptill's hand, who shone a light on them.

The photo showed a collection of black cylinders with yellow marks on them. Fins at the top and bottom. Hellfire missiles. Stacked next to a pile of Pathway missiles. Air-to-surface missiles used in Reaper drones, and also fired from a range of other aircraft. The next photo showed Heckler & Koch 417, and M4 SOPMOD carbines, all modified for Special Operations. But the locations were odd. They were on a mud floor, inside a mud hut.

Guptill said, "A Marine recon platoon chanced upon this in northeast Afghanistan. Inside a Taliban compound. Not controlled by us."

Dan said, "How did it get there?"

Guptill said, "The compound belongs to a senior Al-Qaeda commander, sheltered by the Taliban. That man is now on the run. We know where he is hiding." Guptill looked at Dan.

Dan knew where this was headed. He handed the photos back to Guptill. He said, "No."

Guptill said, "These are our current weapons. Taliban have the capability to fire them from the Russian helicopters they have. It negates a huge tactical advantage for us."

Dan said, "Who is supplying them?"

"That's what I'm trying to find out. But first we need to get this guy, and confiscate the weapons."

Dan said again, "No. Get someone else."

"You'll get paid."

"I've already been paid."

"Not all of it. Plus, this time, you get a bonus."

"You could give anyone a bonus. Why me?"

Deep inside, Dan knew the answer. The man opposite him had been there on the last day of his Delta selection, when Dan almost died of dehydration. The notorious 40-mile hike with a 45-pound backpack through the remotest Appalachian Mountains. A feat that still disabled a soldier or two. Less than ten percent made the grade.

Dan was the first one in his group to make it back. He broke the all-time record for speed of completion of the final stage.

A record that still held firm.

Guptill had seen his potential and taken him under his wing. After his father's death, Guptill was the man who had become a father figure to him.

Guptill said, "The same reason I now have two bodyguards with me."

"You cannot trust anyone."

"Correct."

Dan sighed and rubbed his hands on his face. He said, "What do you know so far?"

"Not much. Somehow these weapons are getting up to Afghanistan. And if they can get up there, shit, they could potentially end up anywhere."

Dan understood. Any number of jihadis would love to get their hands on these weapons.

Guptill said, "Dan, this is a really big deal. JSOC contacted me. Remember Jim McBride?"

Dan nodded. He had heard of Lt. Colonel Jim "Fighter" McBride. One of the head honchos of Joint Special Operations Command at Fort Bragg, NC.

Guptill reached inside and took out another photo. Dan took it. It was a black and white photo of a man lying face-down in a pool of blood.

Guptill said, "That's the CIA agent who got me the photos. The cops found his body in London yesterday. They alerted MI5, who alerted the CIA."

Dan said, "Sir, you know I have left all this behind. If I do this, I get sucked back in."

Guptill leaned forward. "What if it was me in that photo you were holding, Dan?"

Dan stopped. What would he do? What *could* he do?

"I cannot trust anyone else on this. One last time. I swear I'll never call on you again. Not for anything like this."

Dan said, "There's something else. Intercept told you to come looking for me. You're not telling me the whole story."

Guptill sat back in the seat. The wooden slats creaked. He breathed out into the mild spring air. Dan waited.

Guptill said, "This is top secret. Officially, you don't have clearance anymore."

"Officially, you shouldn't be here asking me to go back to work. I quit, remember?"

"Whatever. Just remember what I said."

"I got it."

Guptill lowered his voice. "NSA, and GCHQ over here, have picked up a lot of chatter from online jihadi networks. A big attack is planned. In a European capital. Paris, Frankfurt or London. We don't know when."

"What does that have to do with this compound in 'Stan?"

"People who stashed those weapons there, you don't think they could use them here?"

Dan was quiet for a while. Then he said, "So getting the Al-Qaeda guy would help you to find the missing links."

"Right now, he's the only link we got. We need to get those weapons as well before the Taliban get to use them."

"And then what?"

Guptill asked, "What do you mean?"

Dan said, "What happens to me after the mission is over? Will Intercept cut me loose, or keep an eye on me?"

Dan had not planned to stay in London for long. He thought about the airline tickets he had bought. He had used cash, but someone must be keeping tabs on his bank account. The thought was unnerving. He might never be free of these guys. Dan was trained to be a killer. He seldom felt any emotion. But he did now.

Anger. Anger that they were still following him around, like he was some criminal.

He had done nothing wrong.

Dan stood up. He looked at Guptill who raised himself up slowly.

Dan said, "I guess you know where I'm staying. Well, I'm headed back. But I'm not *going* back, if you know what I mean."

Guptill stared at him for a while, then nodded. "I don't want to force you. It is your decision. I just told you the facts."

Dan said, "Thank you." He looked at the two guys, one of whom who was still rubbing his chin. He raised a hand.

"Sorry about that, guys. Next time, just come up and ask me. It's much easier."

CHAPTER 3

Dan went off to the nearby West End to catch an evening show. The show was enjoyable, but he watched it with half a mind only. After dinner in Chinatown, he headed back to his small hotel in Charing Cross Road. It was opposite Leicester Square, down an alley that dated back to the Victorian times. The front seemed like a shop that had shut down, and the sign was hidden behind a hanging basket of flowers. It was barely visible unless one looked hard. It was a narrow-terraced building, a common finding in London, and the interior was quaint beyond belief.

Dan stepped inside, and a doorbell chimed. The striped blue and gray wallpaper made the place even smaller than it was. Brits loved dark wallpaper. At the reception, the balding head of Rupert St John-Smythe, the proprietor in whose family the building had been for the last three generations, looked up as Dan came in.

"Ah, Mr Roy," Rupert said.

"Hey," Dan replied.

"Nice evening?"

"Caught up with some old friends."

"Splendid. However, and if you don't mind me saying so, you look rather tired."

Dan leaned against the table. "What you trying to say?"

A look of embarrassment passed Rupert's face. "Oh, nothing at all. Perhaps impertinent of me to suggest such a thing. I was merely..."

Dan said, "Rupert."

"Yes?"

"Chill. I was just busting your balls."

Rupert looked confused again, then his face cleared. "Ah, that expression. Means you speak in jest."

"I do."

Rupert said, "May I offer you a nightcap?"

It was just what Dan needed. He did not keep alcohol in his room. He did not want to rely on it. At night when he could not sleep, he went for a walk. The tourist areas of Central London were well lit and safe at night. And common thugs or street gangs did not worry Dan.

Lately, he had spent many nights walking around the lonely streets. It had made him appreciate the city better, without the usual throng of tourists. At night, and on his own, the city was beautiful. He often walked down to Waterloo Bridge, and leaned against the stones, watching the rushing black river underneath. The tall spires of Westminster shone golden yellow like a dream in the street lights. The solitude gave him some respite from the visions in his head.

He said, "I would like that."

Rupert reached behind the desk and pulled out a bottle of Drambuie brandy. He poured two glasses and passed one to Dan.

Rupert said, "You know, this used to be The Queen Mother's favorite drink."

Dan knocked it back. The liquid burned his throat and warmed his insides. He shook his head. If it was good for The Queen Mother, it was good for him.

Rupert smiled, and poured another.

After three shots of Drambuie, Dan was ready for bed. He insisted on paying for the drinks, but Rupert said it was his personal supply. Dan went upstairs, put his sixteen-inch kukri knife under his pillow, and fell into a dark, dreamless sleep.

His eyes flew open when he heard the birds outside. His primal instinct, as always, was to reach for a weapon. A hardwired instinct. Then he relaxed, and sank back on the bed. It was strangely comforting to lie in that old bed in an old English Bed and Breakfast, and listen to the birds tweet outside. The first portent of spring. The first thawing of the ice in his soul. As he lay there, drifting in and out of sleep, he remembered that fateful day in Sanaa, the capital of Yemen.

Sanaa was a medieval fortress city of brown terracotta houses and white minarets. His mission: to blow up a bus carrying a local chapter of Al-Shabaab terrorists. He had staked out the bus garage for two days. He had surveyed the route. In the dead of night, he laid Claymore anti-personnel mines across the stretch of highway the bus would travel on. Next morning, he waited by the highway, hidden in the brush, detonator in hand.

As the bus got closer, he saw something that took the breath out of his chest. Little arms poking out the windows. The cries of children. He saw it clearly with his binoculars. For some reason, the route and transport had changed. This bus was taking kids to school. Thirty or forty kids, playing and screaming. His fingers were on the detonator, gripping it tightly. He had seconds to act. He heard the voice in his earphone.

"Take the bus out, now."

Intercept's support team. Dan's knuckles were white on the detonator. The bus came closer. He could still see it clearly – the eyes of a boy, about 8 years old, leaning out the bus, staring directly at him.

"Take the hit. DO IT!" the voice growled in his ear again.

Dan's eyes opened wide. His nostrils flared. The bus was ten yards away. He could hear the jingles of some music from the radio. Dan had never failed on a mission. A target was as good as dead when their folder was passed to his hands.

The cries of the children got louder. Dan's fingers were like claws. His hand shook. Within seconds, the bus was on him.

Now or never. That boy's eyes never left him. Dan would remember those eyes till the day he died. He saw them now, as he lay still on this English spring morning. Wide, innocent eyes. A face that would never harm him. A child who would never harm anyone. Dan Roy was a killer, but he did not kill children.

His fingers went slack. He lowered the detonator from his hand. The voice on his mic was going crazy. Dan ripped the earpiece off his ears, and lowered his head to the ground.

Early the next day, he was flown back to base. He wanted out. He promised his silence. They didn't like it, but they let him go. Dan knew there would never be a way back in. He had burned his bridges.

Till now. There was something odd about the whole thing. First off, Intercept were following him around. They knew where he was. Intercept always did things for a reason. In his heart of hearts, Dan had not wanted to leave after a failed mission. But he could not have fulfilled his last mission. If that is what Intercept wanted him to do…

But Intercept would know what was going on inside Dan's mind. He had been subjected to days of psychological profiling. Every thought of his was known to them. It had not bothered him before. Now, it made him uneasy as hell.

Guptill was sent for a reason. Dan would not listen to anyone else. They knew that. They also knew a mission like this – to potentially avoid a terrorist attack in a big city – would appeal to Dan. It could be his last chance to leave Intercept with a flawless record.

Well, maybe it was time to prove them wrong.

Dan showered and dried himself. His thick biceps, and the broad muscles of his back rippled as he went through a yoga routine afterwards. Then he dressed and went downstairs for breakfast.

Rupert had got the chef to make him a full English breakfast. He got stuck into sausages (called bangers in London), bacon, beans, tomatoes, toasted bread and black pudding. After breakfast, he slurped on his cup of Earl Grey Assam tea. Earl Grey English tea was cool, but not strong enough for him. Ever since he had started living in London, a whole new world of teas had opened up to him. The stronger ones worked almost like coffee.

As he walked out the door, he felt in his pockets to make sure he had everything. His fingers brushed the piece of paper on which Guptill had written down the cellphone number. Dan walked out towards the subway, or tube station of Leicester Square. He looked around him as he walked.

He picked up his first tail on the tube train as it rumbled through the underground. A middle-aged man with a newspaper. Dan came out on the other side of the river at Embankment, and walked down the river path towards the Tate Modern art gallery. Inside the gallery, it was easier to keep an eye on his tail. There were now two of them.

He had said no to Guptill. Why were they still following him?

CHAPTER 4

It was late afternoon by the time Dan had lunch and returned to Soho. He had managed to lose the two tails, but he was sure there would be others around. Inside the rabbit warren of Soho's narrow streets he could duck and dive, giving his followers the slip. Trained in countersurveillance, Dan used every trick in the book. He changed trains three times, caught a cab and jumped off at a traffic light, and doubled around himself till he got back to Soho.

Now he needed a drink. He watched the entrance of the Duke of Edinburgh pub for ten minutes. It was still early, but there were a fair number of people inside already. Through the windows, he could see Lucy cleaning the tables. She straightened, and tucked a loose strand of her ginger hair behind her ear. Dan could see that she was wearing a yellow tee shirt and jeans. When she leaned over the tables, he could see a flash of her cleavage. He smiled.

Dan took one last look around, then headed for the doors of the pub. Lucy looked up as he opened the door. She was twenty feet away from him. Dan stood at the doors of the pub, and smiled at her. She caught his eyes, put her hands on her hips, and tilted her head. She opened her mouth as if to say something.

The blast of heat exploded in a giant yellow fireball behind her. It ripped apart the long bar, flung tables, chairs and bodyparts out of the windows. Dan was lifted up in the shock wave and flew back from the door, which tore off from its hinges. His back smashed against the wall of a building opposite, more than ten feet away. He crumpled to the floor.

He was still alive. Breathing. He felt something hot and sticky coursing down his face. Glass and wooden debris rained down around him. He covered his head and let the falling fragments subside.

Silence. That total, awful silence immediately after an explosion. He looked up, and groaned as he pulled himself to his feet. There was a black, smoking hole where the doors had been. The two long windows had been smashed out. Hanging from the nearest window, a headless body lay upside down like a rag doll.

Dan's heart wrenched inside. He coughed and belched out smoke. He got to the doorway and leaned in. Black soot covered the floor. It hid the slick of blood, but not the charred, cut human remains. Dan ignored the ghastly sight around him. He limped over to where Lucy had been standing. There was no sign of her. He looked down in the smoke and haze, and heard the few groans that came from a survivor. At his feet, he found a pair of Doc Marten boots with purple laces, still smoking from the explosion. They were Lucy's shoes. Dan picked one up and pressed it against his chest.

A fearful pressure was building inside him. Rage, hurt, sorrow were mixing into a deadly cocktail, ready to burst out like a grenade. His fingers flicked down to his belt line. No, he did not have a weapon. He wanted one. He could smell blood, and felt something wet on his face. Not blood. Something lighter, and coming from his eyes.

He held the shoe tightly in his hand, and walked over to the nearest groaning survivor. His torso was half-blown off, and his left leg was missing. He would not survive long. Dan had done this before, but today it made him sick to the core. He rolled over a few bodies. It was horrible work.

He found her finally, slumped over the legs of a table. The left side of her body – the arm and legs, were missing. He knelt down and passed a hand over her red hair, now burned black. Dan was no stranger to death. He had pulled out corpses from demolished buildings before, and taken photos of kill targets as proof. He had not known Lucy for that long. But seeing her down there moved something inside him. He did not know what it was. Something like pain, an emotion that was alien to him.

He made a guttural, choking noise from his throat and stood up. His lungs were heaving. He opened his mouth, smelling the death and destruction around him. What he had lived for all his adult life. What made him who he was.

Did he bring this upon Lucy? And to the others inside this place – all human beings with a home and a family – now lying in a macabre assortment of flesh and bone. The thought came quickly and left. He could have been killed in any number of ways. Killing him like this would only bring attention upon his assassins.

This was a terrorist attack in the heart of London. The attack that Guptill had warned him about.

Dan heard a groaning noise above him. He looked up as dust fell on his eyes. The sound grew and something crashed down behind him. Dan lifted Lucy's half-body and ran for the door. The building, like most of Soho's structures, was an old one, and the ceiling had wooden rafters. They had cracked in the explosion and the heat was now bending them. A large black beam smashed down in front of him. With a huge groan, the windows started to cave inwards. Dust filled the air.

Dan dodged the falling plaster and bricks, and stumbled out. He laid Lucy's battered body on the road. A crowd had gathered. Sirens wailed, getting louder. Behind him, there was a huge crash, and the building collapsed completely. Dan picked Lucy up again, and stumbled out farther for protection. There was a whistle, and running boots indicated the arrival of policemen.

The next few hours were a blur to Dan. An ambulance arrived, and conducted the grisly task of taking the torn victims away. A paramedic arrived and spoke to Dan. She put a hand on his arm. He was holding Lucy's remaining arm tightly, and the paramedic gently removed it. A stretcher lifted her body into the ambulance.

Dan watched the ambulance thread its way out of the crowd. He knew her family would be notified and they would come down to see her body. Burial would be over the next few days. Dan hung his head. He put his hands inside his pockets.

When he took his right hand out, he was holding the piece of paper with Guptill's number on it.

CHAPTER 5

Guptill answered straight away. Dan was inside a typical, red, London telephone booth. He leaned against the side, wiping the sweat and blood from his face.

"It's me," Guptill said.

Dan swallowed, then said, "The mission. I am in."

Guptill did not answer for a while. Then he said, "Where are you?"

Dan did not reply. "The mission," he repeated like a robot. "I need the file."

Guptill was quiet again. Then he said, "Meet me at the north end of Hyde Park Corner. There's an oak tree next to the statue of Oliver Cromwell. I'll be wearing a black overcoat."

Dan said, "ETA one hour." He hung up.

He watched for a while from the phone booth. Then he slid out, and walked down a series of alleys. People and policemen rushed around him. He could hear human voices screaming, and the wail of more sirens. He stopped at a dead end alley, and walked to the end of it. There was a row of lock-up garages. Dan went to the last one, and inserted a key in the lock. He took one last look around him, then went inside. He shut the door, locked it and turned on the light switch. The space was roughly twenty by ten feet. In the middle rested the rusting hulk of a Austin Minor car from the 1920s.

The Cockney gangster who had sold Dan the garage had said the car was worth a lot of money if it was refurbished. Dan had replied that if it was, then the gangster would be doing it himself. The man had taken his money and left.

Dan knelt by the car, and slid under on his back. He had taken a screwdriver from a toolbox at the side. He worked for the next ten minutes, removing a portion of the chassis. When the last part came off, it showed a hollow space inside. The space was about four feet long. Inside, there was a black metal case. Dan removed the case. Then he crawled out of the car.

He went to the door and looked outside. The cul-de-sac was empty. He went back inside and leaned over the metal case. Inside, there was an M4 carbine rifle, one fitted out to the SOPMOD or Special Operations Peculiar Modifications. Dan checked the night sight, the Underslung Grenade Launcher, and the various objects he could fit on the Picatinny rail. He also had a Sig Sauer P226, his favorite handgun. He expelled the magazine, slid back the breech, then sprung it back. Everything worked.

He checked the five boxes of ammo he had, for each weapon. To one side, he had another curved kukri knife, slightly shorter at eleven inches. He put the knife and the Sig in his belt line, and kept the M4 inside the metal case. He picked up the case, locked the door, and headed out into Soho.

*****

Guptill was waiting for him under the oak tree. He was sat on a bench. Dan couldn't see the other two men, but he knew they would be around.

Guptill looked up as Dan approached. "Jesus," he said. "What happened?"

Dan did not say anything. He sat down. Guptill stared at him for a while then said, "Shit. You were there."

Dan stared stonily ahead. His eyes saw nothing, he felt nothing. The only thing that mattered was the Sig and the kukri in his belt line. They gave him all the comfort he needed. Like an extension of his body that had been missing for a while.

Guptill said, "I'm sorry."

"Did you know?" Dan asked. He was aware that Guptill had turned to look at him, but he ignored it.

Guptill's voice hardened. "If that is what you believe, then walk the fuck away now. Don't come back."

Dan nodded. Guptill had not known about the specific location. That was all the confirmation he needed.

Guptill said, "You knew someone there." It was a statement, not a question. Dan did not respond.

"I can see it in your face," Guptill said. "You should not be on a mission for personal reasons. You know that."

"It's not personal."

"You sure about that?"

"Yes."

Guptill said, "Dan, I had to cover for you last time. Told them to leave you alone. This time around, I can't do that."

"Last time was different," Dan said.

"And this time won't be? Who was she?"

Dan stood up. "Do you want me on the job, or not?"

"Sit down. I need to make sure you are not distracted on this job. It's a big one. We need a kill and intel, or live target capture. You have to be firing on all cylinders."

"You know I will," Dan said. He caught Guptill's eye. He read the look. Guptill knew him well. Now he was seeing something new in Dan's eyes, and it was confusing him. But Guptill did not look angry or disappointed. There was curiosity in his eyes, and what seemed like an acceptance. Dan looked away.

Guptill said, "Give me your word, Dan. I need you to focus. For all our sakes."

Something in his voice made Dan stop. He looked at his old CO's face. There was an earnest plea in Guptill's tone. Dan knew he would not use it without good reason.

"I am focused. What time is the flight?" Dan asked.

"2000 hours. From RAF Brize Norton." Dan had flown on missions from that Royal Air Force base before.

"Who is my contact?"

"An Intercept guy called Rory Burns. Call him Burns. He's a good guy. You can trust him."

Dan had heard of Burns in the past, but never met him. He provided intel, and handled some of the operatives.

Guptill said, "Burns will meet you in Afghanistan. You fly out alone. Your kit will be there. At the RAF base there is a weapon armory. Pick what you want."

Dan said, "I need to pay my hotel bill. Pick me up in half-hour."

"Roger that," Guptill said. They both got up and walked off in different directions.

CHAPTER 6

Jalalabad Air Base
FOB (Forward Operating Base) Fenty
Afghanistan

It was weird being back in Afghanistan. It was dark inside his dorm room, a respite from the blinding yellow heat and relentless dust outside. That was one thing Dan never got used in the 'Stan. The constant dust, powdery and floating around in huge clouds. It got into his eyes, clotted up the valves of weapons, made his skin itch.

In the dead heat of the afternoon, Dan picked up his suppressed Heckler & Koch 416 assault rifle and looked down the ten-inch barrel.

The weapon had an EOTech optical red dot sight with a 3x magnifier mounted on top. He slid back the bolt and chambered a round, made sure the safety was on, and used the laser beam to light a pinpoint at the far end of his tent.

He checked the side pockets of his camouflage pants. In one he had his leather gloves for abseiling down ropes from whichever copter they would be flying in. Chances are it would be a Black Hawk Mi-17 or an Apache. In another pocket he had extra batteries. In the lower Cargo pants he kept his digital camera to take photos of kill targets and for intel. Wrapped round his left ankle he kept a small, snub-nosed, suppressed Sig for emergencies. The butt was thicker due to a rubber grip, and came easily into the hand. It had saved his life in the past.

He stood up and put his vest on. The ceramic armor plates weighed it down and the rest of his gear made it up to a full sixty pounds. On either side of his chest he had a radio. He tested the headphones to make sure he could hear the buzz of static, and the tiny digital microphone embedded in his right ear. Between the two radios he kept four extra magazines for the rifle, and a fragmentation grenade. Below that, on either side of the vest, he kept flashbangs, plastic lights, wire cutters and plastic handcuffs. He reached behind his back to make sure he could get the C-4 explosive fixed to the vest. It came off with a pull. The detonators were in a small pocket on his sleeve.

Then his hands slipped down to the curved, sixteen-inch kukri knife strapped to the belt line on his back. Presented to him by a Gurkha soldier, who had also shown him how to use it.

He hefted the kukri in his hand without taking it out of its black scabbard. Its long edge had been used with spectacular effect on a Taliban chieftain's neck. The head had separated from the body.

"Dan, are you there?" The voice came from outside the open door of his bunker. A tall, wiry man in a crumpled suit came in.

Rory Burns had a sallow, angular face with sunken cheeks. His gray eyes were bright and lit up when he talked. Dan had not met the guy before he had arrived at the base. Burns had taken care of his kit and acted as the liaison between them and the regiment billeted at FOB Fenty.

"Yes," Dan said.

Burns' head was bent, touching the top of the door frame. He stepped inside the room and blinked as his eyes adjusted to the dimness inside.

Burns said, "Time to debrief ten minutes. In HQ."

"Cool."

Burns sat on his haunches on the floor. There was an unexpected look of concern on his face. He said, "You okay?"

Dan could not keep the snap out of his voice. "Why shouldn't I be?"

Burns shrugged. "I spoke to Guptill. He said…"

Dan interrupted. "Said what?"

"Nothing. Just to keep an eye on you. Make sure you were cool."

"I don't need a nanny." Dan stood up, his broad bulk filling up the room. Burns stood up as well. He gave Dan another concerned look. Dan ignored him.

"See you out there," said Burns, and left.

Dan came out of his bunker, locked it, and walked across the dusty courtyard. The flat expanse of the silver hangars loomed in the backyard. He could hear the whine from the rotors of a large Chinook 47 as maintenance guys tested the machine. People in uniform moved in and out of squat buildings around him. There was a cafeteria and, adjacent to it, the military hospital. FOB Fenty was an annex to Jalalabad Airport, and much smaller than the larger camps in Afghanistan such as Camp Bastion. It was easy to spot people here, and as Dan came out he caught sight of Burns again. Burns waved at him and went inside the HQ building.

Dan opened the glass door of HQ and heard the suck of rubber gaskets as the doors shut. He was in an air-conditioned space with carpets and a hallway opening up to an office reception. The reception desk was empty. He turned down the hallway and knocked twice on the first door. Burns opened the door and Dan went in. An older man with salt-and-pepper hair stood next to a screen in the corner of the room. Apart from the three of them, the room was empty.

Dan and the older man stared back at each other. Then Dan remembered. He had seen the man on a TV screen before. Lieutenant Colonel Jim "Fighter" McBride. One of the deputy commanders at Joint Special Operations Command or JSOC, over at Fort Bragg, North Carolina. The guy who had spoken to Guptill about the operation. McBride was dressed in civilian clothes and was not here on official duty. No one in the Pentagon would know he was here, apart from the few who knew of Intercept's existence.

"Come in, Dan," McBride's voice was gentle, but it was obeyed instantly.

This room was soundproof, and secure. Inside this room they were Intercept. The US, or any other government, would deny their existence.

They were a highly secretive branch of elite soldiers, picked from the four squadrons of the Delta Force. The best of the best. Even their Delta colleagues did not know that they existed.

Their specialism was the shadowy world where DoD sanction was not needed, nor asked for. The Pentagon was tired of paying hundreds of millions to private military contractors, or PMCs. It was time they played the same game. The lawyers made sure their activities could never be traced back to the Army.

Dan saw the grid reference map as he sat down. The same map would be used by the support guys at base, hunched over screens showing live images from drone feeds and satellite images.

"The Person of Interest is holed up in the main building of this compound." McBride pointed to the cluster of buildings in the middle of the satellite image on the screen. "POI is a senior foreign fighter, Arab Al-Qaeda, but sheltered by the Taliban. Our mission is to destroy the compound, and take the POI alive if we can. If that's not possible, kill him if you have to. Intel thinks 20-30 fighters are in there. Expect a firefight. You will have air support on standby."

McBride shifted and continued. "You will be dropped two miles away at 2230 hours. Evacuation will be when you call for close air support." He stared at the two men in front of him. "Dan is front and center. Rest of you are backup."

They nodded. It was always like this. Dan would go out, do the recon, and complete the mission on his own. The others stayed back to assist if he landed in trouble.

Apart from the mission in Yemen, Dan Roy had never failed. He had spent several years of his childhood in a village near the base camp of Mount Everest, almost 30,000 feet above sea level. Running up the steepest mountain paths in the world from the age of seven had given him a level of physical fitness most humans did not have.

McBride asked, "Any questions?"

"No," said Dan.

CHAPTER 7

It was dark inside the Black Hawk. The rotor blades spun into a frenzy and the noise drowned out everything. The bird rose vertically, then its nose dipped as it picked up speed and roared through the desert night sky. The Helicopter Landing Site was half an hour's flight away. Dan was near the door and would be quick to rappel down. He checked the safety catch of his rifle. It had happened to some poor bastard once, inside a bird packed with kit and men. Rifle got knocked against wall and a chambered round went off by mistake. It all came down to standard operating procedures.

It was a good hour to the HLS in the Azrow Mountains, south-east from Kabul. Dan used the time to close his eyes and doze.

His mind drifted back to the cloud-wreathed mountains of his childhood. His parents lived as UN workers in a village in remote Nepal, before they had relocated back to the States.

His father waking him up at five o'clock, putting a doko bag around his head, and setting him off on his five-mile run up the goat path. He had the same routine as the hardy mountain men, the Gurkhas who lived in the village. The Gurkhas were renowned as legendary fighters, and made up three regiments of the British Army.

Mother calling him back in the evening, framed against the falling sun at the head of the rice fields. His mom forced him to study in the evenings. It was the only reason he did well in school. She was now dead, and so was his father.

Back in the US, he had joined the Army. After his basic training, he relished joining the 10th Mountain Division at Fort Drum, NY. Then he spent six years at a 75th Rangers Battalion, a proud "Bat Boy", rising from a rifleman to counterterrorism section leader. When the bearded and laid-back Delta Force NCO came calling, US Ranger Dan Roy was ready. He had trained for almost a year, preparing for the ultimate in selection tests.

He earned the Delta patch. It was in his locker, back at home in Virginia. He did not have any US Army-identifiable kit on him. Right now, officially, he did not exist.

Thoughts turned to a black mist in his head. His chin dropped forward onto his chest.

The pilot leaned back from his cockpit, close to Dan. His barking voice got through Dan's thin veil of slumber. The pilot lifted up one finger.

"One minute to HLS!" he shouted.

Dan switched his NVG on and everything became bathed in a green hue. These NVGs were new with a 180-degree field of vision. It was a vast improvement on the older ones, which did not allow any lateral sight. He adjusted the toggles on the side until the hills around him came into sharper focus. His radio chirped for the comms check. They were losing altitude rapidly. Before he knew it, the ground was rushing up to meet them.

Dan shook off the lanyard fixing him to the safety rail and jumped out. The area was deserted, but that didn't mean some resourceful Taliban watchman hadn't seen them coming and raised a signal.

A direct hit from an RPG would be all it took for the bird to go down.

He tried to run, but the rotor wash from the bird flattened him to the ground. He held his weapon ready and lay on his belly. Dust glinted on the rotor blades as the bird hovered inches above the ground, creating fire sparks. This was the most dangerous time. Those sparks were visible from a distance. But within seconds, it seemed, the helicopter raised itself up in a blaze of dust into the night air. Rapidly it became a distant speck in the sky, fading from sight.

Dan lay quietly as silence flooded back around him. The desert ground was hard and the smell of dust was everywhere. The radio came alive in his ears.

"This is Bravo One." That meant Burns, his handler for the mission.

Dan said, "Roger that. Proceeding to target."

He walked almost an hour before the small hills surrounding the compound came into view.

Dan did a last-minute check on his sixty-pound backpack. Breaching charge, check. Comms on the right channel, check. Tactical beacon attached to his left wrist in case he fell, check. Extra ammo, grenades, flashbangs where he could reach them – check, check and check. It was the mantra of all Special Forces warriors.

Never, ever skip on the basics. It made the difference between life and death.

Dan patrolled tactically. He ran a hundred yards, found shelter and scanned 360 degrees with his rifle night sight. Then he moved again. He found a small hillock within seventy yards of the target. Silent as a ghost, he scrambled up it.

Dan dropped to the ground and focused his NVG on the courtyard of the compound. A large building, presumably the residence, stood in the middle, flanked by two smaller buildings. The entire compound was roughly one hundred and fifty square feet in size. As he looked, Dan saw two figures, wearing loose kaftans and headgear typical of the Taliban, stroll out from one of the buildings. He took aim. The head of the first Taliban appeared in his cross hairs.

Soon, another figure came out of the main building. The lights were off, and the figures wouldn't have been visible without his NVGs. Lights flickered briefly, and Dan realized the guards had come out for a cigarette. Dan waited for a few more seconds, then waited some more. He wanted them close to each other again, like when they lit their smokes. In another twenty seconds that happened.

BOP.

The suppressed H&K jerked in Dan's hand once as the 5.56mm ordnance smashed into the head of one Taliban fighter. Dan had already aimed fractionally to his right before the figure hit the ground.

BOP.

Silence came back again. Dan waited. It was all about waiting. Wait for the enemy to show themselves. Wait for them to make the first mistake.

"Proceed to breach," Dan thought to himself.

Dan reached behind his back and detached the C-4 explosive. He slithered down the slopes into the flat ground leading up to the compound gates. A ten-foot-high, six-foot-thick mud wall, typical of Afghani compounds, surrounded the site. Dan went halfway up the open road and dropped, weapon trained on the door. He quickly set the explosives, making sure to dual-charge them, in case one detonator failed. Then he retreated thirty yards and surveyed.

A dog bayed in the distance, but not close. If there were dogs in the compound he was yet to see them. The moon vanished behind clouds making the night pitch black.

Dan slithered forward again, and went around to the rear. There was a small gate there. A black shape slumped near it. His NVG picked it up as a sentry guard. The man was asleep, but even as Dan looked, he straightened and sat up in his chair. He looked around.

Dan cursed. He went down, staying still as a statue. He couldn't aim and fire. First off, it would cause a movement, and nothing attracted more attention than movement.

Second, even the suppressed H&K would make a noise. If the man fell back against the gate he might make a crashing sound. Too risky.

Very slowly, Dan reached behind his back, and took out the sixteen-inch kukri knife.

Dan waited till the man was more settled in his chair. This guy also wore the typical Taliban headgear, and a dishdasha around his body. Something had caught his attention: hence he was looking around. But soon he lost interest. He lowered his head inside his dishdasha for some warmth.

It would be the last mistake of his life. Dan raised himself without a sound. He scurried towards his quarry, faster than a leopard. When he was within two feet of the man, he was startled and looked up. By then it was too late.

The man waking up helped Dan. He looked up and exposed his neck. That fraction of a second was all Dan needed. The kukri flashed in his hand, and buried itself to the hilt into the Taliban's neck. A gurgling, choking sound came, and warm blood pulsed over Dan's gloved hand. The eleven-inch blade cut the neck arteries, smashed the soft bones of the lower skull, and severed the cervical spinal cord at the back.

Apart from a soft pop and the choking, no other sound had been made.

Dan lowered the body to the ground, and checked his G-Shock timer. Forty seconds to go. Hurriedly, he set the second charge, and faded back to his perimeter, circling around to the front of the compound.

The explosion lit up the night sky. A giant yellow and gold fireball erupted, flinging the door apart and crumbling a section of the wall. Shouts and screams came from inside. Dan crouched behind the rubble as he heard the whine of the heavier 7.62mm bullets the Taliban fired from their AK-47s. Some bullets splattered into the rubble in front. Dan lifted his head up briefly and saw muzzle flash up ahead.

He ducked his helmet down just in time to hear a bullet pass overhead. He waited for a lull in the firing, then got up and fired. Some of the guards in front fell and some scattered for cover. Dan took aim and let off some rounds in the direction of a new muzzle flash. He heard a distant scream as his rounds hit target.

The Taliban now poured out of the building and into the compound. Right on cue, the rear explosion shattered the back gate. Part of the compound wall crumbled. The charge had been heavier, and Dan felt the ground shake underneath him. The enemy was now disorientated by the twin front and rear explosions.

Agitated, some turned back. The others ran around, looking for a target. They missed the figure lying silently on the ground, only a few feet away. Dan counted ten Taliban in total. He rose up, and locked onto his targets. He double-tapped the three closest to him. Then he advanced onto the compound. He used the Underslung Grenade Launcher (UGL) attached to the HK417. Three grenades were fired in an arc ahead of him. He took cover, turning around as they exploded.

There was nothing behind him. There was a sudden silence in the compound, punctuated by shrill scream from the wounded lying on the ground. They had never seen anything like this. The speed and ferocity of the attack had taken them by surprise.

Dan took his steps carefully, checking out every shadow in every corner. His senses were on fire. He crouched down and looked at the door of the outhouse. It was locked from the outside. He set his last small breach charge and moved away, out of range. When the charge breached, he went back in, shining his infrared torch. The room was empty. He chucked a couple of plastic chemical lights inside, which meant the room was clear.

It was ominously quiet. Dan didn't like it. If a senior Al-Qaeda was holed up here, where the hell were the other fighters? He had killed seven, maybe eight so far and wounded two or three, maybe more.

He went around the building and into the foyer. It was a two-story, four-bedroom house.

Dan peered against the wall of the first room, then kicked the door down. It fell off its hinges. His rifle light darted around the room. Mud walls. Folded mat in one corner. Two AK-47s. Rest empty. He darted around all the rooms on the ground floor. All clear.

He came out in the hallway and as he was about to go up the staircase, Dan saw a movement at the far end of the hallway. A figure slipped out a doorway in the back. Dan fired a round, but it missed, hitting the door frame. He ran to the back of the house and to the wall next to the doorway. He kicked it open, staying under cover. No gunfire came from outside.

He went out, weapon at the ready. He was in a courtyard, smaller than the front. The tall perimeter wall loomed at the back. Dan saw movement on his extreme right. He fired immediately and saw his target crumple to the ground. He ran forward. As he got closer, his heart jumped in his mouth. The prostrate figure on the ground was wearing a uniform. He recognized the blue shirt of the Afghan National Police. This was all wrong. This was a Taliban compound. What was ANP doing here?

Dan turned the body over. He flicked his light on the face. It looked familiar for some unknown reason. Dan snapped off two photos and looked at the body again. One arm was pointed straight, as if it was reaching for something. He looked, and found a large brass handle embedded in the ground.

The cries of the wounded had died away and the compound was strangely quiet.

Dan checked the trapdoor for any IEDs (Improvised Explosive Device), then grabbed hold and pulled. There was a splintering noise and he stopped.

"It's a cellar," he whispered to himself.

He pulled again, and this time, the loose earth on top fell off, revealing a chasm beneath his feet. He shone his IR torch on wooden steps descending into darkness. Dan leaned down, weapon still at the ready, and checked with the magnifying night scope mounted on his rifle. What he saw took his breath away.

Anti-aircraft guns. The DShKM, known as the Dushka, was a Soviet heavy machine gun on a tripod. There was a whole row of them, with mounds of coiled ammunition chains, on the floor of the basement. Dan had seen them before in Iraq. Insurgents still used them frequently.

He went down the steps. A long, wide room opened up below. Rifles were mounted on the walls and several short-range missiles lay on the floor. They looked Soviet-made with surface-to-air capability. In the corners, he found high, stacked piles of grenades with launchers. He got to the far end of the room and his hair stood up on end. Heckler & Koch rifles. G3, G6, 416,417, all sub-types. MP5 and 7 sub-machine guns.

These *weren't* Soviet-made.

He looked closer at the serial number on one HK. It was indistinct. He could smell the oxyacetylene blowtorch used to remove the serial number. Insurgents did this in Mosul, Iraq. His breath came fast and shallow. He'd found the evidence Guptill was looking for.

He flicked his light to the left. Long, black boxes with missiles inside them. He read the numbers on the Hellfire missiles. Next to it he saw stacks of boxes. The legends on them made him lean closer.

CL-20. State-of-the-art military explosives, more powerful than HMX. It was rumored that they could penetrate a ten-foot steel wall.

The Taliban were still using TNT and PETN, the least stable of all explosive compounds. If they got their hands on these…

Dan turned on his radio. "Bravo One, this is Tango One."

Burns replied immediately. "Receiving, over. What have you found?"

Dan told him. Burns said, "Good work. Take as much photographic intel as you can." Dan switched off and carried on taking photos.

In five minutes, his radio crackled into life again.

"Bravo One calling Tango One, respond. Over."

"Bravo One, this is Tango One. I have…" He didn't finish. Burns' normal calm voice seemed forced.

"Mission aborted. I repeat, mission aborted. Evacuate site and proceed to HLS. Do you copy? Over."

Dan stood in the silent blackness of the basement, thoughts running in his head.

"Roger that, Bravo One," he whispered into his radio.

He put his camera away, and prepared to get out of the basement. He poked his head out. The night air was silent. He heaved himself out, rifle ready to fire. Nothing. He patrolled out, then hurried along to the HLS.

CHAPTER 8

The flight back was quiet. Back at base, Dan clambered off the bird slowly. Burns was waiting. He came over and said, "There was a platoon-strength Taliban force headed your way. We had to evacuate you."

"What happened to the weapons?" Dan asked.

Burns said, "We've got a drone up there now. Any minute, the place will be blown sky-high. You being there would have compromised the mission. You did what you had to."

Dan said, "The POI was not there."

Burns said, "We don't know that for definite as yet. You might have killed him."

Dan shook his head. "This guy is important, right? He wouldn't have ten or twelve Taliban guarding him, there should be around fifty. I reckon he got wind and ran off."

Burns said, "McBride wants to see you. You got the photos?"

"Yes." They walked over to the HQ building. McBride was waiting for them in the same room.

"We are still not sure if the POI was there," McBride said quietly. "But at least you tried. I thank you for that." He looked at Dan and continued. "What did you find in the house?"

Dan reached inside the cargo pockets of his trousers and pulled out folded scrolls of paper. "I found maps, sir, of the large bases we have here and in Baghdad." It was a detailed map of Bagram airport and Camp Bastion.

"I understand you went around the back. Is that right?" McBride's eyes scanned Dan's face.

Dan explained to him about the basement and showed him the photos.

McBride looked at Dan's camera in silence, flicking through the images. He said, "I'm keeping this camera, Dan. I need to send these photos to HQ."

Dan opened his mouth and shut it.

"Yes, sir."

*****

Dan slept fitfully that night. Strange dreams filled his mind. He could see Lucy. Her red hair was falling over her face. Dan was holding her close to him. He bent forward to kiss her and she closed her eyes. The red curls of hair became rivulets of blood, wrapping tightly across her face. Lucy opened her eyes in alarm. She began to choke. She opened her mouth and shouted; Dan could hear a faint scream. She was saying something, and Dan strained his ears. Her voice was weak, faded.

"Let me in. Dan, let me in."

Dan was gasping. He yelled out, *"Yes, I will. I will."*

Lucy's voice came from far away. *"Open the door, Dan. Open the door."*

He awoke with a start. Someone was knocking on his door hard enough to make it rattle. He groaned and checked his watch. Seven o'clock. The sun was already bright. He swung his legs off the bunker and opened the door, stifling a yawn.

He blinked in surprise. Two Military Policemen were standing outside. They were stout, large men with meaty forearms hanging loose at the sides.

"You are Dan Roy?"

Dan rubbed his eyes and shook his head. "Yes. Why?"

"Come with us, now."

Dan held his ground. "What for?"

One of the MPs took a step forward. He was sweating. "Come with us and you'll find out. Now."

Dan put his combat shirt on and followed. They walked down the hallway towards the mess room and a row of lockers. Dan could hear Burns' voice. It was high-pitched, stressed.

Burns was saying, "It makes no sense. This is bullshit, right? Right?"

Dan frowned as he saw McBride and Burns standing next to his locker. McBride gave him a hard stare before looking away. One of the MPs opened his locker and reached inside. He pulled out a collection of folded papers. He opened one of them up. Dan stared in surprise, his heart thudding inside his chest.

It was a map of their base. He had no idea how it had ended up inside his locker, to which only he had keys. Before he could say anything, the MP pulled out another map. This was of Camp Bastion with portions circled in red.

Dan moved closer. "Hold up," he said. The MP had his hand inside the locker again. He stopped and looked at Dan. Dan met his eyes.

"I need to see inside my locker."

The MP moved aside. The locker was almost empty of kit, but Dan was on duty, so that was expected. But there were scrolls of maps, a laptop, and something else below it. Dan didn't touch anything. He turned to the officer and McBride.

"Sir, this stuff is not mine."

McBride said, "That map matches the ones we found in the compound last night. They're hand-drawn and the scale is the same. How did they end up in your locker?"

"I have no idea, sir. Why would you want to look in my locker anyway?"

"We didn't want to, Dan. But after last night's mission, I decided to check everyone's." A strange look passed in McBride's eyes. "We didn't expect to find this."

"It doesn't belong to me, sir," Dan repeated. A whirlwind of thoughts was passing through his head, but he kept his face impassive, giving nothing away.

Burns' face was working. He waved his hands in McBride's face. "Someone is trying to frame him! Damn it, can't you see that? Someone is trying to discredit Intercept." Burns jabbed a forefinger in Dan's direction. "By framing this guy."

McBride said, "Like who?"

Burns said, "Take your pick. The CIA, the government, other PMCs, they are all trying to get in on the act. All they see is the dollars we earn. No one thinks of the risks we take."

"You seriously think CIA will try to sabotage you guys?"

Burns leaned towards McBride. "Believe me, you have no idea how many feathers we have ruffled in the CIA. They call our operations illegal, even when they provide the damn intel!"

McBride gestured to the MP, and he resumed his search of the locker. He lifted the laptop and pulled something out. Dan tightened his jaw. His breath became shorter. It was a flat block of C-4 explosive with detonators on the side. He had used similar charges numerous times to breach into a target zone. But he had never kept anything like this in his locker.

"Where did you get this from, Dan?" McBride's voice seemed to come from far away. So did his own voice, when he finally found the strength to speak. Things were hazy in front of his eyes.

"I don't know, sir," he said.

CHAPTER 9

Dan sat on his bunker bed, his eyes staring straight ahead. A dull ache was gripping his head, like a hangover. His mind went back over the last two days. Arriving at FOB Fenty from Camp Bastion. Finding his barracks, bunker and locker. Debrief of the mission. Meeting the team. He couldn't place any time or event that had been odd, irregular. Apart from the mission itself.

What the hell was going on?

There was a knock on the door, then it pushed open before he could say anything. It was Burns. Their eyes met briefly before Dan looked away. Burns walked over to the corner of the room, lifting the curtain of the small box window to look at the blinding heat outside. Then he sat down on the beanbag in the corner. Neither of them spoke for a while.

"Dan?"

Dan rubbed his eyes and looked at his friend without speaking. Burns had a puzzled expression on his face.

"Who and why?" It was a statement, not a question.

"Damned if I fucking know," Dan whispered. He wasn't a paranoid person. He didn't think someone was out to get him. He killed his enemies. He knew who they were. But inside the barracks…

Burns sat down next to him on the bunk. "You reckon this has something to do with what you saw?"

Dan jerked his head towards him. The thought had appeared in his mind, too, but the potential ramifications were mind-boggling. He didn't want to go there. Dan frowned and focused on a mark on the wall, dead straight.

"Burns, I…I just have no idea right now." For the first time in his life, Dan felt helpless, a feeling he didn't like. Quickly, it turned to anger. He clenched his thick fingers, and slammed one fist into the other palm. The sound echoed in the room.

Burns said, "We will get to the bottom of this, Dan. I'll vouch for you, don't worry. You had nothing to gain from this."

Dan was silent. He did not know which way he could turn. Why had he come back? His thoughts turned to Guptill. If it hadn't been for him…Dan couldn't think anymore. He was getting a headache.

"What happens now?" he asked Burns.

Burns sighed. "Flight back to HQ. For both of us."

Dan's mind was working. "HQ in Virginia?" The Intercept HQ was near Fort Belvoir in Virginia.

Burns said, "I think so, yes."

Dan shook his head. "I need to go to London first, to see Guptill. Can you organize that for me?"

Burns chewed a nail. Then he said, "Leave it with me. I'll be back in a while. Pack your stuff up."

Burns got up and left. Dan stood up. He did not have much to pack. Whatever he had fit inside a small backpack.

Burns came back in fifteen minutes. He said, "I managed to get a deal. They want both of us back in Virginia. But I said Guptill will see you in London. I still have to head out to USA. The two MPs will escort you back to London."

It was better than nothing. Burns had done well to buy him some time. "Thanks," Dan said.

Burns stepped forward. He lowered his voice. "Do you think this has anything to do with what happened in Yemen?"

Dan had been thinking the same thing. Was Intercept betraying him? Maybe they needed to get rid of him. For good. Dan knew the high standards to which Intercept held every agent. Failure was never rewarded. Disobeying a direct order was the same as high treason. That was exactly what he had done in Yemen.

If they could show Dan was guilty, he had no hope of ever serving anywhere again. He might end up in jail. Or even worse, Dan thought grimly.

He said, "You work for Intercept, Burns. Why don't you try and find out?"

Burns said, "I believe you did the right thing in Yemen." He held up a finger. "It was me who asked Guptill to approach you. I knew that you had quit. But you showed in Yemen you had guts. You called Intercept's bluff. I needed a man like that for this mission. Someone who could use his own judgement. You saw what happened in London. This shit is serious, Dan. We need to get to the bottom of it."

Dan said, "There is someone inside Intercept. Someone told the POI we would be raiding the compound. That's why he escaped."

"Correct."

"Who is he, Burns?" Dan stared at Burns intently. The man shifted uneasily.

Burns said, "It's not me, Dan."

Dan said, "How do I know it's not you?"

Burns' face changed. He said, "If it was me, would I go out of the way to get you back in? I would try like hell to cover it up. I wouldn't even be here."

Dan nodded. It made sense. He asked, "What about Guptill?"

"You know your CO better than me, Dan. Do you think he'd do it? He approached you. You saw the photo of the dead CIA agent in London?"

Dan nodded. Burns said, "If Guptill was guilty, why would he show you all the photographic evidence?"

Dan was silent. Intercept was a shadowy, dark place. No one knew the top management or what they got up to. He asked Burns about them, but the fixer shook his head.

He said, "No one knows the top brass, Dan. No one ever will. All I can say is, I wouldn't want to be their enemy." He looked up at Dan. Their eyes met. Each knew what the other was thinking.

"I need to get out of here," Dan said.

Burns said, "You will get some breathing space in London. What you do with it is up to you."

"Yes," Dan said slowly.

*****

Dan had packed his gear the next morning and was waiting when they called for him. The same two MPs knocked on his door. He read their names this time, sewn into their shirts above their breast pockets. Smith and Sullivan.

Sounded like two freaking talk show hosts. His weapons had already been confiscated. The rifles were gone, so were his Sig Sauer P226 handgun, and his 35mm Beretta. Only the kukri was left, and hell, that was all he needed to chop their heads off. He could feel its reassuring presence on his belt, the blade resting against the small of his back.

He hefted the bag on his shoulder and followed them without a word. The courtyard was deserted in the early morning, and the desert sun was just beginning to rear its malicious head. It was 0600 hours. They walked for fifteen minutes until they got to the hangar. In normal situations, they would have taken a bus.

A Chinook 47 was being loaded with supplies. Some were standard military ration boxes, and some weapon stacks for repairs. He clambered aboard. Maintenance guys shouted orders and checked lights, helped load boxes. Dan watched them. He knew his destination already. The two MPs would be traveling with him. It was back to Bagram Air Base, northeast of Kabul, then another plane back to London.

Then he needed to get some answers.

CHAPTER 10

The Ilyushin 76MD cargo plane started to flash its tail lights as it prepared for landing at Heydar Aliyev International Airport, twenty miles northeast of Baku, the capital city of Azerbaijan.

Robert Cranmer came off his seat in the huge, central aisle of the plane, empty now, but wide enough to fit two armored vehicles side by side. He walked towards the rear of the plane. A flight of stairs led down to the observation chamber below the plane's tail.

He stepped into a small room filled with screens of maps on the walls, radars and radio equipment stacked on the side desks. The floor was essentially see-through, a giant window that allowed 360-degree views of the country around. In the Soviet era, the Ilyushin served a dual purpose as the main transport for its airborne divisions, as well as a spy plane. Now, the planes were chartered out to various agencies for freight purposes.

Robert looked at the green mountains of Azerbaijan, and the vast, brown, flat plains stretching beyond them in the distance. To the east lay the gleaming blue waters of Caspian Sea, the largest lake in the world, but called a sea by the ancient Romans because of its salty waters.

The airport appeared, white in the afternoon sunlight reflecting off its domed buildings. Robert enjoyed coming down to the navigation chamber, watching the land below as if he was on a parachute. It gave him a certain sense of privilege.

The pilot's voice came on the loudspeaker. "Seats, *pazhalsta,* comrades. Preparing to land."

Robert clambered out and wobbled back to his seat, strapping his seat belt on. For such a large transport plane, the Ilyushin landed smoothly, its wheels barely bumping the runway. Robert stood up and grabbed his briefcase. Robert Cranmer was not his real name. Not many people knew his real name, and that was the way he liked it.

Robert strode into the check-in area and flashed his diplomatic badge at security. He was waved through. A few guards lounged around, leaning against the walls, AK-74 rifles hung casually round their shoulders. They barely lifted an eye as Robert walked past them. Robert walked to a row of counters in the corner of the Arrivals section and to his company office.

"Living Aid" specialized in transporting food and health items to countries with governments too weak to do it for themselves. Countries like Afghanistan and Angola handed out the logistics to private contractors. To men like Robert Cranmer.

The door was open and the man sitting at the only table, staring at his laptop, looked up and stood, grunting. He was considerably shorter than Robert's lanky six feet one.

"Robert," he extended his hand.

Robert shook the man's hand, feeling the weight.

"Hello, Yevgeny." Yevgeny Lutyenov was going past forty, his hair starting to bald and a pot belly growing on the formerly hard slabs of muscle. Strangely, that didn't mean he was out of shape, as Robert had seen him load huge cartons into pallets for the steel shipping containers. Beneath his eyebrows a pair of light brown eyes glinted, matching the color of his mustache.

Robert gestured at the laptop. "Any news?"

"Yes," said Yevgeny, and rubbed his hands. "New order from Vietnam."

"Good," said Robert, running eyes up and down the spreadsheet quickly, then he turned to Yevgeny and raised his eyebrows.

"Chilli powder?"

Yevgeny shrugged. "Guess they like it hot."

The two men met during the Anglo-Russian Chamber of Commerce Gala night, hosted in the sumptuous India Durbar of the Foreign and Commonwealth Office in Westminster, London. Yevgeny had a background in the KGB, but after 1991 became an importer of Western goods. Business had been slow at first, but as the inflation settled down in the late-1990s, Russia's import-export business went through a prolonged boom. When he heard Robert's business proposition, it hadn't taken them long to become colleagues.

Robert tapped his briefcase. "I have end-user certificates for Kabul, Democratic Republic of Congo and Vietnam."

"*Kharasho*, comrade," Yevgeny smiled.

"And I've put all of our planes on the flight schedule of Bagram and Jalalabad. So, from now on, you won't have any more problems."

Russian planes were not much loved in Afghanistan. The Afghani airports were littered with the rusting hulks of destroyed MiG fighters and a few of the old Ilyushins. One of the Living Aid planes had been boarded by the Afghan Airport Authority after landing in Bagram last month, and the crew arrested. It had taken all of Robert's diplomatic skill to persuade the government to let them go.

"Are you sure about that?" Yevgeny said.

"*Konyeshna,* comrade." Robert switched to Russian when he wanted to make a point with Yevgeny. "Have I not just come back with an empty plane from Jalalabad? You have nothing to worry about anymore."

"I hope you are right," grumbled Yevgeny. "How did it go at the airbase?"

Robert paused for a moment before replying. "Yes, it was all fine."

Yevgeny seemed thoughtful. "Are you sure?"

"Yes, comrade. Don't worry. I am off to London now. See you later."

CHAPTER 11

The Chinook landed at the Royal Air Force base in Brize Norton. Dan yawned as the jolt of the landing bump awakened him. He looked out the window. It was summer, and apart from cloud cover, the weather did not look too bad. He got up, and packed his rucksack.

Dan stared out the black-tinted windows of the armored Range Rover as it speeded through the English countryside. Rolling green fields and gentle hillocks appeared, with white sheep dotted on them. Despite the bucolic surroundings, he couldn't help but wonder what was going to happen.

They suspected him of selling out to the other side. He would be grilled by intelligence officials whose names would never be disclosed.

Would they torture him? His own people?

They entered London. As they went down the old city's narrow streets, Dan recognized some of the sights. Then he saw the large, square building from a distance. He caught his breath. Grosvenor Square, Mayfair. One of the most expensive addresses in the entire world, and the location of the US Embassy in London. It was also the HQ of all clandestine CIA operations inside the UK.

But they drove past it. The car went straight down east, then banked south, heading for the River Thames. They drove past Hyde Park Corner, and the regal old buildings that faced the spacious green expanse. Soon they crossed the river at an unknown bridge, and the scenery changed. Industrial estates appeared, and they took a left after a grimy block of council houses, England's version of the Projects. Dan did not recognize these parts. He knew they were in South London, but not which part exactly.

The car stopped in front of what looked like an abandoned warehouse to the casual observer. But not to Dan. He could see the wide satellite receivers and tall antennas on the roof that marked a major communications hub. He also did not miss the men strolling around the front of the warehouse. Their shoulder bulges were well hidden but they did exist. Their eyes were hard and calculating. Paid mercenaries.

The warehouse backed onto the river. It was a gigantic structure, taking up almost one whole block. A row of warehouses merged into one building. A jetty on the river flashed by as they drove past. Dan could see two black, rigid inflatable boats or RIBs docked at the jetty, the military's choice of water transport. When the car came to a stop, two of the men loitering at the front ambled over.

IDs were checked, and security poked their heads in to look at the occupants—Dan, the driver and the two MPs. The bar lifted, the iron grill gate swung open, and the car swept inside the warehouse awning. Smith and Sullivan, the two MPs, both without uniform, and no doubt working on a private contract, stood on either side of Dan as he got out of the Range Rover.

The two suits gave Dan the once-over. One of them opened his jacket slightly to let Dan see the weapon inside. Dan stared back at the man, then walked past him.

Men were doing a search in front of a conveyor belt and X-ray machine. Dan dumped his rucksack in there and walked to the guards. He spread his arms and was patted down.

Dan looked around him as he walked inside. He was in a cavernous space, but one that crawled with people. Desks had been laid out, and large screens stood on the far walls, frequently changing pictures. Hallways branched off from the main atrium, men and women emerging from them with folders in their hands.

From the outside, he would never have known all these people were crammed inside. But he knew that was always the case in England. The British were masters of subtlety. A tiny building would go on for miles inside. A deserted warehouse by the river would turn out to be the Intercept HQ in London.

Dan was willing to bet money most of the agents inside were transported by riverboats from their homes. That left the roads empty. MI5 was probably on the take and they told local police to stay away.

Dan recognized the figure of Major Guptill walking towards him. He felt a sense of relief at the sight of his old CO. The only man he could trust.

Or could he? Guptill had not traveled to 'Stan with him this time. Burns had acted as his handler. Dan wondered why that was.

Neither man smiled at the other. Guptill glanced at Dan and gestured with his eyes to follow him. Dan walked down one side of the large atrium, looking at the men and women hunched over their screens, talking on phones. In one corner, a teleconference was going on. A man with a military buzz cut, but not in uniform, was telling the assembled group something from a giant screen. The face was well known to anyone who had worked in US Special Forces for any length of time.

Dan felt a surge of adrenaline. This *had* to be the Intercept's European HQ. He had so far been briefed 24 hours before his operations. In random locations. A folder would be left for him on a seat in a diner. It seemed risky, but the diner's staff would be trained. He had meetings with Guptill, his handler, at locations made known to him an hour before by a text. The locations were always different, irrespective of the country he was in. This was the first time he was attending HQ.

They headed off the main drag into a hallway. The two MPs were right behind him. Their boots clicked on the bare cement floor. They went down a flight of stairs and into a basement. Guptill pressed on the digital keypad next to a steel door and it swung open.

Guptill said to the MPs, "Stay here."

Dan walked inside. There was a table with two chairs inside. No windows. In another corner, there was a polygraph machine hooked up to the wall. There was something else in that corner, on another table, covered by a black cloth. A machine, Dan figured. He recognized an interrogation chamber when he saw one.

Dan sat down opposite Guptill.

Guptill said, "The plastic explosives found in your locker had Russian serial numbers."

Dan shrugged. "So do most weapons in Afghanistan."

"Remember your last trip to Russia?"

"Yes, to Belarus. On a reconnaissance mission to check their satellite station."

"Yes. It was an ISR mission with Delta." Intelligence, Surveillance and Recon.

Dan said, "You got me down here to talk about old times?"

Guptill stared at Dan for a while, then wrote something down on a piece of paper.

Then he said, "The investigation is still ongoing. We require you to be in London until it is finished." He fished inside his pocket and took out a cellphone. He slid it across the table to Dan, who did not touch it.

"Use this phone to contact me. And I will contact you. I don't have to remind you what happens if we can't contact you, or if you go AWOL."

He would be hunted down, and killed without hesitation.

It was a truth that was ingrained into the frontal lobe of every Intercept operative. They were the best of the best, but they were also held to a rigid code of silence.

"I know," Dan said.

"For what it's worth, I don't think you did it. Your career record is exceptional. You are one of our highest-value operators. You had nothing to gain."

Dan said, "Glad you see it that way." He pocketed the cellphone from the desk.

Guptill rose without a word. Dan followed. He knew when his former CO was giving him a silent order. Smith and Sullivan were still standing outside, silent and watchful. The four men went up the stairs. They walked back outside, and were waved through when Guptill flashed his badge.

They got back into the armored Range Rover. Guptill said something to one of the MPs and they pulled out into the empty street.

CHAPTER 12

They drove for a while and then joined traffic. Dan read the signs. They were in a part of town called Wandsworth. He did not know the place. They took a left and Dan saw the flash of muddy gray waters of the Thames again. The car came to a stop outside a section of the river that was empty of pedestrians. Guptill got out and Dan followed. The MPs stayed in the car.

There was a railing, beyond which a path ran down alongside the river. Heading up, Dan could see shiny new apartment complexes on both sides of the banks, and a hauling crane at a riverside dockyard. The sun had peeked out, and water rustled at the edges of the bank below them.

They stared at the swirls and eddies for a while.

Dan was the first to break the silence. "I didn't do it, sir."

Guptill didn't say anything. Dan waited.

"I know," Guptill said eventually.

Guptill gave Dan a hard stare, then nodded. Dan breathed out. He had served under Guptill in the Afghan war back in 2002. Then in Iraq and back in Afghanistan. As a Delta operator, then for Intercept. But the man who was his mentor didn't seem like the man standing opposite him now.

Dan said, "What's going on?"

"It's a shit game, this, you know?"

"Always has been. What's new?"

Guptill shook his head.

Dan pressed him. "I saw Special Forces rifles in there. H&Ks, adapted for our use. With NVGs. CL-20 explosives. You saw the photos."

Guptill's head jerked up. Dan held his eyes.

"Where is the camera I took the photos with?"

Guptill sighed. "Gone."

"Gone where?"

Guptill didn't say anything.

Dan said, "You're trying to protect me."

Guptill smiled for the first time. Then it vanished. "I don't know who to trust, Dan. You included."

"I told you. I didn't do it. Besides, if I was dirty, I would never make an error like that, would I?"

"You can't get into this, Dan. They are everywhere, up and down the country…" Guptill stopped, and looked away.

"I'm in this already," Dan said. "What do you want me to do? Roll over and give in?"

"Who's behind this?" he persisted.

Guptill didn't answer. Dan said, "You brought me here to tell me this gibberish?"

"Believe me, son, I have told you a lot more than I should have already."

Dan balled his fist in frustration. He gripped the iron bars of the railing. "What am I supposed to do with this clusterfuck?"

Guptill sighed and frowned. Dan could now see the conflict in his mentor. He wanted to help. But he did not know how far he could go.

Guptill regarded Dan for a few seconds. Then he leaned closer and whispered. "My apartment in Chelsea. Tomorrow evening. 1900 hours. Keep stag." He gave Dan the address.

Keeping stag was something they had picked up from the SAS guys. It meant surveillance. Dan nodded.

He heard a car pulling up. He looked behind him. An SUV had drawn up alongside, and the door was open. Guptill nodded at Dan, then walked to the car. He got in, the door shut, and they drove off.

Dan walked back to the Range Rover. He opened the back door and got in. Smith started the car and they pulled out.

"Where we going to?" Dan asked.

They didn't say anything. Dan figured they would take him back to base, and he would await orders there. He didn't have any money on him. He always traveled without ID. Either he needed to get some money, or Intercept had to find him some accommodation.

They drove for twenty minutes. Dan watched the traffic and read the signs. They were heading out of town and onto a road called the A3. The sign said they were heading for Portsmouth. Dan knew that was the south of England. Portsmouth had big docks and a Royal Navy base.

"Where we going to?" he repeated.

Sullivan replied, "A safe house for you."

Dan settled back in the seat. They got onto a faster dual carriageway. Soon it was countryside again. They hooked a left and went down a narrow, quintessentially English country lane. A car passed by on the opposite lane, inches from the Range Rover's wing mirror. After ten minutes, they pulled into the gravel drive of a country house. The front was shielded by a ten-foot-high fence, with tall pines in the middle. The building was set back and isolated from the road.

They parked, and Smith opened Dan's door. Dan got out. The two guys were flanking him. Dan looked at the house. A gray-brick building, two stories tall, old and imposing. It was very quiet here. He could not hear any cars. Some birds tweeted in the trees, and leaves rustled in a faint breeze.

Dan did not like it. Some unknown tension at the depths of his being was gnawing away inside him.

An instinct for danger. An instinct that had kept him alive all these years.

He met the eyes of the MPs. Eyes like stone. No feeling in them. One of them nodded towards the house. Smith walked ahead, while Sullivan walked behind Dan. Dan walked slowly, then stopped.

"I left something in the car," he said.

Smith, who was in front of Dan, took out his weapon. A suppressed Colt M1911. He flicked the safety off. The gun was pointed at Dan. The round, if fired, was going nowhere but his chest.

Dan turned, and saw Sullivan had drawn his weapon as well. The same Colt.

Sullivan was standing next to the back passenger door. Dan went to reach for the door, and the man was standing very close to it. Dan had already noticed his weapon's safety catch was on.

Dan turned as if he was reaching for the door handle, just as Sullivan stepped back. His right arm reached for the handle, but his left arm lashed out in the same movement, slapping Sullivan's gun arm away from him.

The movement was sudden, vicious and totally unexpected.

Sullivan swore and tried to bring his gun back, but Dan had already pivoted on his heels, and slammed his wide frame directly into Sullivan's chest. The man stumbled back. Dan grabbed his gun wrist, and drove his right fist straight up into the man's chin. The fist slammed against the bone, making a dull thud, and the man's head snapped back. The gun fired, the bullet picking up gravel dust at Dan's feet.

Dan was aware of movement behind his back. He pushed Sullivan backwards to the rear of the car even as a bullet smashed into the glass next to him. Dan dived forward, pulling Sullivan with him. That dive saved Dan, as he felt another round whistle over his head and blast into the side of the armored car. The round pinged off, and Dan rolled over to the other side of the Range Rover, the fallen man's Colt in his hand.

He had no time to stand up, turn around and aim. But he had the car's side as cover momentarily. Dan crawled on the gravel, hearing Smith run up behind him. He flattened himself on the ground, and looked underneath the car. He spotted the feet running up. He squeezed off two rounds, and heard the satisfying scream as they found their mark.

Even as the man fell on the gravel, Dan was up and moving.

He leaped onto the hood. He rolled over it, and came off firing at the figure lying on the gravel. Smith was ex-military, and he was no stranger to combat situations. But Dan's sudden move had taken him by surprise. He was aiming his gun underneath the car, searching for Dan.

Rule number one – Always do what your enemy does not expect.

Dan fired rapidly as he fell, the round streaking into the body on the floor. Smith realized at the last minute, but by then it was too late. Three rounds smashed into his skull and neck, and they erupted in a spurt of blood. His head fell back and he sagged sideways.

Dan fell on the gravel, feeling the stones pinch him sharply on the sides. He was up quickly, resting on one knee, gun arm straight at the elbow, scanning 360 degrees. No one else.

He went over to Sullivan, still lying on the gravel. He was starting to recover. Dan leaned over him, pointing his gun.

"Who sent you?" Dan asked.

In response, Sullivan spat at Dan. Dan turned his head just in time, missing the sputum. He kicked the man hard in the ribs. Sullivan rolled over, getting up on one knee. He reached inside his jacket and pulled out a small, snub-nosed 9mm gun. He never got the chance to use it.

Dan double-tapped him in the face and neck. Sullivan fell backwards, dead before he hit the ground.

Dan spun around, ready for more contact. Blood was roaring in his ears, and his chest was heaving, but inside, he was icy calm. This is what he thrived on.

If twenty men came charging down the road now, if they rappelled down from a Sikorsky bird above his head, he would fight them. He would fire till he ran out of ammo. Then he would pull out his kukri. If the kukri broke he would use his bare hands.

He would kill them all. He always had done.

But the surrounding quiet English countryside gave no indication of further threats. Dan did not let his awareness slip. He pulled the two bodies into the bushes at the side entrance to the garden. The gun had been suppressed, and there weren't any houses nearby, so hopefully he had avoided detection. Then he heard the buzzing sound. For a moment, he thought it was the cellphone that Burns had given him. But after a while he realized it was coming from one of the fallen men. He frisked the two bodies, and found a cellphone inside Smith's jacket.

He held the phone in his hand. Caller ID withheld. As he had expected.

If he answered, he was answering the question.

No, he's not dead.

Dan put the phone back inside the man's jacket. He frisked them both again, expecting to find nothing. Expectation fulfilled, he approached the front door. He nudged the door with his foot without touching it. Locked.

Dan did not want to waste time exploring the place. If these guys had been Intercept enforcers, then he knew they did not travel alone. That unanswered phone call would raise questions. He needed to put distance between himself and them.

He got into the car, and drove out. He headed straight down, looking for a sign. He found one that said "A3, London", and took it. He noted the right-hand drive, and drove carefully.

Once on the road, he allowed himself to think laterally.

Guptill did not travel back with him. Why was that? Burns had left for Virginia. It was Guptill who had wanted to see him in London.

Was Guptill showing fake concern for him?

Why had Guptill asked him to visit his apartment in Chelsea? So that he could finish the job?

Guptill, more than anyone else, would know that Dan could handle these two assassins.

Dan shook his head and gripped the steering wheel hard, till his knuckles were white.

What about Burns? Dan had kept the cellphone Burns had given him before leaving for the USA. But before Dan started the car, he had turned the phone off, and ripped the battery off the back. He kept them separate. His senses told him to throw the phone away. But it was his only link back to Intercept now.

No one had survived an Intercept hunt down. But they had not hunted Dan.

"Fuck you," Dan snarled under his breath. He changed lanes and speeded up on the A3. He was heading for Chelsea.

CHAPTER 13

Robert Cranmer watched the sunlight glinting off the Arghandab River far below his Sikorsky S-92 helicopter.

The Arghandab, one of the main rivers in southern Afghanistan, sprouted further up north in the mountains of Ghazni. It flowed four hundred kilometers down into the fertile valley of Helmand, before watering Panjwayi town, which was Robert's destination.

Robert sighed and looked back at the mountains rising in the distance. Afghanistan certainly had a dramatic landscape. He was in a wide, empty valley. The bare bones land shrugged itself into colossal stacks of granite mountains that rose forebodingly into a blue sky.

They were getting closer to Panjwayi. The first mud-thatched roofs appeared next to the river, with larger compounds of the richer inhabitants strewn around. Panjwayi was an important town in Helmand, not least because it used to be a Taliban stronghold. The Taliban had been beaten away, but only temporarily. Robert had no doubt that when the Allies left, they would move back in.

The rotor blades of the Sikorsky raised a storm of debris and the bird wobbled as it settled in the middle of the biggest compound. Children scattered for the cover of mud huts. It was stifling hot inside the cabin, all the windows shut to fend off the dust. Some of it still seeped in, making Cranmer cough. He put a handkerchief over his mouth. Afghanistan was much nicer from high above.

It was his second time back to the district HQ of the Panjwayi District. The Afghan National Police HQ and the local hospital were situated there—the only hospital in the surrounding hundred square miles—and a community care center, both staffed by US Marines. Scattered around the edges of the compound were residential quarters and storage warehouses. Two figures came out of the police HQ, a yellow, two-story clay building with antennas and satellite dishes. Two ANP snipers kept watch from bullet holes in the roof.

Robert got out of the helicopter. A portly figure in a brown uniform was making his way towards him, flanked by two ANP with AK-74 rifles. He extended his hand as they got closer.

"Mr Cranmer, what a lovely surprise," the fat Afghan man said in perfect English.

"Nice to see you again, Fatullah." The two men smiled and shook hands cordially. Commander Fatullah Zalaf waved expansively towards the police HQ.

"Some nice, cold, rose sherbet and sweets await you, my friend. Please come in."

"Ah, that's all I came for," Robert chuckled. Flanked by the guards again, the two men went inside.

Fatullah Zalaf's office was at the back of the building, on the cooler second floor, shaded by the branches of a pomegranate tree. There was no air conditioning. The windows were open, but it was still too early for the early evening winds. The room was hot and stuffy.

A boy came in carrying a stainless steel tray with two covered glasses and a plate of baklava and halawi sweets. Robert sat down and wiped his forehead with a handkerchief. Fatullah closed the door firmly after the boy. They were alone.

Fatullah organized some papers on the desk, pushed one glass and the plate of sweets towards Robert, then sat back in his chair. Robert took a long sip, watching Fatullah. He looked the same as last time. His cheeks had gone to fat, to match his ponderous belly. His luxurious black beard was longer if anything, and gleamed with oil.

"So, Robert, how is business?"

"Brisk, as it happens. We have orders in Africa and the Far East now. As well as here, of course."

"Good, good. So how can I help?"

"Well, it's about the vaccines. You know what happened with the last shipment."

Fatullah nodded. A Living Aid truck carrying vaccines had been seized by the Taliban three months ago.

Fatullah said. "After what happened in Abbottabad in 2011, any medical supplies are treated with suspicion, especially if they're vaccines."

"Yes," Robert frowned. "But this is us. They should know better."

Fatullah nodded. "Agreed."

When he didn't say any more, Robert said, "So what happened to the vaccines?"

"Robert, we *are* trying our best to find them. Searches are still…"

"I know all of that, Fatullah. But we had an understanding. I have to make excuses to the company directors about this. They're concerned. If it is the Taliban who took them, and not any other *mujaheddin* group, then surely you can talk to them?"

Fatullah was silent. Robert watched him carefully. Fatullah was a former Taliban commander, a mid-ranking one. At his peak, he had close to a hundred men under him. With the US-led war effort now coming to an end, the money for Taliban commanders was dwindling and pouring into the Afghan government instead. For those who joined the Taliban for money, such as Fatullah, it was time to switch sides.

"It is not easy, Robert."

"Then how can I guarantee the flow of supplies to you?"

It was a stalemate. Fatullah grasped and smoothed his beard, then sighed something in Arabic. He shook his head and looked askance at Robert.

"Yes, I know." Fatullah seemed lost in thought for a moment. "Okay, I will speak to them. But…" He raised his eyebrow and lifted a finger. "This remains between me and you, eh, *dost*?"

Robert grinned. "Of course, my friend—I mean, *dost*."

CHAPTER 14

The May sun was fighting with the clouds as Dan stepped out of Sloane Square underground station. Underground or subway stations were called the tube in England. He had ditched the car almost as soon as he entered London and taken the tube. He guessed the car would have a tracking device.

It was six in the evening, surprisingly mild. The daylight would help him keep an eye on the apartment. Major Guptill's rental apartment was in Chelsea, a sought-after address in London. His Intercept salary paid for it.

Georgian colonial mansion houses adorned the street on both sides, with leafy trees at regular intervals. Dan kept one eye on the stunning architecture, and another on the people around him. He stopped every fifty yards, either to admire the scenery or to cross the street. He didn't see anything unusual. He took a left off Chelsea Bridge Road into Royal Hospital Road, heading for the river. Paradise Walk was a little street close to the river, just off Royal Hospital Road.

Did Guptill want him dead? His former CO?

Dan could not stop the question from surfacing in his mind. Snippets of his conversation with Guptill came back.

I don't know who to trust.

Up and down the country. Which country?

Dan came to the turning of Paradise Walk and stopped, looking at the spectacular red-brick, terraced buildings. Commuters were walking back from work. A woman was pushing a pram. Two women jogging. He leaned against the railings of a terrace. After ten minutes, he still saw nothing.

He doubled his way back up the other end of Paradise Walk. He was on the Chelsea Embankment now, opposite the river. Traffic was heavy. The sidewalk was wide on the Embankment, with benches to sit and admire the river scenery. He picked one from where the major's apartment was visible. The graceful, red and white terraced building was sandwiched between two others that looked exactly the same. He waited for longer this time, but again saw nothing unusual. Paradise Walk was a narrow street, and he couldn't monitor the building by getting too close. This was his best spot.

Why did Guptill not come back with him? Why did he get into another car? That car arrived like it had been prearranged.

Like they knew what was going down.

Dan kept watch until the sun was tilting in the west, casting long shadows of Chelsea Bridge over the Thames' muddy waters. Dan checked all around him, then got up. He felt the suppressed Colt against his back belt.

He sauntered along Paradise Walk to the double doors of number fourteen. They were tall and brown, the varnish on them shining, a speakerphone beside them. Dan pressed a button and waited. No response. He pressed again. After his third attempt, he gave up. He checked his watch. 1910 hours. He loitered around another ten minutes, then pressed again. Still no response.

Uneasiness began to eat away inside him. He checked his cellphone. No calls. Guptill would never call him on the phone anyway. Tracer magnets, he used to call them. Dan crossed the street and tried to look up at the third floor. The windows facing the street were open.

He waited. After a while, a woman in her mid-fifties approached the house. Dan stayed in the shadow of a doorway opposite and watched while the woman took out a set of keys. He crossed the street quickly.

The woman turned around in the hallway as she heard Dan come in behind her. Movement sensor lights came on in the ceiling, bathing the place in a white glow.

"Here for John Guptill, number thirty-two," Dan said cheerfully. "Have you seen him around?"

The woman ignored his question, mumbled a hello and turned away.

Dan looked around him carefully. No one present but him. He took the stairs up slowly, the Colt now in his hand, elbow ramrod straight.

Dan stepped off the third-floor landing and into the hallway. Fading sunlight streamed in through long windows at either end. The hallway was empty.

At Guptill's apartment, before he knocked, Dan checked around the door frame and the knob. No signs of breaking and entering. He put the Colt back in his belt. He put an ear to the wood. No sounds from inside. He stood on his tiptoes and passed a hand over the top of the door frame. No keys hidden there.

He knocked, then stepped back against the wall. No answer. He rapped the door again, heavily this time.

All of a sudden, his senses were twitching. His eyes jerked from side to side, up and down. His ears were picking up the faintest of sounds. He balled his fists. Something was wrong. He *knew* it. He considered his options.

If Guptill wanted him dead, he would be dead by now. A sniper would have picked him out. Or he would have been ambushed as soon as he stepped inside. Dan needed to find out what was happening. That was the only option. But he had to be ready for whatever lay behind that door.

He leaned on it hard. There was a splintering sound, but it was muffled. Dan grabbed at the handle, preventing the door from crashing in.

Before he went in, he took out his handkerchief and wiped the door handle. He listened. No sound from inside. Slowly he opened the door, but didn't go in. Still pin-drop silence.

No one would shoot him out here. They would wait for him to get inside.

He could see the hallway with two doors leading off it. One for the bathroom, another for the living room. Straight ahead, he could see the large, open-plan kitchen and reception area. The bedroom led off it. Silently, he closed the door behind him. It wouldn't shut, but that was okay. He bent down and crept along the hallway. His senses were tingling. The Colt was in his hand as he moved forward, pointing straight, ready to fire.

Someone's head. Grey-white hair. On the floor, lying face-down.

Dan felt like a mule had kicked him in the stomach. His chest was suddenly hollow, he couldn't breathe. Although the figure on the carpet was facing the other way, he knew it was Guptill.

Dan forgot everything else. Adrenaline took over. He flattened himself on the hallway carpet and searched for angles of fire.

He checked out the doorways ahead of him. Both doors were shut. No light underneath them. Curtains were drawn. The bathroom was further ahead, and the living room.

If the door opened suddenly, he could fire at the intruder's legs. He commando-crawled forward, elbows bunched by his side. A meter away from the reception, and three meters away from the figure on the floor, he stopped. A sofa was beside the motionless figure.

Next to the sofa, a door leading to the bedroom. It was ajar, and a light was on inside. That made him relax slightly. Only a fool would stand behind a door with a light on in the room. But it was still a possibility.

He rolled to his right. He could see the TV now, turned off. There was a glass bookcase stacked with books and magazines, and a minibar on the lowest shelf. A bottle of Chivas Regal on a tray with two crystal glasses. Guptill's favorite drink. His heart twisted at the memory.

He half-crouched and tried the handle of the living room door. He threw the door open, then sank back. The door banged against the opposite wall. No sound from inside. He peeked in, expecting gunfire. Nothing. Staying down, he moved into the room. It was empty, save for two lots of chairs and two glass bookcases again. He turned the lights on. The room was empty. Clear.

He repeated the same process with the bathroom. Clear.

He rushed to the bedroom. The major's clothes were on the bed, as if he was getting ready to go somewhere.

The whole process had taken a minute and a half. He turned quickly and bent down by the figure on the floor. Major Guptill's face was colorless, blood drained from it, his eyes wide and staring, his mouth open, saliva dribbling out. Dan needed gloves. Damn it. He took out his handkerchief and rolled it round his hand. He felt the carotid. A faint pulse, fast and thread-like. He didn't have long. Dan ran into the bathroom and returned with two small towels, rolling each around his hands, covering his fingers. Then he pulled the major onto his back. There was no blood. No signs of injury or assault. He checked the scalp, looked inside the lips.

"Felix...Felix."

Dan jerked his head back to the major's face. "Sir? Major? It's me, Dan. Dan Roy. What happened?"

Major Guptill's lips moved. Dan put his ear over his lips. "Yes, sir, I'm listening."

He stayed in that position for a few seconds before he realized there was no more sound coming from the major. Guptill's eyes were wide and fixed. His pupils were dilated. There was no flaring of the nostrils and his chest wasn't rising. Dan knew a dead man when he saw one. He didn't need to feel the carotid.

"Goodnight, Major," Dan whispered.

There wasn't anything else to say. He closed the major's eyes. He patted the body down. In the inside pocket of the vest, he found a wad of English banknotes. He put it in his pocket. Behind the notes he found a photo. He took it out. A young woman. Pretty, blond, in her twenties. She was smiling and looking at the camera. Her blue eyes matched Guptill's. She was young enough to be his daughter.

Dan knew that Guptill had an ex-wife who was a Brit. It made sense he could have a daughter.

The window behind looked out on the street, and it was open. A brief breeze blew in. Dan heard the slamming of car doors. He got up and stood to one side of the window behind the curtains, careful not to show his face. Two men in suits stood outside a Ford Mondeo.

They were looking up at the apartment. One of them signaled and they began to walk across the street, toward him. The knot of worry inside Dan's gut was growing, spreading into his limbs, making them ice-cold.

He had to escape. It was too late to go through the major's stuff. He stuffed the two towels in his pocket, and with his handkerchief wiped the handles of the bathroom, the living room and the main doors. He took one last look at the major, and then left. He was out on the landing of the third floor in less than fifteen seconds. One of the elevators was coming up. He looked down the stairwell. Empty, but he couldn't take the chance.

He jogged up one flight of stairs and looked down. He could see the elevator shaft from here. The two suits came out of the elevator. Dan knew he had seconds. He sprinted down the stairwell to the ground floor.

He came out on the street and headed down into the traffic of Chelsea Embankment.

CHAPTER 15

The buzz of the traffic and the pedestrians on Chelsea Embankment were a welcome distraction for Dan. His brain was numb, but his body was alive. He frequently did about-turns to look for danger. No one followed him. He was coiled like a wire spring and forced himself to breathe. Air rushed in from the Thames, smelling of mud and humidity.

He had to figure out what was happening. For that, he needed some space, and for everything to slow down. Briefly, he thought about stopping at one of the pubs to get a drink, but then changed his mind. He must get out of this place. The fewer people saw his face, the better. On the tube train he found a seat, put his head down and closed his eyes. The commuter rush was still going on. He was just another face among many. The crowd gave him some much-needed anonymity.

He changed at Waterloo, then got the train for Clapham Common in South London. He had been there once before, drinking at one of the pubs by the Common with some of his SAS friends. It was reasonably close to Chelsea. After some searching, he found a bed and breakfast. Known locally as a B&B, these places were England's version of a motel.

It was a nice B&B, in a large Victorian mansion by the Common. Dan paid in cash at reception, and went out to buy some cans of beer.

Dan's en suite bedroom was on the first floor, and the front windows opened out onto the green fields outside. He threw the shutters wide, got himself a cold Carlsberg can, and sat down in his armchair with his feet on the windowsill.

The evening sky was shrouding a cloak over the trees at the end of the green park. Darkness was claiming the air, and lights from the bars and pubs on the street were beginning to twinkle. He finished the Carlsberg in three long gulps, then went to the fridge and got himself another.

Major John Guptill. His old CO. One of the sharpest men he knew, and a man with connections. Who had killed him? Dan pressed his hands to his forehead. None of this made any sense.

Guptill had been like a father figure to him. The only man he could have trusted. His death made it unlikely that he had wanted Dan dead.

He thought back to how quickly the two suits had arrived. Who had called them? Had they come to dispose of the evidence, or were they cops?

Too many questions, not enough answers.

Dan forced himself to retrace his steps. Back to when he was trying to get into Guptill's apartment. There was no sign of forced entry in the doors or windows. He had no way of knowing if Guptill had a guest before he came in. Maybe he didn't. Guptill was wearing slippers. Had he stayed in the apartment all day? Had he been outside at all?

Dan remembered the pulse in the major's neck, and his breathing. He was still alive, so whatever happened had taken place shortly before Dan arrived. His lips twisted in frustration. While he was keeping stag, Guptill was dying, slowly…but how? As far as Dan knew, the major had no health conditions, he was fit as a fiddle, running two marathons a year. Dan closed his eyes. Guptill's pallid, white face jumped before his eyes. Very pale, drained of blood. But no sign of injury.

Heart attack? Possible. In a fifty-three-year-old man, non-smoker, minimal alcohol, and with his fitness levels? Maybe.

Then what? No bullet wounds. In the arms, Dan had looked for needle or knife stab marks. Zip. Nada. No blood anywhere.

*****

Dan woke up before sunrise. It was a habit. He was up in an instant, hand reaching for the weapon under his pillow. Then he remembered where he was. He relaxed but still kept his hand on the butt of the gun.

He still had the cellphone powered down, with the battery separate. He picked out the wad of notes and counted the money. One hundred and fifty pounds. That would not get him far in London. He washed his face, and did some yoga, as was his routine.

Then he looked out his open window. He had chosen the first-floor room deliberately. It gave him a good view of the surrounding streets. He could not see any cars that he had seen the night before.

It was 0830 by the time he got off at Sloane Square station. He paid the same attention to his surroundings as he headed down Chelsea Embankment. He walked down to the river end of Paradise Walk, casually passing the turning.

He stayed close to the riverside and looked on from the other side of the road. As he expected, the place was now a crime scene.

Yellow and black cross-marked police tape barricaded the entrance to the street. Two white police vans stood in front. As he watched, two men in white forensic suits came out the main door of the terraced house. A uniformed policeman followed. The forensics men went to the back of one van, took a briefcase out and went back into the house.

Dan sat down on a bench with the river behind him. After a while, he saw a woman. She came out and stood outside on the sidewalk. The uniformed policeman spoke to her.

The woman was in trouble. She covered her face with her hands, then allowed the policeman to help her to the squad car. She didn't get in, but took a tissue from the policeman and dabbed her eyes. Then she said something to the policeman, who nodded. The woman began to walk back up towards Royal Hospital Road.

She was blond and the younger side of thirty, Dan thought. From a distance, he couldn't tell her features very well. She wore a brown roll-neck jumper, and a dark blue skirt with black stockings. Her shoes were dark blue flats.

She looked just like the woman in Guptill's photograph. Dan got up and hurried in her direction.

CHAPTER 16

Dan didn't want to run: that gathered more attention than anything else. As he joined Chelsea Bridge Road, he saw the woman just ahead of him. Dan slowed his pace and kept people between them. The woman was about fifty yards ahead. As the tube station got closer, the number of pedestrians grew. More heads appeared between him and the woman. Dan increased his pace. He figured the woman wanted to get into the station, and if she did, he didn't want to lose her in the crowd. But a hundred yards from the Sloane Square underground, she turned into Sloane Avenue.

Sloane Avenue had tall, Art Deco buildings on either side of the street. They were all apartment blocks now, and Sloane Square being the fashionable heart of London, each apartment was worth millions.

Traffic there was less, and Dan hung back, following the woman at a leisurely pace on the same side of the street. She seemed in no hurry. Dan started feeling warm after a while and unfastened the top two buttons of his shirt. Sloane Avenue became full of elegant red-brick Victorian town houses. The terraced houses had elaborate cornices and balconies with curved railings and shutters in their windows. A maroon Lamborghini Diablo came down the road. Dan kept the woman in his sights.

Sloane Avenue turned into Brompton Road, a double-decker bus route, full of tourists and pedestrians. Boutique shops thronged the sides of the road. Dan increased his pace. They were approaching South Kensington. He was closer to the woman now, about forty yards away, when he saw her go into a clothes shop. He debated crossing the street, but decided against it. She could easily be keeping watch through the glass.

Dan bought a newspaper from a stand and pretended to read it. After a while, he peered inside the shop. He could not see the woman anywhere. He folded the newspaper and walked inside. He walked down the wide aisles. He looked at the back of the shop and saw another street exit.

He watched her shape flash against the door as she ran out into the street.

Dan swore to himself and walked fast. When he was out on the street, he caught sight of her, running down the steps of a tube station. Dan ran after her. She was at the ticket turnstiles, and went through as Dan watched. Without looking back she went quickly down the elevator staircase. As the elevators descended, she turned slightly. Their eyes met and she looked away.

"Son of a bitch," Dan said, and ran towards the ticket counter. He did not have time to buy one: there was a queue in front of every counter. He got to the turnstiles and vaulted over them. He ignored the cries of a ticket collector.

He could not see the woman anywhere on the elevators. He ran down, pushing people out of the way. The elevators were crowded, but Dan managed.

A crowd of people came off the train. Dan pushed past them, searching in the windows for a glimpse. He found her in the fourth compartment, looking out sideways to see if she had been followed. Their eyes met again, and at that instant, the train doors began to shut.

Dan sprung forward. The doors had shut but he forced his hand through the rubber gaskets and prised the doors open. Dan got into the carriage, ignoring the disapproving gaze of the passengers, his eyes searching around.

He could not see her. He pushed past people again, determined not to lose her. He found her in the next compartment along. He could see her through the glass doors that separated one subway carriage from another. She was looking around, but could not see Dan.

That was what Dan wanted. He stayed out of her line of vision. She had found a seat. Dan remained standing, watching her. The train stopped at several stations, but she remained seated. Dan glanced at the map above his head. They were into East London.

The woman got off at a stop called Whitechapel. Dan followed a few people behind her. This time, she did not see him.

At street level, Dan noticed she glanced at her phone, then walked down a side road briskly. Dan followed. The traffic grew thin, then non-existent.

She was headed down an alley with old, derelict office blocks on either side. The alley was empty apart from the two of them. Dan stayed well back.

He stopped behind a garbage can and peeked up just in time to see her vanishing into a building. Dan was against the front of the building in seconds. The entrance was wide, with revolving doors. There was scaffolding up the front of the building and it was undergoing renovation. Dan looked opposite and saw a similar office block with scaffolding.

He slipped in through the doors. The large lobby was empty. There weren't any carpets, and some old, disused chairs littered a corner. The reception desk was dirty and unused. Dan stepped carefully, on his tiptoes. Sound traveled loudly on cement.

The woman was not watching her step. Dan could hear the sound of her heels. He followed it to the stairwell next to the elevators. The elevators were out of order, and she was going up the stairs. Dan listened for a while, then followed her silently.

He heard her stop on the fifth floor, then go in. He stopped at the entrance and looked. There was a wide hallway, which opened out into an empty, open-plan room that was not yet built into an office. Opposite, Dan could see the windows of another office block.

Something lifted the hairs on the back of his neck. Automatically, his fingers curled around the butt of the Colt. He listened as hard as he could. The woman walked out into the middle of the open space, and stopped. She was halfway between Dan and the windows.

Dan came out of the landing and ran softly up to the walls. He raised his weapon up and listened. The woman was walking around. He looked in. She had her back to him and she glanced at her watch. She was waiting for someone.

There was no one there.

The realization hit him a split second before his worst fears were confirmed. A red dot danced around the walls. It came from one of the windows opposite. Quickly, Dan was out in the open. The woman turned around and her mouth opened in shock as her eyes traveled from him to his drawn weapon.

Dan bellowed at the top of his voice. "Get down!"

The red dot came off the walls and settled at the back of the woman's head. She was frozen, her eyes not leaving Dan. He threw caution to the wind and ran for her. She tried to move but Dan was swifter than the wind.

He grabbed her just as he heard the sound of a sharp crack. Then he was on top of her, covering her with his body. A few inches of wall protected them as the whining ricochet of bullets streamed in from the window.

"Get off me!" the woman screamed and fought, but Dan held her down. A bullet shattered a glass above their heads and the shards rained down on them. She stopped fighting.

Dan counted the bullets. Ten had been fired already. Most sniper rifles would have a 30-cartridge magazine.

And most sniper teams worked as a duo. When one ran out of ammo, the other took over, or handed a loaded gun to the shooter.

Dan would have to take those few seconds of respite. Dan counted another twenty rounds. They rolled around on the ground, getting closer to the wall and the hallway that separated them from the stairwell.

"When I say run, go for it. Go down the staircase. Right?" he whispered to the woman. Her fearful but beautiful blue eyes bulged out at him. She nodded in silence. Her blond hair was strewn around her head on the floor.

The bullets stopped suddenly. Dan screamed, "Now!"

The woman got up and ran as fast as she could.

But Dan did not run after her.

He raised himself, and took aim at the window from where he had seen the muzzle flash. A wisp of smoke still curled out of it. He fired three quick shots at it. The building was three hundred feet away at least. The rounds from the Colt would not have stopping power at that distance, but he could at least make them duck. Buy some precious seconds for himself.

He stood up from kneeling, shooting another two rounds at the window. Then he ran for the stairwell. The woman was waiting for him, halfway down the stairs.

They rushed down together. Dan stopped at the bottom of the staircase, and put his finger to his lips. He nudged her to a corner, and motioned to her to get down.

He could hear the faintest of sounds. Most normal men would not hear such sounds. But Dan was not a normal man. His senses were tuned to the movement of air around a body. To the whisper that a rubber-soled foot made on the ground.

Especially if that rubber-soled foot stepped on a piece of broken glass and withdrew quickly.

Dan checked his magazine. Three rounds left. He had another mag in his pocket, but he had no time to reload. Also, the click as the magazine went in would give him away.

Three bullets would have to do.

The footsteps approached the reception desk. Dan went to the ground. He was at an angle to the approaching men. They were to his left, and behind the stairwell door, about ten feet away. It was no good trying to come out of the door. They would shred him with bullets. Better to let them in.

Dan looked at the woman, and pointed upwards. She understood immediately. She got up silently, and took off her shoes. Then she padded up the stairs barefoot.

Dan pasted himself against the wall. He waited. The door opened slowly against him. He flinched backwards for the kick that would slam the door against him. It never came. A gun barrel poked through the door opening. Then a black, rubber-soled foot appeared.

Dan got up silently. As the figure came in through the doorway, Dan grabbed the gun. He pulled with all his strength. The man holding it was no weakling, which had the effect that Dan had desired.

The guy stumbled into the space. Without taking his hand off the gun muzzle, Dan fired point-blank with his other hand. The head mushroomed into a geyser of blood. As soon as he fired, Dan pulled the rifle off the man's hand, and dived for the protection of the wall.

Which was just as well. The wooden doors of the stairwell exploded under an avalanche of bullets. The firing was so ferocious that Dan could not lift up his head. Wooden fragments flew over his head, and covered him with sawdust. Dan knew what was coming next. He knew what he would do after such heavy fire. Lob in a grenade or a flashbang.

He would not give them that chance. He waited for the magazine to unload. The bullets stopped and there was a sudden, unnerving calm.

Dan did not wait. He kicked down the door, and the rattled structure flew off its hinges. He heard a grunt from the other side but he was firing blind already, teeth bared. He fired, then rolled into a ball on the floor, got up on one knee and fired again, moving the barrel side to side.

He stopped when he realized there was no return fire. The air was heavy with smoke and the sound of the rifle had deadened his ears. All he could hear was a ringing sound. As the dense smoke cleared, he looked at the floor.

The door had hit the man outside, and then he had been shredded by the bullets. It had been a two-man team. Enough to kill the woman, maybe.

But not enough for Dan Roy.

The man on the floor lay in a pool of blood. The silence was now total, a blanket of quietness that descends suddenly after vicious fighting. Dan heard a sound and cocked his gun up immediately.

It was the woman. Her forehead was plastered in sweat, and her eyes were wild with fear. Dan lowered the gun.

He said, "It's alright. You can come out."

She stepped out slowly. She stood to one corner, looking at the carnage around her. When her eyes saw the dead body on the floor she averted her gaze. Dan went through the unpleasant task of frisking the two men. He came up with nothing again. He lifted up the shirts from the belt line and then looked at their forearms.

His breath caught when he saw the tattoo on one of the men's deltoid muscles, near the shoulder. A red spearhead with the image of a black knife inside it. The Delta tattoo.

Sick at heart, Dan turned away.

He was used to killing. It did not bother him. He had never knowingly killed a woman or a child. He did not want that on his conscience. And neither had he ever knowingly killed one of his Delta brothers. Well, he had not known. That was what his rational mind told him. But his gut was telling him something else.

It's a shit game, son, John Guptill had said. Now he was lying cold in a grave. He should have added – Get out while you can. Otherwise, it might be you lying there one day.

"Hey, you okay?" It was the woman's voice.

Dan had been kneeling with his head against the wall. He felt nauseous and wanted to get the hell out of this place, more than anything else. He turned and straightened.

"Yes, I'm fine. What's your name?"

"Chloe Guptill."

"I thought so."

Chloe frowned. "What do you mean?"

Dan looked at the main exit, forty feet away, straight down the hallway. He said, "Let's get out of here alive, then I'll tell you."

CHAPTER 17

Chloe stayed behind Dan as they crept out of the building site. Once out, they ran for the main street. Dan felt safer with people around him. They ducked inside a coffee shop. They both used the restroom to make themselves more presentable.

When he came out, Chloe was already ordering. Dan got a large caramel macchiato, and with Chloe's cappuccino, they sat down away from the windows.

Her chest was still heaving up and down, and there was a light film of sweat on her forehead. Her blond hair came down to her shoulders. It wasn't dyed, he could tell by the non-darkened hair roots. Her eyes were wide, with long eyelashes. She had topaz eyes with dark, almost black irises. A small nose spread out into a generous mouth. She wasn't wearing much make-up and didn't have any lipstick on. She was very beautiful. Dan stared at her.

"Who are you?" Her voice was low, but direct. Dan had to admire her. Many people would have panicked and got themselves killed in the near-death situation that they had just been in. But Chloe had known how to handle herself. And right now, she was showing remarkable composure.

Dan didn't answer immediately, thinking of his best response.

"Who are you?" Chloe repeated. She was trying not to look scared.

Dan said, "I saw you coming out of the apartment block where Major Guptill lived. You spoke to the police officers, so I figured you had something to do with the major."

Chloe's face became a mixture of worry and curiosity. "Why were you watching me?"

"I wasn't watching you. I was looking out for the major. He used to be my commanding officer in the Delta Force, Squadron A."

She opened her mouth slightly, as if to say something, then shut it. She frowned heavily, and he could see the sadness in her eyes. Her voice trembled.

"He's dead." She lifted up her chin and sniffed, determined not to show emotion in front of a stranger. Dan could tell she was having a hard time.

"My name is Dan Roy. John Guptill was my mentor, ever since I joined the Force. Almost like a father figure. I'm very sorry."

Dan held her gaze. Eventually, she nodded.

Chloe had composed herself. "You are American, like Dad."

Dan nodded. She asked, "Did you recognize me from the photo?"

"Yes."

"Who told you to be there, Chloe?"

"I got a phone call. A woman's voice. She said Dad wanted me to meet someone. From the address, I didn't realize it was going to be that shithole. But I had to go, to find out what I could about Dad."

"What else did this woman say?"

"She said she was calling from Dad's law firm. I checked, they have a branch in London. They are a global firm. Dad wanted me to have some papers, but he wanted this person to give them to me at the location we were just in."

"Did that not strike you as suspicious?"

"Yes. But Dad did meet me in secret locations when he was in London."

Dan thought about that. "Did he ever tell you why?"

"No. But I got the impression he wanted to keep me away from everything. I know he worked for a firm whose name he couldn't tell me."

Dan nodded. Chloe said, "Do you work for the same firm?"

Dan hesitated. Chloe read his mind. "It's ok," she said, "you don't have to tell me. Need to know, right?"

"Right," Dan said, relieved. She was smart, he thought to himself.

"What happened in there…? You knew what to do."

Dan shrugged. "It's my job."

After a pause, he asked, "You live in London?"

Chloe said, "My parents divorced when I was young. I've lived with my mum and stepfather since then. In Reading, outside London, not far from Heathrow. Now I rent an apartment here, like Dad used to."

Dan asked, "Who called you about your father's death?"

"Scotland Yard. Guess they had my name down as next of kin."

"What did they tell you was the cause of death?" he asked.

"They didn't specify. He was found dead, and there was evidence of a break-in. No injuries on his body, however. They think there might have been an intruder, but they don't know how Dad died. Maybe a heart attack, they said, but no one knows." She grimaced. "They said the body would go to the coroner, and if he couldn't find a cause of death, then there would be an autopsy."

"Did they say it's now a criminal investigation?"

Chloe tucked a loose strand behind her ear as she took a sip of her cappuccino. "Yes, it is."

"Did the cops say how they heard of it?"

Chloe frowned. "Yes. They said a neighbor called when they found the body."

That was a lie. Dan tightened his jaw, but didn't say anything.

How could Guptill answer the door if he was lying dead on the floor? What sort of a neighbor would have keys to the apartment? And why had Dan not seen this neighbor?

Someone else had informed the cops. He thought of how rapidly the two detectives had arrived.

Someone who knew he would be there. Dan looked out the window. He hadn't been followed. But there were many other ways of keeping stag. A drone, for example. High above London's skies, invisible. His head became dizzy at the thought.

To get clearance for a drone feed someone needed access to the highest echelons of the intelligence service. Maybe it wasn't that. Maybe he was thinking about it too much. Maybe this was all fucked up beyond all recognition, and he was being played like a sucker.

Chloe coughed. "What do you make of it?"

"Sorry. I am confused at the moment, I have to say."

"Me, too. Do you really think someone broke into the apartment and…" She stopped. "Hang on, you said that the door was shut when you arrived?"

Dan nodded. Chloe said, "So the cops are lying?"

"No. The person calling them probably said he or she was a neighbor.

Then they saw the door broken in when they came, found the body, and reached their own conclusion."

"Are you going to tell the cops?"

"No."

"But why not? It can help them with their investigation."

Dan shook his head. "There was no neighbor. The cops arrived while I was there. If a neighbor knew, they must have phoned the cops already. I can't see how the neighbor would have got into the apartment, unless…"

"Unless what?"

Unless the neighbor was the killer, Dan thought to himself. He shook his head. "Don't worry about it. What are you going to do now?"

A helpless look passed over Chloe's face. "I don't know. I didn't see Dad that often. I was ten when my parents divorced. But Dad came whenever he was on leave. I used to go on holidays with him." She became quiet.

"Are you staying in your apartment?" Dan asked gently.

"Yes," Chloe said.

"If you don't mind me asking, what do you do for a living?"

"I'm a journalist. I work for the *London Herald*."

"Interesting."

Chloe asked, "Why did Dad want to see you?"

"I don't know. I think it was something important, but not sure."

"What's going on here, Dan? You're holding back, I can tell. I need to know."

Dan sighed and nodded. Yes, she did need to know. But he had a problem. He couldn't tell her about his case, it was confidential.

He said, "I am in the dark as much as you are, Chloe."

She didn't seem convinced but didn't prod any further. "So, what do we do now?"

Dan said, "We need to find a cause of death. As you're next of kin, you have the right to demand an autopsy. Have you seen the body already?"

She lowered her face and nodded.

"I'm sorry," he said.

"Don't be. It's happened now. We need to find out what's going on."

"It's time to visit the morgue," Dan said.

CHAPTER 18

They were out on the street when Dan stopped.

"Do you know which coroner's office they've taken the body to?" he asked.

"Yes. The one next to Chelsea Crown Court. It's close to the Royal Brompton Hospital."

Dan said, "The coroner's report won't be ready for a day or two. I know you've identified the body already. I need to examine it more thoroughly. Are you sure you can handle that?"

If Chloe didn't understand what he meant, she didn't show it. She swallowed and nodded.

"Okay," Dan said. "Just close your eyes, if you find it disturbing. Without you, I can't access the body."

Chloe lifted her chin. "Don't worry about me, Dan. I'll be fine." Her upright posture, and the mild arrogance in the lifted chin suddenly reminded Dan of John Guptill. She certainly was his daughter.

At the morgue, a bored receptionist with a red Tina Turner hairdo stifled a yawn as they approached. Without speaking, she raised her eyebrows.

Chloe did the talking. "I need to see my father's body. His name is John Guptill."

"You are the next of kin?"

"That's right."

"Sign here, please," Tina Turner said. "And who's this?"

"My half-brother," Chloe said without missing a beat. Tina Turner glanced from Chloe to Dan and back to Chloe. The two women stared at each other for a few seconds. Then the receptionist pressed a button underneath the table.

"You'll see a guard at the gate of the basement. He'll take you down there."

"Thanks," Chloe said.

They walked through narrow, white hallways to the uniformed guard at

162

the end. He nodded and opened a door, showing them a staircase.

In the basement below men in green overalls wheeled gurneys around, and pulled bodies out of drawers. It felt cold down there. On the walls, large air-conditioning machines whirred constantly. One of the green overalls approached them as a phone on the wall rang. The man answered it and spoke briefly, eyeing them. He hung up and came over.

"Chloe Guptill?"

"That's me," Chloe said.

"You wish to identify the body?"

"Yes," she said. Dan looked at her approvingly. She had identified the body already, but this guy didn't have to know that.

"Follow me."

They went down another hallway, dodging gurneys with stiffs on them. This nice part of London certainly had its fair share of dead bodies, Dan mused. They got into a cold, white room. The man checked a sheet of paper on a clipboard, running his finger down it. He thumped the clipboard gently, then turned and counted the square drawers on the wall. He found the one he wanted and pulled it out, revealing the white, cloth-covered body on the tray. "Do you just want to see, or spend some time?"

Dan looked at Chloe, who took a deep breath. "Spend some time," she said.

The man shrugged. From underneath the tray, he pulled two collapsible legs and set them on the floor.

"All yours," he said, with an understated cheeriness.

"Moron," Chloe muttered as the man shut the door behind him.

Dan exchanged a sympathetic glance with Chloe, opened his rucksack, and took out the latex gloves. He put them on.

"You don't have to look," he said.

"What are you going to do?" Chloe's voice betrayed her anxiety.

"I checked his body in the apartment. But his legs and arms were covered. I also need to check the spine, ears, and scalp."

"Okay," Chloe gulped.

"The quicker I do it, the sooner we get out of here."

Dan took the sheet off. The body was naked. Chloe had turned her back, facing the door. Dan moved his hand through the scalp. Guptill had a military buzz cut and he could see the scalp between the hair follicles. Perfect place, he knew, to hide an injection mark. A tiny, 28-gauge needle would leave almost no mark. Fieldcraft lessons, taught to him by CIA agents, when they worked together on missions.

He didn't find anything in the scalp. He moved down to the ears, checking the back of the lobes carefully, then looked inside. This was when an auroscope became useful, but he wasn't a doctor. He looked closely, but couldn't see any needle marks in the right ear. In the left ear, there wasn't any either, but he saw something else.

A small, black mark. He went over to the sink and wet a piece of tissue. Very gently, he touched the black spot. It flaked off. A blood clot. Beneath the clot, very close to the entrance of the inner ear, he found the smallest of puncture wounds.

So small, he would have missed it had it not been for the blood. He wondered if he had missed similar needle marks elsewhere. It didn't matter. He had found what he was looking for.

He checked Guptill's legs and between the toes of his feet quickly. There wasn't anything. Then he replaced the sheet, lifted the collapsible legs and trundled the tray back inside its square hole. He tore off his latex gloves, chucked them in the trash and washed his hands.

"Let's talk outside," he whispered to Chloe.

*****

Dan steered Chloe down the busy King's Road towards Fulham Broadway underground station.

He could feel Chloe's impatience.

"What did you find?" she asked eventually.

"I'll tell you later."

She wasn't happy with that. "Where are we going?"

"Back to my place, or to your apartment—it's up to you."

"My apartment, then."

Dan would have preferred his own place. Or a park bench, somewhere in the open.

"In which case," Chloe said, "we need to head down south."

"We'll take the tube," Dan said.

"It's not that long a walk."

Dan shook his head. "No, we take the tube."

The pavement was crowded. Easy for someone to hide and watch them, or for a sniper to pick them off a rooftop. He doubted that would happen in broad daylight on an open street, but after what just happened, he could not take any chances.

"Hold up," he told Chloe. "If someone just tried to kill you, chances are they have your apartment covered."

They had reached the crowded tube station. Chloe stopped, looking weary. "So, what do we do?"

Dan said, "They're after me as well. But all they know so far is that I escaped. They don't know where I am. So, it's best to go to the B&B I'm staying at."

Chloe looked defeated. Dan put a hand on her shoulder. "Hey, I know this is weird. But trust me, we will get to the bottom of this. Ok?"

Chloe nodded, and came off the wall. They took the elevator down to the trains.

At Clapham Common they walked to Dan's B&B. It took them ten minutes.

Chloe looked around the double bedroom, and out the window at the common. A soccer team was practicing outside on the green.

"So, what do we do now?" she asked.

Dan had figured this out already. "We need to find out more about what your father knew. I bet you the clues could be in his apartment already. I need to get back in there to check."

He sat down on a chair facing her and ran his hands through his hair.

"Chloe, have you heard of someone called Felix?"

Chloe frowned. "Felix?"

"Yes. Your dad said that word twice before he died. His last words. He was trying to make a point."

Chloe muttered the words under her breath. Then she looked up. "No. They don't ring a bell."

"I didn't see anyone enter or leave from the main door. Yet he was lying there, almost dead. There were no signs of a break-in."

"So the person who got in and killed my father was someone my father knew?"

"Looks like it, yes. Why would he open the door otherwise?"

"Alright. So how did he escape, if you were keeping watch, and you saw no one entering or leaving the apartment?"

"There's no way out the back, is there?" Dan had scoped this out already. There was a back garden, which led straight into the garden of another terraced apartment block.

"No."

"Two possibilities. He'd done the deed and left before I turned up for surveillance. Or, he left via the roof."

Chloe blinked at him in surprise. "What do you mean?"

Dan told Chloe how he had escaped when the cops turned up.

He asked, "You still have keys?"

"Yes."

"Then tonight I pay the apartment another visit."

CHAPTER 19

Chloe said, "I need to eat something."

"You read my mind," he said. He was famished. Apart from the coffee in the morning, he had had nothing to eat.

Chloe said, "If you need to see the apartment again, let's head down to Chelsea. I know a place where we can eat."

Dan looked at his watch. 1800 hours. He needed to get to the apartment under cover of darkness. The timing would be right. They walked out to the tube station and took the subway to Chelsea.

As they walked down, Chloe pointed down Chelsea Embankment towards the bend in the river. "This place is near Chelsea Harbour. Do you like seafood?"

"I eat any food. How far?"

"Fifteen, maybe twenty minutes' walk."

They crossed over to the riverside and walked down. Dan glanced around at the buildings, looking for open windows with curtains spread, and for sun glinting off metal.

"Tell me about your father," Dan said as they walked.

Chloe shrugged. "Like I said, I only saw him once or twice a year, but he stayed in touch. In many ways, we were close."

"I'm sorry."

"Don't be. He was a quiet person. Kept to himself. Never talked about his work."

Dan smiled. "All Army families have the same story. Soldiers lead crazy lives."

"I know."

The river stayed on their left, and bulbous, new, glass and steel residential and office blocks rose on the opposite bank.

On their side, the vintage buildings of Chelsea couldn't be torn down, but

Battersea opposite was fair game, as most of its river front used to be dilapidated warehouses.

Soon they went past Prince Albert Bridge and the buildings on their side changed subtly. Chelsea Embankment had been left behind, and the graceful red-brick Victorian mansions made way for factories and warehouses that had recently been converted into residential apartment blocks. In between stood rows of smaller residential terraces, from Victorian times, but their less imposing façades meant they were for the clerks and servants of the lords and ladies who lived in Chelsea.

Chloe pointed at the smaller houses. "Three hundred years ago, this is where the normal people lived. The rich lot lived back there."

Dan smiled. "Not much has changed, then."

"Nope."

They reached Chelsea Harbour and a restaurant called Fisherman's Friend. The décor inside was dark and velvety, with oil paintings of marine life. Dim lights dotted the floor discreetly, lighting up the ceiling with soft haloes.

"Looks nice," Dan whispered as the waitress approached.

"It is."

It was Dan's turn to ask questions as they waited for their starters.

"Tell me about your job."

Chloe's eyes glinted in the low light. "I enjoy it, I have to say. Right now, the *Herald* is looking into the weapons industry."

Something distant tightened in Dan's mind. A sudden flash of the weapons catchment in that basement in Afghanistan. Then it was gone. He focused on Chloe.

"That sounds interesting. Tell me more."

"It *is* interesting. The weapon manufacturers in the UK are a very privileged group of private companies. The government has a support organization designed to help them sell their stuff to the rest of the world. It's called the Defence Support Organisation or the DSO."

"Surely the government helps other industries in the same way?"

Chloe shook her head. "I'm not talking about tax breaks or financial help here. The UK government actually does the marketing, publicizing and getting them contracts from foreign countries. What other industry does the government do that for?"

"So, what does the government actually do?"

"Diplomats speak to the Defense Ministers of Middle East countries. The Saudis are our biggest weapon buyers. There is even a so-called Export Support Team, a group of ex-military men who advise foreign governments which weapons to buy from us."

Dan had heard about this. "But that's all above board. What's your angle?"

"The angle is Britain's huge arms sales to Middle East countries that are using these arms to fight their own wars. Just pick one. The fight against ISIS, in Syria against the government, in Yemen against the Houthi rebels."

Dan pursed his lips. "I don't want to sound insensitive. But if there is a war, then someone has to supply the weapons, right?"

"That's not the point, Dan. Anyone can supply weapons. The point is, when the regimes we supply weapons to use them in blatant human rights violations, then we're doing something illegal. There is actually a law that prohibits us from doing that. So why do we keep doing it?"

Dan lifted his eyebrows. "When these countries buy the weapons from us, they don't tell us they'll bomb civilians, do they? So how is it our fault?"

Chloe sighed. "Dan, even a ten-year-old child will tell you which countries in the world we shouldn't be selling weapons to. And yet, they happen to be our biggest customers. In fact, they make us the second-largest exporter of weapons in the world."

"Okay. I get it. But let's come back to your angle."

"Right. We have concrete evidence that British-made cluster bombs, now declared illegal by NATO, have landed in farms in Yemen."

Dan kept quiet. Delivering weapons and training to rebel groups was something Special Forces had always done. Dan himself had played a part in training Afghan Special Forces when he was with Delta. No one ever asked where the weapons came from. It was a given that they would be there when needed.

Chloe continued. "As the cluster bombs are banned, several newspapers in the UK are putting pressure on the DSO to negotiate their return from the countries they sold them to originally."

Their starters had arrived and they tucked in. "I doubt that's going to work," Dan said, taking a mouthful of squid.

Chloe wiped her lips and waved her hands. "Maybe. Maybe not. But Dad was going to introduce me to someone in the US Embassy who knows about this."

Dan stopped chewing his food. He swallowed quickly and refocused.

"Wait," he said. "Your father said someone in the Embassy would talk to you about this?"

"Yes."

"Why?"

"What do you mean why? Because he's my dad."

"No. I mean why would this person speak to you?"

Chloe shrugged. "I guessed that he would speak anonymously. It happens a lot."

Dan frowned. "Yeah, but if this guy *works* in the US Embassy, I bet my bottom dollar he's actually CIA. What's his name?"

"Simon Renwick."

Dan thought about the name. It did not mean anything to him. But he felt uneasy. His mind was tangled up in knots.

Chloe sipped her white wine.

"Penny for your thoughts," she said.

Dan said, "Did you ring the Embassy asking for this guy, Renwick?"

Chloe pursed her lips. "Why do you ask?"

"Because I need to know. Did you, Chloe?"

"Yes."

"When?"

"Two days ago."

"When did this woman ring you from your dad's law firm?"

"Yesterday. You think there's a connection?"

Dan sat back in his chair. His brows were furrowed. "Maybe."

CHAPTER 20

By the time they came out of the restaurant, it was past nine o'clock.

"Did you ever know your father's lawyer?"

"No. Why?"

"Call them tomorrow. Ask them about this woman who called you. See if this call was genuine."

Chloe said, "I checked already. I never got the woman's name. The partner who's looking after Dad's assets in the UK is going to get in touch with me."

"But they don't know about what happened this afternoon."

"No. I spoke to them yesterday."

Dan said, "You need to call a cab now. Head back to the B&B. I'll see you tomorrow morning."

"I thought you were going back to Dad's apartment."

"I am. And I need the keys." Dan stretched his hand out.

"Maybe I should come with you," Chloe said. An image flashed before Dan's eyes. Lucy, standing with her hands on her hips inside the pub. Just before *it* happened. With an effort, he suppressed the sense of dread that rose up inside him.

Dan shook his head. "No. There's every chance someone is keeping an eye on the place. If there's any trouble I don't want you to get caught up in it."

"Will you be okay?" she asked softly. Dan looked at her and smiled.

"Don't worry about me. I know how to take care of myself."

*****

Dan watched the tail light of Chloe's cab glow a dull red in the distance, then fade from view. He retreated to the cement balustrades by the river, and reached inside his pocket. He took out the cellphone Guptill had given him. He stuck the battery on and powered the phone up.

He had one missed call.

He thumbed down the list of contacts. There was always only one number stored in these phones. Dan dialed it, and heard it ring four times before he heard Burns' voice.

Dan said, "It's me."

Burns said, "Been trying to get hold of you."

"Guptill's dead."

Burns asked, "I know. How did you find out?"

"He told me to meet him at his apartment. He was dead when I turned up."

Burns said, "Shit. This has to be the same guy who killed the CIA agent."

Dan asked, "What happened in Virginia?"

"Not good, Dan. They want to see you, and find out what the hell is going on. With Guptill now dead, things are more dicey. What are you gonna do?"

Dan thought for a while. He could run, but Intercept would come after him. He had no wish to go back. He wanted to be free. But free on his own terms. Not with a death sentence hanging over him.

He said, "I need to resolve this first. I need to clear my name."

Burns said softly, "Ok, I get that. But you have to be careful."

After a pause, Burns asked, "Who killed the guards who went with you to the safe house?"

"I did. They tried to kill me."

Burns whispered, "Jesus." He paused and said, "We need to meet."

"Yes," Dan said. "Where are you?"

"At the office."

There was a large hotel opposite where Dan was standing. Its lights fell on the Thames, reflecting in the waters. The Millennium & Copthorne Hotel. A Rolls-Royce Phantom V16 came to a stop outside as Dan watched. A man in an expensive tuxedo helped out a woman in a tiny red dress. The woman pouted and smiled. Then she swung her shapely bottom up the marble staircase. She was half her escort's age.

"Meet me inside the Millennium & Copthorne Hotel lobby. Chelsea." Dan hung up.

When Burns turned up in half an hour, Dan was inside the hotel, waiting at the bar. They found two armchairs behind an enormous vase containing a palm tree. Shaded from the other guests, but surrounded by people. Just what Dan wanted.

"Talk," Burns said.

Dan told him what happened. Burns leaned back in his chair. "Fuck."

He looked at Dan. "We've been infiltrated. Let me state the obvious here. Someone is trying to silence you. They got to Guptill already."

"Because of what I saw in that compound. And maybe because of what happened in Yemen."

Burns said, "Yes. Unless there is something else from the past."

Dan racked his brains. Making enemies was a by-product of what he did. He had killed one of the biggest heroin dealers in Iran six months ago. Blown up their factory, too. Iran had become one of the largest conduits of heroin from Afghanistan into Europe. This dealer had been close to the Ayatollah's Republican Guards, who had put a price on Dan's head.

Dan asked, "What did Guptill know?"

Burns shook his head slowly. "I don't know. Now we'll never find out."

"I think you can, if you try."

Burns' tone was sharp. "What do you mean?"

"I reckon you are our connection to the US Government. Maybe you worked for the CIA in the past."

Burns' tone was soft. "How do you figure that?"

"You were there when the shit hit the fan with me. You sort these things out, right?"

"Even if that were true, what's your point?"

Dan said, "So I think you are tight with the powers that be. You can ask favors. Find out what Guptill was up to."

They stared at each other for a few seconds. Then Burns smiled. "Guptill and McBride spoke highly of you. I can see why."

"So will you ask around about Guptill?"

Burns said, "Alright. I'll ask around, I promise. But remember, someone is inside Intercept. The camera you took photos with has disappeared. I could have taken that straight to the CIA."

"I know that."

"Dan, you need to be careful of who you trust. So do I. I don't know which way this thing's gonna go next."

Dan was thinking about Burns. "What are you gonna do?"

Burns said, "This shit is deep. I mean, without clearance no can even access these weapons, right? And I'm talking about a base that we control."

Dan nodded. "Yes. I checked the Hellfire missiles in 'Stan. Sure as hell said 'US Army' on the side."

Burns said, "So we are dealing with someone high up. I need to go back to Virginia soon, to give them a report. Intercept suspect you, Dan. But I know they are looking all around, too. If there is someone inside, they will find him."

Dan said, "I need money. I can access my checking account, but I would rather use the expenses." Every Intercept agent had an expenses account.

"And I also need a weapon. A Sig Sauer P226, with a box of extra ammo. 7.62mm NATO rounds. A Heckler & Koch 417 rifle with all the mod cons we are used to. NVGs and a compass. Can you get that?"

Burns nodded. "We need to be careful with our phones. You shouldn't call me again from the one I gave you."

"Makes sense."

"Use a new one with a new SIM card for every call you make to me from now on."

Dan rose. Burns rose with him. He said, "See you back here tomorrow, same time. I will have the money and a bag with the weapons with me. Do not meet anyone else from Intercept apart from me."

Dan said, "Roger that."

Burns said, "I got something for you." He pulled out a briefcase and opened the lid a fraction. Dan peered inside and smiled. He pulled out his eleven-inch-long, curved kukri knife. He stuffed the knife in his back pocket.

"Thanks."

Burns asked, "Where you headed now?"

"To find the infiltrator."

*****

Dan waited for ten minutes after Burns left.

At 2200 hours, he came down the stairs. He was out the main door in less than five seconds, and on the street immediately after that.

He didn't see any cars waiting at the curb opposite, and he relaxed. He walked quickly, keeping his face low. No one followed him. Orange street lights glowed brightly in the warm night air. He slowed down as he approached Paradise Walk. The yellow and orange police tape was still strung from one end of the street to the other. He kept watch again. After ten minutes, he hadn't seen anything unusual. A couple of residents sauntered out of one of the apartments and then went back in. A couple came out for a walk along the Embankment. Dan stayed in the shadow of a tree, almost invisible in the darkness.

Half an hour later he made his move. He strolled casually up to Paradise Walk, and did what the residents had done. He bent below the police tape and walked on, keeping to the same side of the street as Guptill's apartment. Some of the lights were on in the windows of the four-story building. There was a light on at the main entrance as well, but he didn't see any security cameras.

He let himself in with the key. The hallway was deserted. He padded up the staircase to the second floor. The landing was in darkness. The elevator shaft was open and the lights indicated an elevator was waiting. He went to the double doors and peered through the glass box. The hallway to the apartments was empty. Lights were placed on the wall at regular intervals. Dan waited for a minute. He didn't want to wait too long in case someone came up the stairs or the elevator. He put his latex gloves on.

Three lines of the police tape were stuck across the door frame of Guptill's apartment. The door was ajar. Beyond the door—total blackness. Dan knelt down and removed the tape rather than break it. Staying down, he pushed the door gently. It swung open into silence. He let his eyes adjust.

Then he was inside the apartment. He took the ends of the sticky tape and reattached them to the door frame. He would have to repeat that procedure when he left. He reached into his bag and took out the flashlight, putting it in his pocket for future use.

He could make out shapes. He saw the doors on his right and left. Bathroom and living room. He opened each one and peered inside. Then he went inside each one and, staying down, turned the flashlight around. Clear again.

In total silence, he moved into the reception area. A faint ray of street light let itself in through the window shutters. He saw the furniture, but nothing else. He crept towards the bedroom. At the door, he listened. If there was anyone inside, they were being very quiet. It was almost impossible that they had heard him.

Almost. There was always a danger. He couldn't afford to be complacent. Slowly, he reached out a gloved hand and turned the door handle. It was well oiled. He opened the door soundlessly, and shrank back from the opening, back against the wall. Then he looked inside. Darkness again, but in the broken shafts of street light falling in the reception area, he could make out the bed. The clothes were gone. Staying crouched, holding the flashlight in his hand, Dan walked into the bedroom. He left the door open behind him, so he could escape if something happened.

There was a wardrobe. Dan stood up and shifted his kukri scabbard from his back belt to the front of his waist. He could remove it easily from the scabbard now if he needed to. He opened the wardrobe door and looked inside. An array of suits were neatly arranged inside. Below that, a similar collection of dress shoes. Dan moved the suits and found some shirts. He looked under and, apart from the shoes, he found some slippers. Two travel bags for the suits, both of which were empty. He found two shoeboxes as well, with nothing inside them. He stood up and looked at the suits again. Savile Row. Bespoke and expensive.

He lifted up each suit jacket, shook them slightly, then put them back in. There were six suit jackets in total, and the fourth one seemed heavier. Dan passed his hands over it. Not much there. He turned the torchlight off and put the jacket on. Immediately he felt it. On his left, something inside the lining. He peeled the jacket off and slashed at the sides of the expensive fabric. The lining fell open. Inside, he found a silver wig that would suit an older man. He also found an envelope with three passports inside. A red EU, a navy blue American, and a maroon Egyptian. He used his phone to take photos of everything, then stuffed the passports and wig inside his bag.

Then he heard the noise. He froze.

CHAPTER 21

It had been very faint, maybe a creak of a footstep, Dan thought. But it was definitely something. On the balls of his feet, swift but silent, he moved to the door.

There was no further sound from outside. Whoever was out there had gone quiet. He felt for the kukri. He balled his fists, dropped his shoulders. How many? One or two? Maybe another waiting outside on the landing. If this was a full team, then another in the car.

The darkness suddenly exploded. The bedroom door was savagely kicked open. It smashed against him, and he had his arms lifted up like a boxer's. As the door bounced off him, he saw the gun appear and the hand holding it. Dan grabbed it and pulled up and away from him, and a round went off whining into the ceiling. A suppressed gun, he hardly heard the sound.

Dan kicked the door shut, making the man stumble into the room. Keeping his hand firmly on the gun wrist, Dan punched the man as hard as he could in the stomach. He heard the groan, but by that time his other hand had found the man's hair. Dan grabbed hold of a generous grip and pulled the head down to his rising knee with lethal force. Another round went off into the ceiling. There was a squelching sound, like a large grape being squashed under a shoe, and a muffled scream. The man would need a new nasal septum.

The man used his body weight to crash into Dan, throwing him off balance. They both fell backwards, landing on the bed. The man was on top, blood dripping onto Dan's face. Dan still had a vice-like grip on the man's right wrist holding the gun. With his free hand, the man clawed Dan's face, reaching for his eyes. Dan punched the man in the jaw. He connected solidly and felt the bone crunch. He delivered the same blow again. This time with a soft pop, he heard the TMJ snap. The man screamed this time, loudly. It sounded strange and guttural, like he had lost his voice. Dan rolled on top of him and punched him once more to render him unconscious. He felt the body go slack and the gun came out in Dan's hand. Dan lowered the body gently off the bed. The man might be out cold, but not for long. And if he had backup…

Dan rolled off the bed and, gun in hand, listened by the doorway. Total silence again. His eyes bore into shadows, searching movement: his ears listened to every sound in the night. He could hear water dripping somewhere, a cat's meow. But nothing else. He gripped the unfamiliar butt of the gun. He fell to the floor and crawled his way out into the living room. He was now in a direct straight line with the open door, and he didn't like it. He rolled over and stood up near the window, staying away from the frame, and peered down the side into the street.

He saw the car. On the same side, further down. Lights and engine off, but he hadn't seen the car before he came in. It was a foreign make, probably a Lada or Škoda. He took a deep breath. For a few seconds, he kept his eyes on the car. Then he saw the movement inside. The driver, who took out a cellphone, stared at the screen, then put the phone down. Dan got an idea. He crept over to the glass shelf at the other end of the room. He found a bottle of whiskey. Staying below the window, he opened it a fraction, just enough to put the bottle on the ledge. Then he walked to the doorway and loosened the police tapes. He came back to the window and tipped the full bottle of whiskey out. It fell, landing with a crash on the empty street below.

Dan ran. He came out of the apartment, sprinted down the landing, and took the steps four at a time. In ten seconds, he was at the ground floor. He ran to the wall next to the main door and flattened himself against it, sinking down to the floor. He still had the gun in his hand. He didn't know what type it was, but it had a level of suppression he hadn't come across before. Which was unusual, because he had used most of the common, suppressed handguns.

Ten seconds for the guy in the car to figure out something was wrong. Another ten seconds to get out of the car, lock it and hurry down. Dan counted down. He had ten seconds in hand. Right on cue, there was a sound at the door. A key turned. The door opened gently. A shaft of dull yellow street light fell into the hallway. Dan tightened his grip on the weapon. He couldn't extend his elbow to raise it, but he turned it so it was facing the open door.

A tall, wide man stepped in. Black jacket falling to his knees. He kicked the door shut gently with his heel. Dan got a flash of his face in the street light. Swarthy, dark hair, and with a weapon in his right hand. Only six feet separated Dan from him. Dan could hear his heart squeeze against his ribs. A trickle of sweat found its way past his eyebrows into his left eye. He couldn't move to wipe it off.

The man stared into the darkness ahead, then strode forward. He put a hand on the stair railings, ready to climb upstairs. Then he waited. Dan couldn't see him anymore. He knew the man had one foot on the stair. Listening and waiting. Dan extended his right elbow and moved slightly forward. He would get the first round in.

He heard a stair creak. Then another. Dan kept his elbow extended, and moved it up along the underside of the staircase. The steps kept going further up. Dan listened till he couldn't hear any more.

Then he got to his feet quickly. He opened the door with his key, shutting it gently behind him. He ran over to the car and took a photo of the license plates. Then he turned towards the rustling waters of the Thames and sprinted down the road.

CHAPTER 22

Dan ran down the side streets, avoiding the main avenues of Chelsea Bridge and Royal Hospital Road. As he got near Sloane Square tube station, he was able to flag down a minicab. The driver rolled down his window. He was of Middle Eastern origin, in his late-forties, his teeth stained yellow. Dan looked him over quickly. Then he jumped in the back and gave him directions to Clapham, straight down Chelsea Bridge.

He got out of the cab five hundred yards from the hotel, paid the driver, and walked the rest of the way. It was 0100 hours. He slowed down as he approached the hotel, watching for a minute. The reception light was on. The rest of the building was sunk in darkness, including his room.

Dan stepped into the reception. The owner was dozing at the desk, but he looked up with a start as Dan approached. He recognized Dan and smiled. Dan went up to his room and knocked. Chloe opened the door on the chain, and relaxed when she saw Dan.

Dan felt Chloe's eyes on him as he peeled off his sweaty black vest and went into the bathroom for a quick shower. He put on a dressing gown, then sat down with the bag on his lap. Chloe put the table lamp on and sat down next to him.

Dan told her what had happened. Chloe's hand went to her throat. She looked beautiful in that small gesture of vulnerability. Dan stared at her, then looked away, embarrassed.

She said, "But you are ok, aren't you?"

Something in her voice made Dan look up. "Yes, I am." Chloe did not meet his eyes. She looked down and said, "This is what you do, right? I mean, for a living."

"You mean kill people."

"I didn't say that."

She said, "You are good at what you do."

"I'll take that as a compliment. Thanks."

Chloe looked away. Dan felt a little bad, he was being defensive. This was a big deal for her, and she had probably never met anyone like him.

Dan said, "I grew up in the highest mountain ranges in the world. In Nepal. The Himalayas. Not far from the base camp of Mount Everest. The Gurkhas live there, and they have a fitness beyond the average human being. The reason is the low concentration of oxygen at those levels. I trained myself to do what they did. I ran five miles up and down the mountain path every day from when I was seven years old, till I came back to Bethesda."

"Jesus. That sounds hard."

"I know. But you should see the Gurkha kids. They carried forty-pound weights on their backs and did the same distance as me in the same time. I could, too, but only after hard training. It gave me a level of fitness most humans don't have, and one of the reasons I got picked to join, uh, where your dad worked."

Dan fell silent. He had already said too much. He did not wish to speak about his operations. He never could. The things he had seen and done...he would take them to his grave.

Dan exhaled, stretched, then picked up the passports from the bedside table.

"You got this from my dad's place?" Chloe asked.

"Yes," Dan said.

He took out the gun first. He held the butt with a kitchen towel, not touching the weapon. It was a squat, ugly thing. Almost snub-nosed in appearance. For a small handgun, it was heavy. Using the towel, he pressed the magazine switch. Six-round clip—small for a modern handgun. But his eyes widened when he saw the size of the rounds. 7.62mm standard NATO issue ordnance. This small gun packed a punch. He remembered the soft whistling sound the gun made, far softer than any gun he had used.

He put the gun to one side and took out the wig and the passports.

John Guptill's face stared out of the American passport's photo page. He looked through the Egyptian passport. Guptill again, with a beard, glasses, and the wig. He peered closely at the photo. Guptill's eyes looked different.

Contact lenses. His normal light gray eyes looked black. His face was also more tanned: he looked darker. Overall, one would assume the man in the photo was Middle Eastern.

Dan looked at the red EU passport last. He had lost the glasses, and had brown contacts to disguise his blue eyes, along with a light beard. He wasn't wearing the wig.

Chloe reached out and took the three passports from where Dan had put them. Her face was a mask of shock as she looked through them.

She said, "What did Dad do with these?"

"We do all sorts of clandestine work, Chloe. Most of our actions are deniable if we are caught. But that still means trouble. For us and our country. Hence, we often have fake identities when we are abroad. But, I have to say, you father was very well prepared."

"For what?"

"I don't know. What with the disguise and these passports, I have a feeling he was working for some intelligence agency."

"Like the CIA?"

"Maybe."

Dan looked at Chloe. "Listen," he said softly. "Get some sleep. We can talk about this in the morning." He looked at the bed.

"You sleep on the bed," he said, feeling awkward. "I'll take the couch."

Chloe took the bed, and turned the lights out. She was asleep soon. Dan closed his eyes, but he saw one of two faces constantly. Lucy, then Guptill. He tossed and turned, the two faces keeping him awake.

*****

When Dan woke up, Chloe was up already. She was wearing a light pink, knee-length skirt, a lilac, sleeveless vest with a light blue cardigan that almost matched her eyes. Her hair was tied back in a ponytail. Her eyes had make-up on, but they were lined with lack of sleep.

"Hey, Dan," she said brightly.

Dan made an attempt at a smile. He got up from the couch. "Sleep well?"

A shadow passed across her face.

Chloe waved her hands. "It's nothing. I need to get busy with the funeral, and do my job assignment as well. It will be good for me. But last night," she looked at him, "I just kept thinking about Dad, and…"

She was being brave, holding it in. He remembered how he felt when his father had died.

"It's alright. It gets better, I promise. My dad died, too."

She sniffed and wiped her nose with a tissue, and took a deep breath. "You know, he spoke about you."

"What? Really?"

"Yes. He said you were very tough. And loyal. A good friend to have in a fight."

"Did he mention anyone else?"

"Yes. He spoke once about an older man, Colonel McBride?"

Fighter McBride. Dan remembered him from the night of the debrief in Afghanistan, before the botched operation.

"What did he say about him?"

"Said he was a good man. He enjoyed working with him."

Dan thought for a moment. "I know this is hard for you, Chloe. But I want you to think about something for a moment. Did your father ever mention something, or someone, called Felix?"

Chloe frowned. "You asked me this before, right?"

"Yes."

"No, don't think so."

"Alright."

"Chloe, there's something else I have to tell you."

"About what?"

Dan told her about what happened on his mission in Afghanistan. When he finished, she looked shocked. "Dad suspended you?"

"I don't think it was his decision."

"But he didn't believe you?"

"At the time, maybe he didn't. But, later when we talked by the river, he knew. He wanted to tell me something. That moment never came."

Dan leaned forward. "Something happened last night when I was at your dad's apartment." Dan told her about the men inside. Her face was a mask of shock again.

Dan said, "Chloe, all of this stays between you and me. You understand that? We need to tread very carefully now. I might even have to disappear for a while, in order to find things out."

CHAPTER 23

Dan walked out of the hotel on his own. He walked to the tube station, and got off at Westminster. He went inside a red telephone booth and dialed the landline number that Burns had given him. He answered on the first ring.

Burns said, "We have a problem."

His tone was urgent. Dan asked, "What?"

"Scotland Yard have put out a circular on TV and print media for a man who matches your description. You were seen the first night you went there. An old woman saw you. I rang MI5 and made some discreet enquiries."

Dan remembered the old woman. He had snuck in behind her.

"Shit," he said.

"Yup. Not good. You need to lie low."

Dan told Burns briefly what had happened the night before.

Burns was silent for a while and said, "You got the number plate of the car?"

Dan read it out to him. Burns said, "That sounds like a diplomatic number plate."

"And I got some weapons off them, too. Do we still have our armory guy?"

"Yes."

The armory guy was an old man who supplied them with unmarked weapons. His name was Spikey, and he was an SAS veteran. He had his own makeshift ballistics lab in his backyard. English laws made it difficult for soldiers in the UK to purchase weapons. Spikey got around that problem. He supplied some of the PMCs in London, and soon he had come under Intercept's radar.

Dan asked, "You got his address?"

Burns gave it to him.

Dan broke the connection, but he waited for a while inside the booth, keeping the phone receiver to his ear. He looked around. It took him almost three minutes, but finally he saw it. The one car that wasn't moving. A black car, and it looked like a Lada or a Škoda. Eastern European, probably Russian. Very similar to what he'd seen on Paradise Walk last night. A man got out of the driving seat. Even from a distance, Dan could see the white bandage on his nose. Someone else was in the car in the passenger seat.

The same two men who had been at the apartment last night. Dan had come here by tube and hadn't been followed, he knew that. How did they know he was here?

Dan came out of the booth and walked towards Waterloo Bridge. Sure enough, the black car moved out into the traffic to follow. He could see the two men clearly now.

Dan turned around and ran.

*****

Chloe caught the look on his face as she opened the door. Dan brushed past her into the hotel room.

"What's the matter, Dan?"

Dan went over to the windows and pulled the curtains. The room became dark. He flicked the light switches.

"They were waiting for me," he said.

"Who?"

Dan told her about the two men, and then about the police.

Chloe said, "So they're calling you a suspect in Dad's death?"

Dan shrugged. "Apparently, it was natural causes. We need to see the coroner."

"Why?"

Dan decided Chloe needed to know. Things were getting worse very quickly. When he wasn't around, she needed to be able to protect herself.

"Chloe, I think your father was killed."

Chloe's face went rigid. "How do you know?"

"I don't, but when I examined his body in the morgue, I found a small needle puncture wound in his left ear. I remembered one of the CIA guys talking about it once. Toxic compounds can be injected through needles in places like the scalp, ears, between toes, in the rectum. Where it can be hard for the coroner to find."

Chloe had her arms wrapped around herself. "And you found something like that on my father?"

"I'm sorry. Yes, I did. In his left ear, there was a puncture wound at the entrance of the inner ear. Very hard to see, even with a microscope. The guy who told me about this mentioned how the KGB used this as a killing tactic."

"The *KGB?*"

Dan held his hands up. "Don't run with that. We don't know anything for certain as yet. But those two guys following me, the gun they had, the car they drive, all of it does point to something foreign."

Chloe sat down on the bed and clasped her hands in her lap. "You know the car registration, don't you?"

"I remember it."

"Our newspaper has a database of car registration numbers. I can ring them and find out, or call the Driver and Vehicle Licensing Agency."

"Burns is looking for it already. The DVLA will tell us about the car, but not where it comes from or who it's registered to."

"Good point," Chloe said.

She opened her cellphone and made the call. She scribbled something as she spoke. Then she thanked the person and hung up.

"It's a diplomatic corps number," she said. "The car is registered to Kensington Palace Gardens, London."

"The Russian Embassy," he said softly. Burns had been right. "Ok, let's do this in order. Did you go through your father's bank statements?"

Chloe's eyes brightened. "For the last three months, I did, yes. You'll never guess what I found."

"Hit me."

"Apart from his monthly pay from the organization you both worked for, he was also getting paid a lump sum every quarter from a company called Wellington. I looked into it. The money was transferred by a BACS payment, like most salaries in the UK. I called HSBC and they gave me the identifier for the BACS. It turns out Wellington International Services is an overseas company, based in Jersey."

"Jersey is a tax haven for the super-rich."

"Yes, but not just for the super-rich and hedge funds. The island belongs to the British Crown, but doesn't have to answer to British laws. A huge number of companies are based in Jersey, because they can enjoy offshore status, buy and sell tax-free, and not have to disclose their business to anyone."

"These guys run more scams than any criminal I know. But sounds like you hit a barrier there."

"Yup," Chloe grimaced. "Wellington International Services is run by a board of trustees. Exactly who the bloody trustees are, no one seems to know. But finally, I did find something. The board of trustees are represented by a law firm."

"And?"

"Well, the law firm happens to be based in London. I'm going to visit them tomorrow."

Dan considered this. "You have to be careful. People like these—they don't like people like you who ask questions."

"Hey, I'm a journalist. It's my job to ask questions." Chloe smiled and Dan couldn't help smiling back.

"Anything else?" he asked. "Emails, cellphone?"

"I can't get into his email. It's a dot Army domain, so I rang the Ministry of Defence. They're looking into it."

Dan raised his eyebrows. "You *have* been busy."

"Totally. Cellphone, similar story. Held by Scotland Yard right now."

"They should hand it back, if they're saying this is *not* a murder investigation."

"There's something else. Dad had a car."

"He did?"

"It's still in the garage. Not sure if the police have looked at it. But from his papers I found the address where it was last sent for repairs. I'm guessing it's still there."

Dan's mind was turning over. "We need to get to the car before the police do. And at the same time, we need to visit the coroner. I want to ask him about the cause of death."

He sat down in front of Chloe, crossing his arms. He was wearing a half-sleeve, button-down shirt and he noticed Chloe stare at his forearms. Her cheeks flared a little rosier, then the color died. She smelled nice, Dan thought. He didn't know what the hell it was, but it was flowery and fresh.

He said, "Right. The way I see it, we need to find out about those passport identities that your father had. Maybe you could make some phone calls, ask some questions. But please be very careful about who you go to see. Don't go to the garage, for instance. I want to come with you."

"And what will you do?"

Dan pointed at the plastic bag containing the pistol. He grinned, then his face became serious. "I need to get myself a gun."

Chloe said, "I need to see this man at the US Embassy. Simon Renwick."

"Whoa. You think that's a good idea?"

"It's the US Embassy, Dan. Who's going to kill me there?"

Dan considered this. The logic was irrefutable. Nobody wanted an international incident on their hands.

"Ok," he said. "Just be careful."

*****

Chloe Guptill got off the tube station at Hyde Park Corner and walked to Mayfair. She was heading for Grosvenor Square, to the US Embassy.

She was looking forward to meeting Simon Renwick.

Chloe was one step below becoming a subeditor for her newspaper. A big feature story on this would make her career. Deep inside, Chloe felt her father, despite his military background, had supported her. John Guptill had been a soldier, through and through. He fought his wars on the battlefield. Politics had never been his cup of tea. He had an intense dislike of the DoD in America, and the MOD in England, whose budget cuts, Guptill said, hurt a soldier's life more than a bullet did.

She felt a tug in her heart as she thought of her dad. A constant emptiness. He was gone. She would never see him again or hear his voice. The sunlight turned to rust, and the breeze flowing in from the Thames turned cold and frosty. Chloe hastily put her sunglasses on. She blinked away tears.

At Grosvenor Square, there was a steel barricade, and a ring of US Marines with MP5 sub-machine guns. They stopped every pedestrian attempting to enter the steel barricade. The checkpoints were busy. Chloe waited in the queue for half an hour, getting impatient. When she finally got inside, and showed her newspaper ID and the letter her dad had written for Simon Renwick, she was asked to take a seat.

Soon she was led from her seat and taken to a bank of elevators. She went up to the third floor and stood in front of a door that blocked a hallway. She had to press the buzzer three times before it was answered. A middle-aged, bespectacled woman opened the door. She told Chloe to sit in the reception while she went to look for Mr Renwick. Chloe hadn't expected anything glamorous, but the plain green chairs, the dying plants on the window ledge, and the slightly musty air of the old building all pointed to an atmosphere that could be improved.

An array of posters adorned the wall. Exhibitions and event advertisements. There was an aircraft exhibition coming up at Farnborough, and an armored car expo in Kent. For both events, the DSO would act as brokers to introduce defense companies to the relevant officials in foreign Defense Ministries.

"Miss Guptill?"

The voice came from behind her. Chloe turned around. The man she saw was younger than she had imagined. She'd only spoken to him on the phone, and the man had a heavy voice.

"Simon Renwick. How do you do?"

Mr Renwick had a sallow complexion, sunken cheeks and square glasses. The glasses gave him a slightly nerdy look, but his smart suit and easy manners made up for that. His dark hair was short and brushed back. When he smiled, his eyes remained blank. His face was tanned, with lines in the forehead from the sun. He had an American accent, as she had expected. She imagined he was a well-travelled man. She shook hands with him, and then followed him up to his office.

A large desk in the middle of the room took up most of the available space. A set of windows looked over one of the many Grosvenor courtyards.

"Have a seat please, Miss Guptill."

"Thank you."

He tapped a few buttons on the keyboard in front of him and looked at the screen briefly before turning to her. He was smiling, but his eyes remained untouched by mirth.

"How can I help?"

"Well, my father advised me to see you. His name was John Guptill."

The smile vanished slowly from Renwick's face. "You are John Guptill's daughter?"

"Yes," Chloe said slowly.

Renwick's face cleared. "Ah, right, I see. What is it that you want to know?"

Chloe said, "You knew my father, right?"

"Yes, I did."

"He asked me to see you about the weapons industry in the UK. About the DSO in particular."

Renwick said, "I am sorry, Miss Guptill. I am an American. It would not be wise to comment on UK policy."

"Your name does not have to be mentioned. Ever read a newspaper article quoting a source in Washington or London? You could be that source."

"I know that. But these things have a habit of coming around. Like I said, I am sorry. And I am sorry about your father, too. I will miss him."

Chloe stared intently at the man. "Exactly how did you know my father?"

"That information is classified. But we became friends. We played golf together." Renwick pressed his lips and looked out the window. Then he glanced at Chloe.

Chloe got the impression that she was done here. It was a blind alley. She would not get anything more out of Renwick, and nor did she care about his attitude. She got up.

"Goodbye, Mr Renwick."

"Thank you for coming, Miss Guptill."

CHAPTER 24

Dan took the bus to the far south-east corner of London. It was more run-down here, a grimy collection of tall, brown-brick council estate buildings, all built in the 1960s, designed to herd as many deprived families into one place as they could. Upturned shopping trolleys and trash cans littered the streets. In a basketball court, teenagers smoked cannabis and played their MP3 players loudly. Rap music blasted at Dan, along with a few taunting calls asking him if he was scared. He walked on.

After fifteen minutes he came to a shabby building called Ferguson House. The timber- and glass-paneled doorway had been kicked a few times. Glass lay scattered on the floor. Graffiti adorned the walls, inside and outside. Dan approached the doorway and looked at the calling buttons for the apartments. The building had seventy-four apartments. He pressed the buzzer and waited. After the second buzz, a voice came crackling on the intercom.

"Who is this?"

"Spikey, it's Dan."

"Dan who?"

"Dan Roy. The one with the kukri."

Dan took the cramped elevator to the fifth floor and knocked on number forty-three. After a fumble with the lock, the door opened.

The man who stared at Dan was well into his sixties. He was shorter than Dan, but even now, his impressive girth was a reminder of how physically strong he had once been. His eyes were hooded but attentive. His scalp was bald, and his skin wizened and leathery from many years of service in deserts and jungles. Spikey Dobson, so called because he was short and an expert in using the bayonet to kill at close quarters, smirked at Dan and walked back slowly, leaving the door open.

The apartment was cramped. Photographs of old escapades hung on the walls. Dan pushed his way past two tables overflowing with papers and books, and two sofas with foam leaking out of them. Spikey slouched in an armchair, the TV on some game show.

"To what do I owe the pleasure of this visit, Mr Shady American?" Spikey said, moving his head from the TV screen to stare at Dan.

Spikey was an old boy. A former SAS man, he served in the 22nd Regiment in Northern Ireland, the Falklands, and the Balkans. He also had a lot of decommissioned weapons in his personal possession that he'd accumulated over the years.

Spikey had become an institution, known only to a handful of men. If any of that select few needed a weapon, they came to Spikey. No questions asked, no answers given.

Dan suspected Spikey had contacts with the criminal underworld as well, but he never asked. He had wanted a Dragunov sniper rifle as a memento once, having used a discarded one in Afghanistan a few times. Spikey had been the man to get him one.

Dan took out the plastic bag containing the handgun and threw it on Spikey's lap.

"Hey!" Spikey looked up with a frown. "What you playing at?"

"Don't worry. The safety's on."

Spikey sat up in his chair, grumbling. "To hell with safety." He took the gun out and caressed the butt, looking at the weapon closely. Then he whistled.

"Wow," Spikey said. "Where the hell did you get this?"

Dan tapped the side of his nose. "That would be telling, Spikey. Can you tell me what it is?"

"This is a PSS silent pistol. Jacketed, steel core outside, internal automatic bolt mechanism inside. It's designed for use by a certain country's Special Forces. It's one of the most silent guns in the market. Do you want to know why?"

"Why?"

"It uses a heavy 7.62mm cartridge. But the cartridge is coated with a chemical called SP-4, which absorbs all the gas that explodes when the cartridge is fired. Hence, unlike a traditional suppressed gun, none of the exploding gasses are released. So, the sound you get is more like a soft whistle than a loud BOP or BAM from a suppressed gun."

"So the gun only works with this special ammunition."

"Yup. It's called the 7.62x41mm, SP-4 ordnance." Spikey's voice was suddenly quiet. "Do you know who it's used by?"

Dan had an inkling of the answer already, but he didn't like it. He really didn't like it.

"Go on, then," he said.

"Spetsnaz," Spikey said.

Russian Special Forces. The Spetsnaz were equivalent to the Delta, Navy SEALS and the SAS.

Dan sat down on the tattered sofa. "Yes, that figures."

If Spikey wondered what Dan was talking about, he kept it to himself.

Dan said, "So after these four bullets have gone, I can't get any more."

"I didn't say that. If you know anyone in the Russian Mafia, I'm sure they can sort you out. I don't think the Spetsnaz will give you any, though, even if you ask them nicely."

Dan rolled his eyes, then looked at Spikey carefully. "I need a weapon."

"What do you want?"

"A Sig Sauer really. P226 if possible. Or a Glock. If neither of those two available, then I'll settle for a Beretta or an H&K handgun. But not too old."

"Don't ask for much, do you?"

"Have you got anything?"

"Yes. A Sig Sauer P226, as it happens. But a few years old. Automatic, sixteen-cartridge magazine, good condition. Cost ya."

"How much?"

"Two hundred."

"Come on, Spikey. It's a handgun, not a rifle."

"I know, but you're asking for a specific gun you lads use. They're harder to find. You want a Glock or a Colt, I can get one for less than hundred."

They settled for one hundred and seventy-five, with extra ammunition. As Dan was leaving, Spikey shuffled closer to him. The old man lifted his face to Dan. "Be careful, kiddo. The Spetsnaz don't like their weapons being nicked."

"Yeah, well," Dan pulled the rucksack on his shoulders. "Neither do I. See you around, Spikey."

*****

As Dan approached the hotel on Clapham Common he saw a black Lada car parked nearby. It looked brand new with gleaming, metallic paint. The car was facing away from him. The number plate was different this time and he tried hard to read it. Another diplomatic number. He could make out two men seated in the front. The car was parked on the same side of the road as his apartment, a few doors behind.

Dan walked past the car, keeping his eyes straight ahead. He got into his room quickly, looked around, it was empty.

Chloe was still at the US Embassy. That was good.

From his bag he took out the PSS silent gun and put it in his front jeans pocket. He stripped off, put the Sig Sauer in a shoulder holster and wore a brown shirt on top. He took two extra magazines and stuck them in his sock. His kukri remained on his back-belt line. He stashed the remainder of the 5.56mm ammunition underneath a floorboard in the room.

He got his rental bike from the hallway, locked the door and made his way north-west, towards the river and Battersea Park.

CHAPTER 25

As he put foot on the pedal, Dan heard the growl of the engine behind him. Traffic was moderately heavy, evening peak hour was approaching. Around most of London, the next two hours would see its narrow roads gridlocked.

Battersea Bridge rose up ahead, but Dan was heading right. The road ended in a T-junction underneath another railway bridge. To the right, next to the railway bridge, there was a disused factory. Dan turned right.

He heard the Lada's engine: it was catching up on him to see which way he would turn. Dan speeded up, and as he came up to the gate of the derelict factory, he skidded off his bike.

Leaving the bike on the pavement, he ran into the factory. The building was large, and its corrugated-iron roof extended back more than a hundred yards.

There was a pair of large, iron double doors in the front covered in moss and plants. Broken pipes and smashed beer bottles littered the floor around. A smaller workers' entrance lay to one side. It was rusty as hell and one solid kick was all it took for the door to fall off its hinges. It would clearly give his position away, but that was exactly what Dan wanted. He heard the Lada screech to a stop behind him, car doors slamming and running footsteps. He didn't have much time.

He did a SitRep. The floor in front of him was about fifty yards wide and more than a hundred yards long. Three hulking, rusting machinery blocks lay in the middle. Fire escape stairs led up into a balcony snaking around the entire periphery of the upper floor. Shafts of dull sunlight came in from the broken skylights above and through gaps in the roof.

Dan ran inside. He came to the first machine. It had chains and pulleys, and an old tractor sat in the middle. Everything smelled of old grease and stale urine. Dan ran around the back, took out the PSS silent pistol and lay down flat on the floor, gun arm extended. To anyone coming in through the door, he would be practically invisible on the garbage-strewn floor, hidden behind the machine. But someone entering through that doorway would be framed in the sunlight, presenting an ideal target.

He waited. His ears were attuned to the sides of the warehouse and behind him. If these guys had any sense they would split up and one of them would come either from behind or down the side.

They didn't. Dan saw the small guy enter first, crouching down, holding his weapon straight. Dan fired, gripping the PSS gun tightly with both hands, as he couldn't guess the recoil. It was just as well. The butt jumped in Dan's grip. The sound was like a soft squelch of air from his bike tire. The man crouching in the doorway screamed and went down. Dan fired two more rounds, both of which hit the door.

The taller man leaned his weapon into the entrance and fired a burst inside the warehouse. The ordnance splintered across the warehouse, chopping up dust and whining as they ricocheted against the scattered metal. The sound was suppressed, but Dan still recognized the firepower. An MP5 or MP7, set to automatic. In an enclosed space, a firefight would be deadly. With his Sig Sauer, he wouldn't win.

Dan had already dropped back into cover behind the tractor. He took out his trusted Sig. A foot crunched on paper, followed by another burst of gunfire. Dan slid further down the floor, the rounds whining above his head. He used the noise to turn around.

Now he could see the taller man. He was inside the warehouse, but he had backed into a corner. His gun was pointed up and he was looking around the balcony, jerking his arm around. That made sense. If Dan had the time to go up the fire escapes, laying down fire from a height could be fatal for the man.

The man had his gun pointed to the walkway above. Dan picked up the PSS pistol. Lying on his back, he threw the gun as hard as he could, upwards and to the left. It clattered against one of the iron fire escapes, making a sound that echoed around in the silence. The man turned to his right immediately and let loose a burst from his MP7. At the same time, Dan rolled on the ground to his right.

He was out in the open now. He came to a rest on his chest, both hands gripping the Sig. He had the man straight in his sights.

Because of his height, he was an easy target. The man saw the flash of movement from the corner of his eye. He started to bring the MP7 around, but he wasn't quick enough. Two 5.56mm rounds slammed into his chest, pushing him back against the wall. He grunted and still tried to raise his weapon. Dan squeezed the trigger again. This time the bullet found the head. Blood and bone splattered in a red eruption on the wall behind him. The man slid down to the floor. Dan rolled back to the cover of the machine. He listened for three seconds. No sound.

He crouched and came out into the open. The man he shot first was still on the floor, but he was moving. Dan could see him trying to raise his arm to reach his gun, a few inches away from him. He saw Dan coming and made a desperate lunge. Dan fired instinctively. The bullet went in the man's neck. He shuddered once, then was still. Dan swore and ran forward. He wanted one of them alive—to make them talk. He felt the carotid pulse. Gone. The other attacker had half his head blown away. He wasn't talking to anyone.

Dan frisked the body and found no ID. Dan searched the man thoroughly. In a shoulder holster he found a larger weapon. He whistled as he took it out. He had seen this little monster before, in an operation against government forces in Syria.

It was a KEDR, perhaps the most compact and lightweight sub-machine gun in the world. He hefted the thing in his hand. It was like a feather compared to an MP7. He took the magazine box out. It had 9x18mm ordnance in a thirty-box mag. Capable of firing 800 rounds per minute. An absolute killer in close quarters battle. The KEDR was exclusively used by the Russian secret service and Spetsnaz.

He put the KEDR under his arm and went over to the other corpse. An MP7 lay on the ground next to him. In this man's pocket Dan found something interesting. A small, dark glass bottle with a liquid inside it. Dan held it up to the light, but he couldn't see a great deal. The bottle had a tight screw top. He put it in his pocket.

Dan went back and picked up the PSS. He wiped the butt clean. He did the same with the KEDR. He put the PSS in his back pocket and the KEDR, which had a strap, over his shoulder.

The street outside was empty. He got on his bike and pedaled away, fast.

CHAPTER 26

Dan stashed the bike in the hallway, and paid the hotel manager for its rental. He was relieved he hadn't damaged the bike.

Chloe was waiting for him when he got up to the room.

"Guess what I found?" Chloe said as soon as Dan walked in.

"Tell me."

Chloe held out the fake American passport that belonged to one of her father's identities. "This man's name is Lee Hill."

"So?"

"So I looked him up in the telephone directory. There are three American Lee Hills in London who have the same DOBs. Only one of them wasn't available to talk to me. I spoke to the others. In fact, I spoke to their wives first. They were both at home, enjoying some time off with the family."

"And the third?"

"The third lives at Hyde Park Corner. I visited the apartment. No one has lived there for the last six months, according to the landlady."

"Interesting."

"It gets better." Chloe waved the passport under Dan's nose. "Where do you think this Lee Hill works?"

Dan thought for a while, then frowned. "Same place your dad gets all the money from?"

"Yes, Wellington International Services. They even have a damn motto—relationships are our business." Chloe rolled her eyes.

"How did you find out where he worked?"

Chloe narrowed her eyes. "You need to keep a secret."

Dan smiled. "Sure."

"I saw a letter poking out of his letter box. Actually, there was a bundle of them. They'd been gathering dust for the last few months, I guess. I picked up the whole bunch. Most of it was mail order crap, but I did find a letter from his employer. It shows his tax return for the year."

"Quite the detective, aren't you? Or should I say journalist?"

"Tricks of the trade, nothing more."

Dan sat down on the bed, thinking. "Wellington International Services," he said to himself.

Chloe came and sat down in front of him. "I haven't finished," she said. "I rang the lawyer firm of Wellington as well. No reply from them. I left several messages."

"Don't bother. We need to visit them. It might need more direct action."

"Where have *you* been?"

"I went up to see an old friend."

"Were you followed?"

Dan hesitated. "Yes," he said shortly.

"What happened?"

Dan stood up and went to the window. "I guess you can say they've retired from their jobs."

Chloe didn't say anything for a while. "What's going on, Dan?"

Dan paused. "Something weird. A mixed bunch. All I know is that we need to get to the bottom of it, and fast."

"Something strange is going on, that's for sure."

Dan picked up the newspaper on the desk. It was one of London's daily tabloids. He read the screaming headline with the lurid photo of a bearded Taliban soldier holding a rocket launcher on his shoulder:

"Senior Taliban commander responsible for bombing stadium in Peshawar killed by drone strike."

Dan read a few lines of the report, then threw the newspaper back on the table. Chloe was sitting on the bed with her legs folded under her. Dan stared for longer than he intended, he couldn't help it. He met her eyes, then looked away to pace the room. Eventually he stopped and looked at her again. He didn't miss the faint blush on her cheeks, which made her look prettier, he thought.

"Okay, so let's see what we have." He made a fist and he flicked one finger up after another. "We have Wellington, the car, the coroner, and the passports."

"Right. Let's do this. In that order?"

"Yes, there's something about Wellington that I don't like. But I need to speak to the coroner first. Then let's hit their lawyer."

"Sure."

Dan took the small bottle he had got from the dead Spetsnaz agent, and wrapped it carefully in some tissue. He put the bottle in his inside pocket. They walked to the tube station, and traveled to Chelsea and Westminster Hospital, which was a short walk from Fulham Broadway tube station.

They went inside the large, sunny atrium of the hospital and followed signs to Pathology. At the reception, Chloe asked for Dr Sherman, the coroner who had given the cause of death. They were provided with a copy of the death certificate. Chloe took a while to go through it while they waited to see the doctor. Dan frowned as he read. "Septic shock following alcohol toxicity. Leading to cardiac arrest."

Chloe was surprised and saddened. "So he'd been drinking?"

Dan shook his head. "I didn't smell alcohol on him. And I got up pretty close." He needed to ask the doctor some questions. He reached into his pocket and took out the small bottle.

Dr Sherman arrived. They both stood up as the white-coated figure approached them. The doctor was into his fifties, with a mop of white hair. He had kind, blue eyes that crinkled into crow's-feet at the corners. He smiled gravely at them.

"Sorry for your loss, Miss Guptill," Sherman said. "What did you wish to speak to me about?"

Dan said, "My name is Dan Roy. I'm a member of the same Army unit the major belonged to." They shook hands.

"Yes, Mr Roy. Did you wish to say anything?"

"Would it be possible to speak in your office, Dr Sherman?"

"Yes, of course," the doctor said.

In his office they sat facing the doctor across his desk. A life-size skeleton stood next to Dan's chair.

Dan couldn't tell the truth. Not without implicating himself in the murder. He held out the bottle. "I need to find out what this is, Dr Sherman.

The major gave it to me the last time I visited him. He wanted me to have it tested to see what it was. He was helping in an investigation with contraband drugs."

The doctor took the bottle, turned it around.

"I see. Sure. I need to run a couple of tests on it. I can tell the lab guys to do it right now. Are you okay to wait for a few minutes?"

"Is there a coffee place around here?" Chloe asked. "I could use some."

The doctor said, "Ground floor on your right. There's a Starbucks."

Dan and Chloe went to get their coffees. The main atrium in the hospital was busy. They stood in a queue to get their coffee, then went back to the office. Chloe nervously sipped her coffee. Dan squeezed her shoulders. "Hey, it's going to be alright, don't worry."

Chloe's face was pale and drawn. "Let's face it. It can't get much worse than now."

Dan sighed and held her hand. In a few minutes, Sherman returned. He looked at Dan, a curious expression on his face. Dan stood up.

"What did you find, doc?"

Sherman closed the door and sat down slowly in his chair. He steepled his fingers in front of his face. "Where did the major find this bottle, Mr Roy?"

"He received it during the course of an investigation. I believe he was trying to get it checked, but you know what happened. Could you please tell me what it might be?"

Sherman paused for effect before continuing.

"The liquid in the bottle is a chemical called diphenhydramine. It can be used as a sedative antihistamine in the right dose. What people take for hay fever, right?" Dan and Chloe nodded.

"But in such pure form as what you have here, and injected in the right amount, it can cause respiratory and cardiac arrest. Its effect is potentiated by the presence of alcohol. But the critical thing about diphenhydramine is this—the molecule disintegrates in the body very quickly. About an hour after injection into the bloodstream, there's no further trace of the chemical. It simply breaks down."

"So, no trace of it is found in the body?" Dan asked.

"None whatsoever."

Dan and Chloe rose and shook hands with the doctor. Dan said, "Thank you very much, Dr Sherman. You've been a great help."

They left the office and went out to the back of the building where there was a garden and a seating area. Dan breathed out and spoke first.

"Right, let's suppose that the major was drinking that afternoon. With someone who came to see him. Maybe more than one person. I'm going out on limb here. He became sleepy, maybe they put something in his drink."

"A few drops of that stuff would do the job," Chloe whispered.

"Then, when he was drowsy, they put the drug in a syringe and injected him in the ear. The effect was enhanced by the alcohol. He stopped breathing. The drug broke down and no trace of it was found in the post-mortem."

Chloe and Dan sat in silence, thinking. After a while, Chloe spoke.

"Who was it?"

"Probably the man I got it from. There were two of them. The same two I met in the apartment the night before."

Chloe looked at the floor when she asked the next question. "What happened to them, Dan?"

"They're dead, Chloe," Dan said quietly.

Chloe leaned back in her seat. After a while, she stood up and walked away. Dan drained his cup, threw it in the trash, and followed.

He caught up as she was coming out of the main hospital exit. He settled into a walk next to her and when the street was quieter, he touched her arm.

"Chloe, wait."

She stopped and looked at him, rubbing her arm.

"Look," Dan said. "I know this is weird. But someone framed me in Afghanistan, and then someone killed your dad. I took photos of what I found in Afghanistan and that camera has disappeared. I'm not saying they're connected. But there are a lot of loose ends we need to tie up. I don't know where this is going to lead to. But I know it's going to get a lot worse before it gets better."

"I know that. But shouldn't we tell the police?"

"I'm under investigation already. They won't believe me. Trust me, we need to do this ourselves. Once I get enough evidence, then we involve the cops."

Chloe looked vulnerable. Dan put his arm around her shoulders gently, and she didn't resist.

"We'll get to the bottom of this, I promise you."

They walked in silence for a while. "Where to now?" Chloe asked.

"We need to check out Wellington."

"I have the address of their law firm."

CHAPTER 27

The law firm was called Overmeyer and Sons, and it was close to a tube station called Temple, in the financial district of London. Temple was on the eastern edge of the city and it took them a while to get there. The tube station was packed and it was slow coming out onto street level. They walked for ten minutes, going past the shining tower blocks with clumps of young men and women in suits standing outside smoking. Finally, they came to an alleyway, at the corner of a street with a pub. The alleyway looked empty.

Dan asked, "This is the place?"

Chloe checked her phone. "That's what it says on the website."

They went into the alley. London was full of small alleys such as these, often a conduit from one large street to another, sometimes merely a dead end that might have been a courtyard in the distant past.

The back-end of the pub took up most of the alley, and behind it, there was a small, two-story building with a glass door and a small, silver plaque beside it. Chloe bent down to read the names.

"Here it is. Overmeyer and Sons. That's Wellington's lawyers."

She pressed the buzzer and the door slid open soundlessly. Inside, plush green carpet swallowed their footsteps. Air conditioning hummed unobtrusively and sculptures on pedestals adorned the small lobby. Beyond that, Dan could see the reception. A thin blond, dressed in a tight dress suit, looked up as they approached.

Chloe told her, "We would like to see Mr Overmeyer, please."

"Certainly. And the name is…?"

"Chloe Guptill."

"Please take a seat."

The reception area was recessed into the wall. They sat down in a corner from where they could watch the reception desk, but they couldn't be seen. After five minutes, Chloe suddenly clutched Dan's arm.

"Look!" she whispered.

A man was passing through reception to the outside. Dan only saw him from the back.

Chloe stood up. "What is it?" Dan asked. She started for the door.

"It's that man I met at the Embassy."

"Who?" Dan was still confused.

"Simon Renwick. The man who knew Dad."

The secretary saw them leaving and reached for the telephone.

Dan followed Chloe as she rushed into the alley. They saw a flash of the dark suit as Renwick turned the corner, heading right into the road. Dan lowered his voice.

"We might have to split up. Two of us following him looks suspicious." Chloe nodded.

"You go first, then," she said. "He knows what I look like and you can guard me, if he turns around."

The crowd was helping Dan keep out of sight, but he also kept losing sight of Renwick, who was heading for the trains. For the moment everyone was at a standstill, waiting for the pedestrian lights to change. Renwick smoothed his hair back, then turned round to look, checking. The traffic lights changed. The mass of commuters surged forward.

Dan saw Renwick turn up ahead. He took a sharp left, leaving the crowd of commuters. Chloe was now ahead of Dan, and he saw her turn and follow. Renwick was walking faster now, glancing at his watch. Chloe speeded up.

Renwick took another turn off the main thoroughfare. This road was quieter, facing the back of large department stores and some restaurants. Dan caught sight of Chloe before she disappeared round another right corner at the end of the road.

Dan broke into a run. It was a maze of streets. Original old City, as the financial district was known. Ahead, he was just in time to see Chloe turn another corner. The sounds of traffic had faded now. Dan surged forward and took the turn Chloe had just taken.

Then he stopped short.

It was a dead end. A tall brick wall blocked the alley. He had no hope of scaling it. Against the wall there was a row of three men holding KEDR sub-machine guns. They were heavy, swarthy, similar to the Spetsnaz men he had seen. The guns had suppressors attached. Chloe was standing in front of them. As Dan came skidding to a halt, she turned around, her mouth open in shock.

Renwick was nowhere to be seen.

Dan heard a screech of tires behind him. A black SUV had come to a stop, and men piled out of it. These men were bearded, heavily armed and agile. They held MP7s, and handguns tucked in their waistbands. Three of them. Not Russian. But with the Russians, they formed a combined team.

Six in total. He was held in a crossfire, with Chloe in the middle.

"Put your gun down," came the shout from behind Dan. Dan stood still, watching around him. Chloe stood near him. Six men circled them, guns pointed. Dan did not recognize any faces. He felt a barrel poke him in the back. In the next instant, the heavy butt of a gun smashed against the side of his skull. The sound of the impact was like a pistol going off, reverberating against the walls of the alley.

Most men would have fallen unconscious. Not Dan Roy.

A yellow ball of pain zoomed across his head, and he felt his eyes get hazy. He stumbled forward, but did not fall. He rectified himself quickly, and swung around, fist raised. Another blow, from something similarly heavy, crashed against the other side of his neck.

Agony exploded inside his brain. Dan grunted, and lurched forward, feeling a wave of nausea. He shook his head, bent at the waist. Through blurry eyes, he saw two of the men grab Chloe from behind. They tied her hands. A shape appeared before him. Tall and dressed entirely in black. Dan stood up but he was too late.

A heavy fist swung and brushed against his right jaw, aimed to poleaxe him. Dan had leaned back at the last minute, and he did not feel the full impact of the blow.

His instinct was to fight back. But his head was telling him he needed to be calm. If Chloe had not been here, he would have gone for it. They were too close to him. Bunched together. With his Sig he could have unleashed mayhem.

The man in front of Dan raised his fist again.

"Enough!" A voice rang out.

Dan turned. One of the men from the car was out, and he seemed to be in charge. His face was bearded, and he wore black glasses, hiding his face. A black cap hid his hair.

"We need him alive. Put him in the car, with the girl." The accent was American.

Dan felt his hands being tied behind his back. He was patted down, and his guns and knife were removed. He shook his head twice again. The ringing sound was less, and his eyes were clearing. The left side of his face felt numb. He saw Chloe being bundled into the car. Anger flared inside him. But he controlled it. His time would come.

As usual, they had made a mistake by not killing him.

The three Russians got into another car and waited, engine purring. This car was a ZiL limousine, Dan noted. Beloved of the Kremlin upper classes. In the SUV, he saw a driver up front, with a man in the passenger seat. Chloe was in the back, next to a man by the window. One man got into the rear seat of the SUV by lifting the trunk door. Dan was shoved next to Chloe, and the other man, who seemed to be the leader, got inside next to Dan. Dan watched them carefully. He noted the knife in its scabbard, and the keys of the plastic cuff next to it, in the man's belt.

"Go," the man ordered.

There were two men up front, including the driver. Two in the back with them, and one in the rear. Total five, in this car. Four in the Zil. Dan glanced at Chloe. Her eyes were wide with fear. Dan pointed down with his eyes. She gave an imperceptible nod. In the rear-view mirror, Dan could see the Zil following them.

The driver was playing with the sat nav. The leader lifted up a hand.

"Take the left," he said. They drove fast, threading their way through traffic. Dan saw the flash of water. They were in a deserted stretch of disused factories by the river. Somewhere in East London. The cars came to a halt.

Dan was covered by an MP7 from the front, rear and sides as he alighted. Chloe came after him. The factory had a steel roller door. One of the men lifted it up. Inside was a large area with old, rusting machines. Clumps of grass grew in the deserted space. They entered. Two more men with MP7 sub-machine guns were waiting for them.

Dan said, "I need to pee."

The leader gestured to one of his men. A gun barrel prodded Dan in the back. Another man moved to his front. The leader faced Dan. He still had his black glasses on.

He said, "You try anything funny, we kill the girl." Chloe was thrust forward into his vision, a gun to her head. Dan nodded, his cold eyes giving nothing away.

The gun shoved Dan further down the yard. Dan walked slowly, looking up at the ceiling, taking in the surroundings. There was no walkway up there, it was bare, corrugated-iron roof with great holes poking out to the sky. They went outside through a rickety door. Shrubs and weeds grew tall around them.

One of the men faced Dan. His back was slouched. His finger was not on the trigger. Dan felt the gun shift behind him, and keys slot into his handcuffs. He felt them turn. His handcuffs fell away. The man in front of Dan was in the process of lighting a cigarette.

Amateurs.

As soon as his arms were free, Dan spun on his heels. He crashed into the man behind him, moving the gun barrel away from his back. He grabbed a handful of the man's shirt, leaned his head back, then slammed his wide, thick forehead into the man's face. Teeth and bone fragments exploded out of the man's mouth. Dan repeated the process, and the man sagged to one side, unconscious.

Dan picked up the knife from the man's belt as he fell. The other guy had dropped his cigarette and lighter and tried to rush Dan.

Dan let him come. He stood half-turned, and still. When the man was about to grab him, Dan ducked down, and used his attacker's momentum to lift him above his shoulders. Then he slammed him down on the ground, the soft grass absorbing the sound. The knife stabbed deep inside the man's neck, severing his trachea. Blood spurted in an arch. Dan held his face down, avoiding any sounds.

The whole thing had taken no more than five seconds.

Like a cat, he crouched and turned. Observed. Waited. No sounds, no witness. But they would come out soon.

He picked up both rifles, and strapped one on his back, and checked the other one. Heckler & Koch 416, both with 30-round mags. A waste of a weapon on these jokers, but a weapon he liked using.

There was a fire escape going up the side. He thought about it, but then decided against it. He needed to be on the same level as Chloe.

He opened the door a fraction and peered in. They had not moved. The man with his gun to Chloe's head was farthest from him. But he had a clear shot. The leader was to his side, looking around, alert. The rest of the men were lounging around. The Russians were on the floor, leaning against a wall, smoking. Five in total.

Dan spreadeagled himself on the floor, and extended the rifle across the crack of the doorway. He had the man holding the gun to Chloe's head in the gunsight. His finger caressed the trigger.

But the man moved. Dan jerked his eyes off the rifle. The leader shouted an order, and was heading straight for the door. His eyes had still not fallen on the gun barrel sticking up from the floor. Any second now, he would.

Worse, his body was now blocking Chloe. As the leader's eyes moved down the door, he shouted again. He had seen the rifle. The leader drew his weapon, pointing it at Dan.

Dan had no time. He fired. The 5.56mm ordnance hit the man in the chest, and Dan followed it up with a headshot as he fell.

The shouts had already alerted the men, and they had their weapons out. Dan ignored them. He had a few seconds in which to take decisive action.

In these split-second situations, it came down to priorities.

He shifted his attention to Chloe. The man holding her had turned his back to him. Dan fired, and saw the head erupt in a cloud of red mist. He shot him again in the back, and the body toppled forward. He saw Chloe spread out on the floor, lying very still.

Dan's heart jumped in his mouth.

A bullet jarred the iron door above him. Dan turned the gun a fraction. Three men were aiming at him, but they never stood a chance. Dan was partially concealed, and they were out in the open. Dan double-tapped them twice in the chest, and they went down like they had been hit by sledgehammers.

The remaining gunman had hidden himself behind an old oil barrel. He fired, and the round smashed inches past Dan's right arm into the ground, kicking up dust. Dan swore, and aimed at the source. Two of his bullets hit the top and base of the barrel. Then he stopped, and waited. Waiting in a firefight was often the best option.

It worked. The man thought Dan was out of ammo, or loading his weapon. He lifted his head up to aim and fire, but Dan was waiting. The round made a mockery of the man's face. He fell backwards, dead instantly.

Dan scrambled up and ran towards Chloe. A horrible, sick emptiness was clutching his guts. There was no blood around her body, save what was seeping out from the skull of the man lying dead next to her.

Gently, Dan supported her neck and turned her over. Her eyes were shut. The chest was rising and falling. He checked her head, neck and scalp. No injuries. He ran his hands and eyes down the rest of her.

Then he lifted her off the floor, and held her against him. Her eyelids fluttered open. Dan heaved a huge sigh of relief. She had fainted.

She blinked. "Dan?"

"Can you stand up?" Dan asked. She could. Once her eyes were open, she was steady on her feet, and alert. Dan ran around the dead bodies, frisking them quickly. No ID, as usual. He found a six-inch knife on one of them and took that. He took off the dead leader's glasses. Caucasian, but no one he knew. He checked him for tattoos. Nothing. But he did find a Sig P226 handgun on him. Dan discarded the rifle and checked the Sig's magazine. It was full. He put the gun in his back belt.

Chloe followed him outside. Dan had concealed the rifle inside his jacket.

They came out of the disused industrial area. They skirted around old, broken warehouses, and came out onto the main road. Traffic was flowing and the pavement was busy with pedestrians.

Hand in hand, they walked quickly to the nearest tube station. Traffic grew in volume. They walked till they came to a station called Shoreditch.

"Where now?" Chloe asked.

Dan's face was tight. "You are going back to the hotel. I need to see Simon Renwick at the Embassy."

CHAPTER 28

They sat down at a café on the pavement opposite the US Embassy, from where they had a good view of the building. Chloe stirred her cappuccino and took a long sip.

"I needed that."

Dan looked at her critically. He was worried about her. She had never lived the life he had. She was a civilian. It was a lot for her to go through. Either she was hiding her true feelings, or she had some of her father's natural toughness.

He decided it was the latter. Chloe put her cup down.

"No, I'm not going back to the hotel," she said.

"Excuse me?" They had had this conversation already, and they weren't getting anywhere.

"I told you about this guy. Now I want to see it through."

"What if we get ambushed again?"

"I didn't pay attention last time. I lost him too easily. It won't happen again."

Dan's voice was gentle but firm. "No, Chloe. I cannot have that on my conscience. Do you understand?"

Chloe said, "I can look after myself."

Dan looked down at his cup. The vision of carrying out Lucy's torn body rose up like a nightmare, shrouding his mind in a black shadow. A frown passed across his face.

Chloe said, "What is it, Dan?"

Dan stirred his cup in silence. He did not answer. He raised the cup and finished his drink.

He said, "It's nothing."

He stared at the hulking building opposite. They had been sitting there for half an hour. One car had left the entrance in that time.

Dan told her, "There is something you can help me with. If you keep watch for five minutes, I need to do some shopping."

"Shopping? Really?"

Dan stood up. "Five minutes. Call me, if you see him leave."

He returned wearing a new black tee shirt, baseball cap and sunglasses. He had gone into a nearby sportswear shop, and got changed inside a McDonald's toilet.

"You look different," she said.

"Good. That's the impression I need to give this guy. If he's a CIA field agent, he will notice patterns."

Dan glanced at his watch. 1400 hours. "Let's move," he said. They paid the bill and left.

"Shall I head back to the hotel, then?" Chloe asked. Dan nodded. Chloe took Dan's discarded jacket and vest and Dan waved her goodbye at the train station. Then he walked around.

Further across from the Embassy there was a building site, which looked empty. A two-meter-high wooden enclosure surrounded it. Dan could see the top of a large, earth-digging JCB machine poking above the enclosure. As he approached the building site he kept a close eye on movement in and out of it. There was a door to the enclosure, but it was probably locked.

Dan pulled out his knife. To anyone looking from the street, it would look as if he was reaching for his key. The lock on the door was flimsy. He leaned on the door with his hands. It gave way slightly. Dan pushed harder and there was a crack. A splinter appeared at the top of the makeshift doorway, and it swung open. Dan stepped in quickly.

Dan put a brick against the bottom of the door. That would have to do for now. The area was a rough rectangular shape, thirty by fifty yards approximately. The ground was being dug up, no doubt to put down foundations for yet another building. The giant claw of the JCB machine yawned in front of him like the jaws of a Tyrannosaurus. Dan went to the eastern edge of the enclosure and climbed a small mound. From here, over the fence, he had a good view of the sidewalk ahead and the Embassy building

Dan settled down to wait. It was 1500 hours. A fresh breeze across the

Thames dragged in black clouds that scuttled across the sun. A few drops of rain fell on Dan's face. Well, if he had to get wet, then so be it. He took out his kukri and began to sharpen the blade against a stone. Time passed slowly. His knees grew stiff. Once his kukri was razor-sharp at the tip, he climbed down from the mound and carved an eyehole at the base of the fence. He could lie down spreadeagled now and keep watch on the street ahead of him. With any luck, no one would notice it.

Half an hour later two figures emerged from the Embassy gates. One of them was Simon Renwick. His colleague said something to Renwick, then turned and walked away. Dan watched as Renwick pressed the button on the traffic light.

Dan didn't wait any longer. Renwick was heading back to Vauxhall station. Dan got up, dusted himself clean, adjusted the baseball cap and his sunglasses, then left.

Traffic was heavy. The lights wouldn't turn red, despite him pushing the button repeatedly. Ahead of him, Renwick reached the other end of the four-lane road and was walking towards the station concourse. Dan sprinted across to the island in the middle, dodging cars. One driver put his window down and shook his fist at him, shouting. At the station steps Dan couldn't see Renwick anymore.

He took his sunglasses off, and walked slowly into the station lobby. Without moving his head, he swiveled his eyes back and forth. There was a crowd of commuters. Dan took his time and inched forward.

Renwick was in the queue at the automated counter. Dan sighed in relief. He made sure it was Renwick, then he put the sunglasses in his pocket. Renwick took the Victoria line headed north. Dan stayed in the same carriage. He got off at Notting Hill Gate following his target.

Dan bought himself a newspaper, letting Renwick get ahead of him as he walked up Holland Park Avenue. It was getting quieter, and Dan was hanging back forty yards now to make sure he wasn't spotted. Renwick passed a small park and turned into a cul-de-sac. Dan hesitated. A blind ending. Was Renwick creating a trap for him again?

Dan walked past, watching. Renwick was fumbling with house keys. But he wasn't alone. Opposite him, the doors of a car were opening. Renwick was oblivious. Dan's breath caught as he recognized the type of car.

A black Lada. He didn't recognize the number plates. The two men who came out wore black suits, and Dan could see the telltale bulge of shoulder holsters. Russians. Probably Spetsnaz: Dan knew just by looking at them. Arms hanging loose at their sides, walking lightly on the balls of their feet, they approached Renwick, who had his back to them.

They didn't lock the car, and the engine was running.

CHAPTER 29

Dan took the kukri out and shoved it into his front waistband. The Sig would make too much noise. The men had got to Renwick now and he turned around, a mixture of alarm and surprise on his face. Dan knew exactly what was going to happen if he didn't act fast.

"Simon!" Dan cried out, waving his arms. His face broke into a wide grin. "Hey, man, how are you?"

All three faces turned to look at Dan. He kept the smile on his face and let a friendly gaze pass over them. He had been ten yards away and closed the gap quickly. Five. Three. He saw one of the men frown and reach inside his suit jacket.

Two yards. Dan spread his arms wide. "Simon, how long has it been?"

Renwick was to his left, and the two men were to his right. Dan catapulted into the man closest to him, wrapping his arms around the man's waist. He stayed low and propelled his shoulders forward, the momentum pushing the man onto his companion who was trying to get his weapon out. Dan felt Renwick scatter backwards, falling against the steps.

The two Russians collided into each other, tripping up and falling. Dan and the two men went down in a tangle of bodies. Dan felt a blow land on his side, crashing into his ribs. It was a good hit, into his kidneys, and it made him wince. He pushed his knee into the man below him, pinning him down, and punched him hard on the jaw, snapping his head back, hitting concrete. The man grunted and tried to get up, but Dan followed through with his fist, making a bone-crunching connection just below the man's forehead. His eyes rolled back.

Like a sumo wrestler, the other guy crashed into Dan. Dan saw him coming and crouched down. The man's head smashed into Dan's chest, exploding air out of it. They rolled back, tumbling onto the ground. Dan was trapped between the man's legs. He was above Dan, and brought his fist down for the knockout blow. Dan moved his head at the last instant and the knuckles glanced off the side of his ear.

It jarred his skull. Dan heaved with his waist, trying to dislodge the man. He was fat and bulky.

He managed to get an arm below the man's thigh. But the man had got his weapon out. Dan recognized the menacing, snub-nosed barrel of the PSS silent pistol. With every ounce of strength in his body, Dan heaved up with his arm, bucking his waist at the same time. The man fired, but the bullet went whistling above Dan's head.

His body fell backwards and Dan leaped on top of him. He grabbed the gun hand, forcing it back, and brought his forehead down on the man's face with savage force. The man fired again, and screamed as his nose was smashed. He hit Dan on the side, but it bounced off Dan's midriff. It was Dan's turn to deliver the knockout punch. He pushed his knee forward and trapped the man's arm. He hit the man with an uppercut, jolting his chin back with a cracking sound.

The man's eyes clouded over and closed. The gun became loose in his fist and Dan took it.

He looked behind him, and his blood turned to ice.

Renwick was lying in a pool of blood. He was looking at Dan, the glasses still on his face. Dan checked the other thug quickly. He was out cold. Dan removed his weapon, the same PSS silent gun. Then he crouched next to Renwick. He had been hit in the abdomen and Dan could see two entry wounds.

Dan ripped open the blood-soaked shirt. He checked the back. No exit wounds. Damn. Damn it all. The large arteries in the abdomen were probably shredded by the 7.62mm bullets. Dan felt the neck pulse. Almost non-existent. Dan took out his phone and dialed 999.

Dan pressed on the wounds, trying to stem the flow of blood. He crooked his elbow underneath Renwick's neck and lifted his head up.

"Simon, my name is Dan Roy. I work for Intercept."

Renwick's face was mottled gray. Dan could feel the body turning cold. The man didn't have long left. Slowly, he nodded. "I know who you are. The man who worked with John."

"How did you know John Guptill?"

"We were…" Renwick closed his eyes then opened them again. "We worked together." His chest heaved and he was getting exhausted. Dan spoke urgently.

"Who is Felix?"

Renwick's eyes flew open. His mouth opened. Fright covered his face, then a look of anguish. "Felix…"

Dan leaned closer. "Who is he, Simon? Tell me."

"Dangerous. Very…very dangerous."

Simon's eyes closed again. Dan shook him, but Simon didn't wake up. He was still breathing. Dan felt his neck again. The pulse was present, but fast and threading, implying significant loss of blood. If Renwick could get to a trauma surgeon quickly he might still live. Dan heard sirens in the distance. He took one last look at Renwick and checked his pockets. He found his wallet and pocketed it.

The cul-de-sac was still deserted. If someone had passed by they hadn't stopped. Dan took one last look around him. He picked up his baseball cap and put it on.

"Good luck, Simon," he whispered.

*****

Dan retraced his steps back towards Notting Hill. When he was in a secluded, leafy street, he stood underneath a tree with low branches and took his phone out. He flicked to his self-image and looked himself up and down. There was blood on his hands, his jeans and the black tee shirt. He couldn't go back like this. He walked another five minutes and found a phone booth. He didn't want to use his own phone to call Chloe. Opposite the phone booth was a café. He gave Chloe the address and hung up.

He went into the café, ordered a beer and used their toilet to get changed. He peeled off the tee shirt and washed it under the tap. He took off his jeans, where the bloodstains were turning black and were obvious. He washed the blood patches the best he could, then put the jeans and tee shirt back on. When he came out, he took the beer and sat down near the window, watching the street. He heard police sirens. Two patrol cars rushed down the road, heading for the crime scene.

Dan lifted the beer and in a long gulp half-emptied the pint glass. He needed that. One of the waiters looked out the door as another police car screamed past. Dan breathed softly. The waiter smiled at Dan, then turned and went back to the counter. Dan took out Simon Renwick's wallet. He counted one hundred pounds in twenty-pound notes. He took out the cards. Credit and bank cards, along with an ID card for the US Embassy. Dan stopped at the next card and studied it carefully.

It was a Royal Air Force card, printed for a base in Welford, near Berkshire. Dan hadn't known that the RAF had a base in Welford.

The name on the card was Major John Guptill, SFOD-D. An old card bearing the major's old job title.

He wondered why a Delta Force major had an ID card for an RAF base.

There was no photo on the card, but there was a magnetic strip on the back, which he knew would contain most of the holder's personal details. Dan put the card in his pocket, and the rest of the money and cards back in the wallet.

He saw Chloe peering in from the door. He waved her over. Chloe spoke to the waiter and ordered a cappuccino. Dan took his vest, jacket and a pair of slacks from her and disappeared into the bathroom. When he came out, Chloe was sitting at the table, sipping her drink.

The café had three more customers, but more were coming in for evening meals. He slid in next to Chloe and downed the rest of his beer.

"What happened?" Chloe asked.

"Simon Renwick might be dead. I couldn't save him." Her mouth was open in shock. She looked down at her coffee in silence. Another couple came in. Dan took a twenty-pound note from the wallet and put it on the table. He brushed Chloe's arm.

"We need to get out of here," Dan said.

They headed towards Holland Park tube station. Their train was tunneling towards Chelsea within minutes. They got off at Victoria station and by the time they were back in the B&B it was nearly eight o'clock. Dan had a shower and came out to find Chloe sitting at the mirror, combing her hair. She put the comb down and looked at Dan as he came out, fully dressed. He was toweling his hair.

"What happened out there, Dan?"

Dan told her the best he could. Chloe gripped her forehead. "But why? Why would someone want to abduct or kill him?"

"He knew something. I'm guessing it's about Felix. Whoever that is."

"But did Renwick not try to lead us into an ambush?"

Dan had been thinking about that. He sat down. "Did you actually see Renwick's face when we left the lawyer's office?"

"No, just his side profile and back. It looked like him."

"So, someone could have been impersonating him."

Chloe frowned. "But why?"

Dan said, "To get more information out of the lawyers."

Dan sat down on the bed. He didn't like the way people were being taken out. First Guptill, now Renwick. Chloe or he would be next. He hardened his jaw. It would not be Chloe. He would take a bullet to his brain to save her.

He asked, "Your dad's car. Do you know exactly where it is?"

"Yes, I have the address."

"Good. Tomorrow we get the car. Then I have to drive to a place. I have a feeling I'll find something there."

"Where?"

"RAF Welford," Dan said quietly.

He said, "Better get some sleep. I need to go and see a friend." Dan needed to see Burns.

She stared at him for a while without speaking. Dan didn't look away.

Chloe whispered, "Would you mind not going out tonight?" She brushed her hair back and Dan could see the redness working its way up her neck. "It's just with what's been happening, I...I just wonder if someone is looking for us, too...maybe we're finding out more than we can handle and..."

Dan held her. She was shivering, and her breathing was rapid. She placed her head against his chest and Dan tucked it under his chin. She smelled nice, that same flowery, soft scent that suffused his tense muscles with a looseness, uncoiling his tight sinews.

She looked up at him, her eyes shining in the light, lips inches from his mouth. He couldn't take his eyes away from her face. Faintly, he was aware of his own breathing, suddenly labored and harsh.

"Stay tonight, Dan," Chloe whispered.

Dan's lips were pulled to hers. The first touch was electric, it sent shivers down his body and spine. She gripped him tighter, her hand pressing on his wide chest, fingers digging in gently. Her mouth opened further, and slowly their tongues met and entwined. Dan lost himself in the sensation. He stood up without realizing, lifting her up, too, their lips still locked in a kiss. He put her gently down on the bed, then Chloe pulled him down on top of her.

CHAPTER 30

Dan woke early the next morning. He looked over at Chloe, who was still asleep, her head nestled in her folded arm. He leaned over and moved a strand of hair away from her face. She was beautiful.

He looked out the window. The spring sunlight was brightening up the room. Despite all that had happened in the last few days, he felt a strange peace. Like he was floating in a warm swimming pool on his own. The cold cage that enclosed his heart was melting. The hard edges were blurred, softened.

But an anxiety burned inside him. He could not let Chloe be harmed. Come what may, he had to protect her.

He lay there thinking for a while, preparing himself for the day ahead. He needed to meet Burns. There he was a lot he had to discuss with him.

He got up, splashed water on his face, and performed his yoga routine. He did it most mornings, particularly when he didn't have time to go on his usual five-mile run.

"Wow. Never knew you were into yoga." Chloe was still in bed, watching him.

"Yup, don't blink."

Chloe went for a shower, and when she returned, Dan was looking through his phone.

"Where is the car garage?" Dan asked.

"A place called Balham, in South London."

"Yes, I know it. Not far from Clapham and Battersea. Who gave you the address?"

"Mr Mortimer, the lawyer."

"Okay. Is it as simple as showing your ID and picking it up?"

"Nope, not even that. It's a lock-up garage. We just need to pick it up." Chloe finished latching her earrings and picked up a set of keys from the dressing table.

"Excellent."

As Chloe got dressed, Dan came up behind her. Chloe saw him in the mirror. "What is it?" she asked.

"Do you have a hat? Or anything, to hide your blond hair?"

Dan was the first one to leave, and he spent some time as usual checking out the lobby. The road opposite was empty except for a few tourists. Dan walked ahead on his own, then sat down on a bench, keeping an eye on Chloe. No one followed her.

It took them almost half an hour to get to the garage. The road was lined with Victorian terraced houses, but suddenly gave way in the middle to an apartment block.

"This is it." Chloe said, checking the address. The car park was behind the block. Rows of lock-up garages lined the space.

"Number 55," Chloe said. They found the right one and unlocked the single door, then slid the garage door up. The space was for a single car. A maroon-colored Toyota Celica stood inside. The car was a two-door coupe. It looked new, but had a sheen of dust, like it had traveled but not been touched in a while. Dan saw flecks of mud on the bumpers. The tires looked good. There weren't any dents in the bodywork. Chloe handed the keys to Dan.

"Thanks," he said. "But wait." In the cramped space, it was difficult for him to get down. Something bugged him. In Iraq and 'Stan, it was a favorite ploy of the enemy to put improvised explosive devices in cars. Grunting, he poked his head underneath the car, then lay down and slid under. He couldn't see any obvious wires, scratch marks or tampering.

"Let's go outside." He shut the garage door and moved twenty meters away. "Stand behind me."

Dan pressed the unlock button. The Toyota beeped once, and the car unlocked. Dan opened the garage door again. Lights had come on inside the vehicle. He looked at the car one last time, then opened the driver's side carefully. The leather seat was worn with use. He slid in, while Chloe got in the passenger side.

He turned the ignition on. Half a tank full. Dan flicked his eyes to the sat nav and went through the controls. He found the stored addresses.

The first one said, Bickersteth Road. EC14 0RN. East Central 14. That meant somewhere in East London. He could look that up later. He went through the list. Two other addresses made up the bulk of the list, interspersed with Bickersteth Road.

Neither of the two addresses that turned up frequently had road names, only zip codes. One was RG20 7EY. The other, IP11 3ST. Dan scrolled down the list, but he couldn't see any other addresses.

"Looks like this car traveled between these three addresses a lot," he said.

Chloe was leaning over to him, looking at the screen. "Yes."

"Did your dad have another car?"

"Not that I know of."

Dan looked at her raised eyebrows and smiled. She had taken off the wide-brim straw hat and her hair fell on her shoulder.

He said, "It will be fun driving this car. But it will be me alone." Chloe's face clouded over.

"It's for the best," Dan said gently. "Look, I can hire a car, if you want. But I still need to see where your dad went."

Chloe shrugged. "I'm not worried about the car."

He reached across and put his hand on her thigh. She covered it with her own, her lips pressed together.

"I don't want anything to happen to you."

"Nothing will. Don't worry."

As they drove back Dan did a Google search for the zip codes. He didn't find the exact location, but he did find a location on RG20 that got his attention.

RAF Welford. Something prickled the back of his neck.

The ID card he had got from Simon Renwick. It belonged to the major, and it was for RAF Welford.

He did a search for the base. It was run by the US Air Force. USAF 420th Munitions Squadron, to be specific. It was the largest depot of heavy ammunition for the USAF in Western Europe.

A black cloud of worry was beginning to form at the edge of Dan's mind.

He did a search for the second address. It was in Ipswich, near the coast of Norfolk, in the east of England.

He had to make some urgent phone calls when he got back to the hotel.

*****

After they parked and paid a royal ransom in parking fees for one whole hour, Dan jogged to the nearest tube station. He got off after ten minutes and made a phone call to Burns.

He got back on the tube and came off at Piccadilly Circus. He walked on foot, passing the Royal Academy of Arts. He went to the nearest hotel on Regent Street. He waited outside, watching.

Burns drove up in a black BMW. He parked and went inside the lobby. Dan watched around him for a while, then followed him inside.

Burns was sitting next to a piano. He was facing the doors and saw Dan coming in. This hotel was smaller but still had plenty of people around. Burns had a briefcase on his lap.

Dan sat down facing him and the door. He asked, "You know of an RAF base called Welford, in Berkshire?"

Burns nodded. "Big place. Missile storage. Hellfire, Pathfinders, for Apaches, MiGs, F-35s. Also light ammunition, rifles, handguns. It's the 501st Tactical Missile Wing of the USAF and NATO Air Force."

Dan digested the information. A tactical missile wing was a big deal.

"Is it true that RAF Welford is the largest heavy ammunition depot for the USAF in Western Europe?"

"Yes, mainly for the missiles and heavy ordnance. Why do you want to know?"

Dan hesitated. Burns said, "I'm not liking this, Dan. Not liking this at all."

"Neither am I. We found Guptill's car. He traveled to this place on a regular basis."

Dan told Burns about Chloe and what happened last night. He did not mention Simon Renwick by name. When he finished, Burns said, "Anything else?"

"No."

Burns said, "Jesus Christ, Dan, you could have told me. Guptill's daughter. You know we've been looking for her. Thought she was dead, damn it."

"The first time I met her, she had a red dot dancing on her head. I didn't know who I could trust. What could I have done?"

Burns clicked open his briefcase. He took out some photos and gave them to Dan. They were photos of Simon Renwick.

Dan said, "Shit."

Burns looked up. "You know this guy?"

Dan told him. Burns was angry. "Come on, Dan. What else you holding back? We got the Russians on our tail, someone's hunting you down, Guptill's dead, what the fuck?"

Dan told him about the Delta tattoo on the man who had tried to kill Chloe. Burns said, "Are you sure?"

"Positive."

Burns was thoughtful. He asked, "Do you have a photo?"

"No. Did not have a phone on me that day. You think that two-man team for Chloe came from Intercept?"

Burns frowned and stroked his chin. "Where else would it be from?"

Dan said, "Tell me about Renwick."

"We did a global search on face recognition software for Guptill. We found a match at the US Embassy here. The Embassy let us look at their photos. That's what you have in your hands."

"Why did they try to kill Renwick?"

Burns said, "He led you into an ambush, right?"

"Maybe."

"Once he did his job, they took him out. To silence him. Unfortunately for them, you were there."

"What's happened to Renwick now?"

Burns flipped out his cell. He read Dan's look. "It's not traceable, don't worry." He talked on the phone for a few minutes.

Then he said, "Renwick is alive. In an intensive care unit, but still breathing."

Burns reached inside his briefcase and took out a wad of notes.

"I figured you would want cash instead of plastic." Dan nodded.

"Thanks."

"Now what?"

"I need to check out the RAF base in Welford. Can you get me in?"

Burns nodded. "No problem. Give me till tomorrow morning."

Dan said, "Tell me where you're gonna be. I can pick up the creds on my way in." He tossed the ID card that Guptill had. "This might not work."

Burns inspected the card. "This is an MOD card. British Ministry of Defence. It means Guptill had clearance from MI6."

"That's what I thought."

"And Simon Renwick had it in his possession. A CIA agent."

"So Simon used this card, or he had clearance from the MOD as well. Have you checked with MI6?"

Burns said, "Yes. But MI6 are keeping a lid on it. Thanks for this. Now I can go back to them and say hey, how the hell does an ex-Delta major get RAF creds?" Burns smiled. "That should crack them."

Dan rose up. "You better tell them we are on the same side on this one. Otherwise the cracks are gonna spread."

*****

Dan got back to the hotel and told Chloe of his plans for the next day.

Chloe said, "While you're away, I'm going to find out what happened to Simon Renwick."

"Whoa."

"What?"

"You think the men who tried to kill or abduct him won't be keeping watch?"

Chloe shrugged. "He's going to be in a hospital, right? If he's still alive. Even if he died, he would have been taken to a hospital. The closest hospital is Chelsea and Westminster. Chances are someone there will know."

"Are you sure about this?"

Chloe nodded. Her features hardened. "Don't forget that I met this guy.

I think he wanted to tell me more than he could. He knew Dad well. I need to see him."

"In that case, I can get someone to help. I know which hospital he's at."

Chloe raised her eyebrows. "Someone from your organization told you?"

"Yes."

Dan rubbed her shoulder. "Don't go as yourself. Do something to change the way you look."

"Yes, I know." She spread her arms. "Besides, he might not be in a state to talk anyway. If he's still alive."

"Exactly. So no point in taking risks yourself." He fixed her with a stare. "If anything happens to you, Chelsea will burn down. You know that, right?"

Chloe hugged him. "Yes, I know."

CHAPTER 31

Dan pressed on the gas and the engine growled. Not been let out in a while, Dan thought with satisfaction. He met Burns at Shepherd's Bush, a place in West London.

Burns parked his car and walked over to the Nissan. He sat down and said, "I don't like this, Dan. I don't think you should go to this RAF base."

"Why not?"

"For starters, even with the MOD creds, you are an outsider. You will be noticed. Think of what's happened so far. These guys know what you saw in that compound in Afghanistan. Only you saw it. You were the only witness. These guys are hunting you down. You don't think they're gonna be waiting for you at the RAF base?"

"There's no other way."

"That's not all. Scotland Yard have an alert out for you. They will have your details at every Army depot in the UK."

Dan was silent. Burns leaned over and handed him a small, black cylindrical object.

"What's this?"

"A GPS beacon. In case you're in trouble, and you need exfiltration. Just press the switch, we'll pick the signal up at HQ."

Burns handed over the creds to Dan as well. He said, "Be careful, and get the hell out if there's trouble."

*****

Traffic was heavy heading down west towards the M25. He traveled north, then took the exit for the M4, heading out towards Berkshire and the West Country.

Something about the zip code bothered him. It wasn't on Google Maps, but the surrounding area was. On the sat nav map it was blacked out. He could see where it was. Close to Welford village, whose surrounding land had been converted into the RAF base during the Second World War.

It was in Berkshire county, which began roughly forty miles outside the western edge of London. Small and gently rolling hills appeared on either side of the M4 as the car cruised. Cattle dotted the green land around him.

In half an hour, Dan was getting close to his destination. He took the traffic circle, and as his exit approached, he frowned. It was marked, NO ACCESS, WORK UNITS ONLY. Normally with an RAF base, there would be a clear sign to mention the base. What the hell was this works unit sign for?

Dan drove in. After driving for more than fifteen minutes, he saw the familiar gray iron grill fence that surrounded an RAF base. Sentry boxes at regular intervals. It looked similar to RAF Credenhill, where the SAS HQ was based.

He was coming down the slope of a hill and he could see large, rectangular structures in the middle of the base, which looked like giant Lego box shapes arranged neatly in a line next to each other. There were four or five rows of these, extending almost all the way across the base. They looked strange.

He got to the gates. Two guards with M4 carbines stopped him. Dan gave them the ID that he got from Burns. The guard looked at it, and showed it to his friend. He nodded.

The bar lifted and he waved the car in. Dan drove slowly. Cylindrical dome-shaped mess houses with corrugated-iron roofs appeared on his left. To his right, another electric barrier, this time unmanned. He took the left at the T-junction. Right in front was the football pitch. Next to it, a canteen with a large sign that said, "American Diner".

Dan drove past the canteen. Two men in gray RAF overalls strolled past the canteen, eyeing Dan and the car. Dan drove around the football pitch. A bunch of men, some in uniform and some in soccer football kit, walked down the road towards the office and the spectator stands. Dan drove past them until he found the soccer pitch car park.

Three cars were parked already, all empty. Dan got out and locked the car. A two-story brick building lay ahead, next to a clubhouse and bar area. The stands were next to it. The men from the road walked in, and Dan fell in behind them, smiling in greeting to the few looks cast in his direction. There was a reception area inside, and double doors leading to the bar opposite. The men turned towards the bar, but Dan followed the sign that said "Changing Rooms". He almost barged into two men in soccer gear coming out.

"Sorry," Dan said, and walked past them into the changing rooms. One person was getting changed. A row of lockers along the periphery of the room. Benches all around and in the middle. Dan instantly saw what he was looking for.

Gray overalls hanging on a wall hook. Dan started taking his clothes off. The man on the other side of the room finished dressing and left. Dan stripped quickly and tried the overalls on. It was a tight fit. He packed his clothes under his arm and went back to the car, putting his clothes in the trunk.

He went past the canteen and kept going until a clearing appeared. He could see the giant Lego box structures in front of him, and they looked extraordinary. What he had thought were rectangular boxes were in fact a neatly lined row of hillocks. Each one about ten yards wide and separated by about the same distance. A road ran alongside.

Each hillock opened out to a hollow in the middle, like a giant claw had eaten half the hill away. A truck rumbled past Dan, stopping at the first hillock and reversing into the hollow. Two men opened the rear and jumped out of the tailgate.

The truck was unmarked. Rows of artillery shells were stacked out in the middle of the hollow. He recognized them—155mm shells for heavy guns, like the self-propelled AS-90. One hell of a monster. He had seen rows of them pummel the life out of the Iraqi Army outside Baghdad, back in '03. Steel rain, bring the pain, baby. His lips twitched at the memory.

The two men were pulling down cages of more shells from the truck. At the back of the hollow, carved into the green hillock, were two giant doors. The doors were open, and Dan could see the cages stacked in order inside.

Another hillock also had a truck in front being unloaded. These weapons had three familiar yellow stripes at equal intervals on the black body. The three black fins at the back. He had seen these strapped under wings of attack Apache and Cobra helicopters.

Hellfire missiles. The best air-to-surface missiles he knew. One of the men unloading looked over at him and waved. Dan waved back. Opposite, the same long stretch of the hillocks. Dan saw another truck in the distance and walked towards it. He moved to the back of the truck.

"You guys need a hand?" he asked the two sweating men taking the cages out. Each missile took two or three men to lift. And these were packed inside their gray metal cases, which made them heavier.

"No, we're okay, pal," one of the men said.

Dan gave them a thumbs-up and went to the front of the truck. Instead of going back on the road he sat down near the front wheel of the truck to tie his shoelaces. From here, he had a side-angle view.

The storage was being emptied, loaded on the truck. The reverse of what was happening in the other sites around him. That could be normal, ammunition being transferred from one site to another. Dan thought about weapons moving out of a large munitions base. A base that Guptill traveled to frequently, maybe with Renwick. He decided to see where this truck was going to.

The two men wore RAF overalls and were loading the truck with artillery shells, SAMs and flat black boxes, which, judging from their size, contained light weapons. Probably rifles. The two men didn't look familiar. The manner in which they worked suggested they had done this job before, and knew the place well.

Dan knew he couldn't stay here for long. He watched as the two men finished loading the truck and shut the tailgates. They got into the cabin, slammed the doors shut and reversed out onto the road. The truck beeped its horn once and the men opposite waved back. Dan remained behind the truck, following slowly on the opposite side of the road.

CHAPTER 32

Dan watched the truck lumber out in front of the soccer pitch of RAF Welford, and turn towards the American Diner. It was moving slowly. Dan hurried back to his car. As he drove out on the road circling the pitch, he saw the truck in the distance stopping at the diner. Dan parked nearby, walked in and ordered a burger. He came back out while the order was being made.

The truck driver's door was open. One of the men was checking the lashings around the side. He went around and checked the tailgate as well. Dan went back inside, picked up his order and ran back to the car. The truck was still standing by the road. Dan watched it as he munched on his burger.

There was rumble of multiple engines. A convoy appeared on the main road leading out to the gates. He counted six trucks, all unmarked and identical. One by one, they left the base. The driver of the truck Dan was following waited for another five minutes. Dan was slurping on his Coke when the truck got into gear and drove towards the main gate. Dan put his drink down and eased the Toyota out onto the main road.

Once he was out on the main perimeter road, Dan could see the truck ahead of him. The rear red lights of the convoy were getting dimmer in the distance. The barrier lifted and the truck swung out on the road directly ahead. Dan gunned his engine. He approached the barrier slowly. The same guard leaned in the window. He frowned at Dan, pointing at his overalls.

"Borrowing some clothes, are we?"

"We had a knock around on the pitch and my civvies got dirty."

The young man didn't seem convinced, but lifted the barrier and waved Dan through.

He couldn't see the truck anymore. But the truck could only go one way at the end of the road—the M4 motorway.

He continued, rarely raising the speed above thirty mph. The country lane, with empty fields on either side, came to an end. Dan could hear the rush of the motorway traffic as he wound the window down. He couldn't see the truck anymore. He speeded up slightly. The motorway was ahead of him, cars zipping across at breakneck speed.

He was impatient to join up, and find where the truck had gone. He was about to pull out when out of the corner of his eye, he saw the truck speeding along the other side of the motorway, heading in the opposite direction.

Dan swore and pulled out into the traffic. He put pedal to metal and the engine responded, growling as it picked up speed. Dan got into the fast lane and accelerated. In a minute, he could see an exit approaching. He veered to the left, and at the traffic circle joined the motorway headed west into London. The truck couldn't have gone far, he figured, unless it had gone into an exit.

For five minutes, he didn't speed. It attracted attention, and police cars patrolled this road often. He kept a steady pace in the middle lane, overtaking the slower cars. Finally, he saw the truck, four cars ahead, in the slower left lane. Dan breathed in relief.

The truck trundled on and the mass of machines and humans grew denser as the M4 approached London. But the truck headed north on the London Orbital M25, the motorway surrounding the capital like a spider's web. Dan almost missed the truck as it veered off to the left. He stayed four or five vehicles behind. The truck traveled onto the west of the country towards the coast. They joined a single-lane road, stopping frequently in the traffic.

Two and a half hours later they were close to Ipswich. He sat up straighter. One of the addresses on the sat nav of Guptill's car had been near Ipswich. He opened the screen and scrolled down.

Ipswich came and went as the truck drove past it. After fifteen minutes, they neared Felixstowe Port, the UK's largest container port. But the name had never meant much to him until now.

Felixstowe. *Felix.*

Dan clutched the steering wheel tightly. He was two trucks behind his mark, and watched as all three trucks indicated for the Port exit. Thoughts were swarming around his head. He got a flashback of Major Guptill's contorted face as he died.

The last word he spoke.

Felix.

A chill ran down Dan's spine.

Guptill had traveled down here from Welford and London several times. That was clear from the sat nav. Why? Had he followed a similar truck? Or had he been tailing someone?

The truck Dan was following now was filled with weapons and missiles. Felixstowe was a civilian port, and it dealt with civilian goods. The realization hit him suddenly like a screaming train crashing into his head.

There was hardly any security in Felixstowe.

True, he couldn't just waltz in, but no way would there be armed guards or customs checks. Container ports were famous for being porous. Most contraband drugs found their way into the country through ports such as Felixstowe. The port workers were in the pay of organized gangs that delivered these drugs to their larger networks.

Dan bared his teeth.

That lax security was the reason why this truck was headed into the port. No one would search inside. No one would question where the goods were going.

From Felixstowe, the contents of that truck could go anywhere in the world.

Into that compound in Afghanistan.

Felix.

Is that what Guptill had tried to tell him? About the port? Yes, and something more. Dan let out a ragged breath. It was a code name. Foreign agents were often given names like these. Felix was the cover for a spy. Possibly a double agent, and Guptill had discovered his identity.

He remembered what Burns had told him. *We have an infiltrator.*

Dan bunched his jaws tight and gripped the wheel. He was getting closer to some answers.

He watched as the trucks ahead slowed and turned left into a lane that said "Delivery-Arrivals Only". A number of other trucks had formed a queue in the wide, multi-lane space. Counters stood at each lane, like tollbooths on a bridge.

Drivers leaned out from the cabins and handed over paperwork or shouted out numbers to the people inside the booths. Some drivers disembarked, and so did the booth operators. The Volvo truck swung down the side and stopped at a far lane behind a bigger vehicle. Dan memorized the registration.

Dan knew he couldn't get in. As the only car, he would be spotted instantly. Traffic was slow, and he moved forward at barely twenty mph, straight past the exit for the trucks. He needed to get out of this road and turn back on himself to get into the port. After ten minutes' driving, he saw the sign he needed. "Non-delivery and other vehicles."

Dan took the exit. Traffic was lighter here and he soon approached the tollbooth. The bar remained lowered as a woman in a Port Authority uniform approached him.

"What's your VRN?" she asked, looking at Dan and the car.

"Sorry, what's that?"

"First time here?"

Dan smiled. "It shows, doesn't it?"

"You American?"

"Yup."

"Hope you're having a good time here."

"I am, thanks." *One hell of a good time.*

"You need a vehicle registration number in order to get in here. Register at the website."

"I see. Is there any other way, like a tourist section? I don't have to get inside, but just wanted to see the large freighters."

The woman nodded. "If you keep going down the way you came, there's a sign for the Port Authority Education Trust. It's for school trips and families, but it's on the water, with a café, benches and so on. You can see the ships docking and sailing up and down as well."

Dan thanked the woman and turned the car around. Another fifteen minutes later he saw the sign. There was no traffic here and he speeded up. Then Dan saw the glimmer of water. The broad sweep of the rivers Stour and Orwell, according to his sat nav, joining the great wash of the North Sea.

Dan parked in the visitors' car park and went over to the café and Port

Museum building. Waves lapped at the pebbly beach. Large freighters were docked at the port. Giant rigs rose high in the air over the berthed ships, picking up shipping containers from their decks in steel claws.

A monstrous floating castle was putting slowly in from the North Sea, its deck and forecastle stacked high with multicolored shipping containers. The ship blotted out the sun as it got closer. On amphibian tours of duty Dan had seen large destroyer vessels, and he'd been on the USS *Nimrod*, the US Navy aircraft carrier in the Persian Gulf. The ship he was watching seemed as big as the aircraft carrier.

The courtyard of the café was sprinkled with people watching the ships. The pebbly beach of Felixstowe Port stretched out towards the fence, separating the beach from the first deep berths.

CHAPTER 33

It was 1845 hours. Another hour and a half of light, if that. He needed to see what was happening with the truck inside the port.

Dan made his mind up. He went back to the car park and bought an overnight ticket. He opened the trunk and took his clothes out. He put the Sig on his back belt, next to the kukri. He lifted the floor of the trunk and peered inside the wheel well. He took the floor out, and unscrewed the reserve wheel.

He took the KEDR sub-machine gun, and slotted out the breech, magazine and barrel. He stored the individual parts in the corners of the wheel well, then refixed the wheel and put the floor back on. He put an extra magazine of the Sig in his pocket, and the Nite-Glo torch in the other. He shut the car and went to the bathroom in the café. He used one of the cubicles to get changed into his jeans and button-down shirt. He dropped off the RAF overalls in the trunk of the car, and then looked around him. The car park was empty.

He walked to the side of the parking lot. The fence was low there and he vaulted across it to the low ground that led to the pebble beach. He cut straight across, heading to the port, walking quickly across the shrub and grassland. A line of low trees near the port fence gave him cover. He studied the wire fence. It was about ten feet tall, with regularly spaced posts, and he couldn't see any signs of electricity. There wasn't any barbed wire at the top, which made his life a lot easier.

He grabbed the wire mesh and shook it. It was firm and would take his weight. He wrapped his legs around a post and pulled himself up with both hands, using it like a fast rope. He crouched over the top and jumped down. The brick wall of a building lay in front of him. He could hear an engine wheezing and what sounded like train railway tracks. Then he saw the freight trains. A small path went past several buildings to the first berth.

The brick wall had a sign. Wickenden House. He came out onto a wide-pitched road. Men in high-visibility, red overalls and hats walked along. He looked at them carefully. They wore steel-toe boots with ID badges dangling from the neck. Opposite him there stood a cluster of buildings, one of them belonging to the Port Authority Police.

Dan headed back out towards the fence. He could keep going down the back of the buildings instead of the road. Eventually he found a clearing with a train station. A freight train was being loaded by fixed electric rigs on the side. A stack of twenty-foot-long, ten-foot-high shipping containers lay opposite, arranged in rows as far as the eye could see. Signs on the containers read: China Shipping, MSC, Lundberg, Evergreen—and many were labeled Maersk.

"You alright there, mate?" a voice called out from behind him.

Dan turned around. A worker with his sleeveless, high-visibility jacket, helmet and glasses stood there smoking a cigarette. He looked Dan up and down.

"Fine, thanks," Dan said. "I came with my brother who is a hauler. He gave me the number of a container in the train docks, and asked me to check if it's arrived. Then I got lost."

The man walked closer. He kept puffing on his cigarette.

"What truck is he driving?"

"A black Volvo."

"So, you don't work here?"

Dan shook his head. "No."

"You American?"

Dan smiled. "Yeah. Not seen my bro in years, so thought I'd come down and see where he worked. Going for a beer with the guys later."

"I see," the man said.

Dan asked, "Do you know how I get back to back to the truck loading zone?"

The man threw his cigarette away. "Yeah. Follow me."

They walked past the train platform. A container landed with a soft thud and screech on the train. The huge claws separated and lifted up.

They crossed a clearing with more buildings. HMRC Office, and then Tomlinson House, P&O Shipping lines. Beyond that, Dan found himself in an open space the size of multiple football fields, all stacked with shipping containers in their white marked berths. Far to his left lay the rigs and waters of the port. The man stopped and pointed.

"Head for behind the containers. That's where the main hauler route comes in. The stations are numbered. Which one were you?"

"Eight."

"One of the last ones then. Keep walking."

Dan pointed to the man's high-visibility jacket. "Do you know where I can find one like that?"

"At the reception desk beside the Customs center." He jerked his thumb backwards.

"Thanks," Dan said. He breathed out a sigh of relief, and watched the man disappear behind a row of containers. Then he went to the reception desk. A surly, old woman jabbed a finger at a stack of old and dusty red jackets piled up on the floor. He found an old white helmet, too. Dan picked one up, thanked the woman and left.

A few trucks were standing in line, and a forklift loading transporter moved between them. The transporter stopped at one truck and lowered its long arm from which hung a wide, double-pronged hook. The hook clanged around the sides of the container on the truck and lifted it up. The transporter drove up to the stack of containers, the container swaying in the air between the two hooks on either side.

It took Dan twenty minutes to find the Volvo truck. It was in the middle hauler park. More trucks stood side-by-side, with enough space in between for another forklift transporter to maneuver.

Dan stepped in behind a truck opposite and watched the Volvo. The cabin was empty. The lashings had been taken off, and the cover removed from a shipping container that bore the legend *"Living Aid"* on its sides. The name didn't ring any bells. There was a sound of gears clashing and the forklift transporter moved past him to the first truck in the line, at the far end. It lifted the container off the truck and moved away.

He could find out where the container was destined for, if he followed the transporter. And maybe, what cargo the Volvo would be taking back. Most of the trucks had empty cabins. The two on either side of the Volvo were definitely vacant. He crossed the distance quickly.

When he was between two vehicles, he looked below the truck. Two sets of legs at the far end, where he could hear the transporter coming back with its load. Dan reached up and tried the handle of the Volvo. Locked. He walked around the back and tried the passenger side. Locked as well.

He heard a sound from the other end. Another forklift transporter was making its way up the line. The driver climbed off. Then he heard voices. Very close. Coming up to the Volvo, and getting louder. Dan was trapped. He dropped to the ground and rolled underneath the truck.

He went forward and pressed himself against the underside of the front chassis. The two drivers came up to the Volvo. One threw down a cigarette on the ground and stamped on it. The cabin door opened on the passenger side. Before the man could get on, Dan heard another voice. A man came up from the rear of the truck.

"Hello, chaps. What have we got here today, then?" The forklift operator. Dan could see up to the man's belt line. He pressed himself further against the chassis.

"The usual cargo. Vaccines."

The forklift guy scribbled something on the clipboard he was holding. "Oh yes. For Karachi again?"

"Yes, Karachi."

"And what about the pick-up?"

The same voice spoke again. Dan assumed it was the driver. "Same again." There was a slight delay, then the voice said, "Container number PV 346756 from Karachi."

Forklift scribbled again. "Yes, got that, too. Okay, chaps, looks like you're third in line now. Just wait." The man was about to turn away when the driver spoke to him again.

"We need to check it. Like last time."

Forklift came forward again. "Now chaps, you know I can't let you do that."

Dan could see the driver reach into his pants pocket and pull out a wad of notes. He peeled off several and handed them to the forklift operator. His voice was lower now, almost a whisper. "We can make it worth your while. Just like last time."

Forklift hesitated. Then he put the money into his pocket. His voice was now a whisper as well.

"Alright. But we go before I take the vaccines off. Come with me when I'm unloading the second truck. Yeah, the MAN truck. Check what you have to, then I come back to take this bitch off. Don't follow me, come back your own way."

Forklift sauntered off. Dan watched the driver and his helper walk down to the rear wheels of the Volvo. They stopped there, watching the second truck being offloaded at the front of the queue. They lit cigarettes and waited. Dan kept himself plastered against the chassis. Silently, he took the Sig out and screwed the suppressor on. He held the butt in both hands, finger loose on the trigger.

He tracked the men as they moved around the truck. If they peeped in, or checked the tires, Dan would shoot first. He would get a headshot on one. No more than one shot would be necessary. Then he could drag the body inside.

CHAPTER 34

The whine of the forklift transporter got louder. One truck along, the container was being lifted. That was the signal. Dan watched as the men threw their cigarettes away and walked after the transporter. The long shaft raised itself from the body of the transporter like the turret of a machine gun. It's widely spaced claws at either end held the container securely, but that didn't stop it from swaying slightly. Dan gave the men a head start, then he rolled out the side of the Volvo and followed.

They moved into a miniature city of shipping containers, piled up to five high. Dan craned his neck up and around. They went around a block of Maersk containers. Dan stopped at the edge. He heard the gears of the transporter shifting, then a loud clang as the container was deposited. The engine died down. He heard the forklift guy speaking in a low voice, but couldn't make out any words. Footsteps receded and he tiptoed around. He caught them just as they were coming out the far end. He ran, and poked his neck past the last container.

The damn place was like a rabbit warren. After another turn, he heard them stop. Dan flattened himself against a container and peered across. The three men were standing in front of a dark blue container. He watched as they unlocked it. The driver lifted some bolts in the front of each door, pulled the long camshafts, and opened both doors. Then the driver and his helper went inside.

Dan shifted back. He was just in time. The forklift guy was looking around fearfully. He called out to them. They emerged in five minutes. They said something to the forklift guy, then locked the doors. Dan got ready to sprint back. To his relief, the men didn't retrace their steps. They went left and Dan followed. They were headed back to the trucks. He ducked back inside the container city.

Dan found the blue container quickly. The bolts were down, but the

245

central lock was still open. He opened one door like he had seen the forklift guy do, stepped inside, and shut it without locking it. He needed to be quick. Mr Forklift operator would be back soon.

It was pitch black inside. He shone his torch around.

Bicycles. Piled on one another, up to the ceiling. Mostly mountain bikes with fat wheels and tubes.

What the hell?

Mountain bikes from Karachi? It didn't make sense. He got closer to the bikes. He put the flashlight between his teeth and grabbed the nearest. It weighed like a mountain bike should. Admittedly, these were sturdy bikes, with wheels larger than normal...

Hold it.

Dan shone the torch down the bike carefully. He tapped the steel tubes. A dull sound. His heart beat faster. He got down to the fat tires. He squeezed one. Tight as a bamboo pole. Ok, it might be pressured. But still... he took his kukri out and stabbed the tire. There was a hiss of air, but only slightly. Dan cut down with the kukri, slashing the rubber. He felt something inside. He shone the torch. Pay dirt.

A plastic tube was wrapped around the inside of the tire. Dan used the tip of the kukri to cut it. Under the torchlight, a gray-brown dusty material poured out. Dan sniffed at it—a pungent, sharp smell. He had smelled this before. When the memory jogged, his spine whiplashed straight.

Eight years ago. Helmand Province, Afghanistan, inside a poppy farmer's hut. The poppy harvest had just finished and farmers were gathering the poppy resin to be sold in the market. Some farmers, like the one whose hut they were raiding, went further. They actually reduced the resin and boiled it with chemicals, then dried it in the sun to form a dry powder.

Heroin.

Dan stared at the powder in his hand, then at the plastic tube hanging from the inside of the tire. Powder was still pouring out, forming a conical tower on the floor. He got up and tapped the steel tubes. The handlebars came off with some effort. More plastic tubes with the same gray-brown stuff inside...

Bicycles were packed inside the container. The HMRC (Her Majesty's Revenue and Customs) man would look at the bikes, tick a box and move on. No one would suspect the millions of dollars' worth of heroin secreted inside the frames and tires.

Dan poked around in the back of the container, but it was all the same. He listened at the door for five seconds, then stuck his head out. He heard the sound of an engine. The forklift transporter was returning. He came out and locked the doors quickly, went around the corner and hid. The forklift made a massive moaning sound as it trundled into the space.

It was carrying the *Living Aid* container. With a loud sound and a cloud of dust, it put the container on the ground. The crane lifted up from the middle of the transporter, and the two claws on either side grabbed the container above the one that Dan had just been in. Finally, the forklift lifted the container from Karachi, and the transporter turned around and left for the hauler park. Dan watched it go around the corner and vanish from view.

He ran over to the *Living Aid* container, got in and took his flashlight out. Shelves lined the space inside. He had a small area in the middle to move around in.

He noted the Hellfire and Pathfinder missiles. H&K rifles lined one whole wall. He swore under his breath when he saw the NVGs. They were the older generation, but they were still of key tactical advantage.

Why the hell were these bound for Karachi? Pakistan's largest port? Now he knew the answer.

He had just discovered a weapon-smuggling ring. From the RAF base, via Felixstowe Port, to Karachi, and then into Taliban hands.

The weapons were paid for by contraband drugs, and cash. He suspected the contraband was worth more than the cash was.

Dan felt sick inside. He thought of the men he had seen die in Afghanistan. He had carried back the wounded from the battlefield. Many of them, for the last time. Is this what those men had died for?

He thought of the young men on the streets, wasting their lives as junkies.

Someone was profiting from this. These weapons would be worth a lot of money to the Taliban.

A rage grew inside him, and so did a conviction. He would get them for this. Dead or alive, he would get them. He was the scapegoat, being framed for smuggling weapons. But they had picked on the wrong person.

He flashed the torch around, searching. Finally, on the lowest rung of a back shelf he found it. The entire shelf was lined with suitcases of C-4 explosives. He picked a hundred-pound bag and opened it. The putty-like explosive was lined in one corner with a fuse wire, a timer and detonator. As explosives went, it was pretty basic, but it would more than do the job.

Dan picked the suitcase up. It was heavy, but he could manage. He was about to step out when he heard the sound outside. It was the forklift operator again, but he was much closer this time.

Dan cursed. He had taken too long to check the equipment. He opened the door a fraction. The forklift transporter was coming around the bend. The wide jaws of its crane were empty, possibly the reason why it had come back quicker. It was now going to stack the containers back in their place, ready to be picked up when their ship was ready.

Dan shut the door almost fully, leaving a small sliver through which he could see. The transporter went slowly past the *Living Aid* container. Dan heard it stop. Footsteps approached. Slowly, Dan put the suitcase down. It would take the forklift driver a few seconds to realize the door was ajar.

Dan had those few seconds in which to act.

He waited until the man came right up to the door and stopped. In that instant Dan pushed the door back with all his might. There was dull thwack as the heavy steel door smashed into the forklift driver's face. Dan pivoted on his feet, and hopped out of the container at the same time. The driver was on the ground, his face a bloody mess. Dan knelt down. The man was out cold.

Then he heard another voice behind him.

"Well, well, what do we have here?"

CHAPTER 35

Dan got up, and slowly turned around.

Four men circled him.

"You didn't think you would get away that easy, did ya?" the tallest of the men smirked. Cockney accent. From London's East End, where most of its criminal underworld congregated.

Dan stood there silently, watching the men form a ring around him.

The tall man was about two inches shorter than him. He was wide at the shoulders, and his long arms hung loose at the sides. He carried himself on the balls of his feet, suggesting a boxer's stance. Dan wondered who had sent them.

The two men on either side of him were shorter and squatter, thick around the neck and shoulders. Their shifting eyes and pock-marked faces identified them as veterans of street fighting. Part of the dockside gang, maybe, who had been hired as protection. They did not have the cold, calculating eyes of men like Dan.

If they had, Dan would have been dead by now.

One of them had stepped behind Dan. He was not worried, he had his measure already. Similar to the two in front, on either side of their leader. He knew they were armed, and that they would not hesitate to use it if necessary.

He was not worried about that. He was more worried about the passage of time.

He needed to get on that damned truck. It would lead him to the source of all his troubles.

He calculated how much time he needed to get through these men, and stayed silent like a statue, watching them closely.

"Throw your weapon and empty your pockets!" the leader snarled, taking a step closer.

Without moving his body, Dan shook his head slowly from side to side. *No. Come closer to me, asshole.*

He watched the leader's hands. The gangster's right hand snaked inside his right coat pocket. He lunged forward suddenly, a gun appearing like magic in his right fist. Looked like a Glock 19. Dan was prepared. He stepped back quickly. With his left hand he struck the gangster's right hand down, hard as he could. The gun went scattering on the floor, out of sight underneath a container box.

Immediately he felt the man behind him hook his elbow around his neck. Dan did not mind that. He had a broad neck, with thick muscles. He bunched his neck muscles, bringing his head down. The man was strong, and he tried to bring Dan down with a wrestler's grip round his neck.

Dan allowed the man to pull him back, but only till he was leaning against the man. Then he used his support to heave his legs off the ground.

His boots smashed into the leader's face, blood erupting from his broken nose. The other foot hit another man in the chest, sending him sprawling against some rattling garbage bins.

Dan hooked his fingers round the elbow that was gripping his neck. He went down on his knees, kneeling forward like he was doing a somersault. The forward jerk made the man fly off him, landing on his friend on the floor, who was still winded from Dan's foot landing on his chest.

It had all happened in the blink of an eye.

The leader was slowly getting off his knees, searching for his gun on the ground, clutching his bleeding nose with his left hand.

The remaining gangster uttered a vile oath and flew in with his fists. Big mistake. The man was wide and thick, and all his power was in his shoulders and neck. His knockout punch sailed harmlessly past Dan's face as he calmly sidestepped. The man stumbled and Dan kicked his feet, bringing him down. Dan quickly stepped behind him and grabbed his hair, bending his neck back. He hit the man as hard as he could just below the right ear, aiming for the jaw angle.

The man screamed and jerked, but Dan held him tight by the hair, and hit him again, in exactly the same spot, feeling the blow reverberate up his forearm this time. Dan let go of the man. Screaming, he went down to the floor.

From the corner of his eye, Dan saw the leader. Blood flowed like a pair of curtains down either side of his face, covering his mouth and chin in a red mask. His eyes were wide, and a knife had appeared in his right hand. He circled Dan, hatred filling his face. The two others had got off the floor as well, and joined their leader. Then they rushed Dan in a triangle formation.

This time, the leader slashed at Dan from below, aiming for his midriff. Dan high-kicked with his left leg, a move that surprised the leader. It surprised most knife fighters, who rely on their arms to parry and block.

The leader cried out as the kick flung his right hand out of the way, dislodging the knife. The cry died in his throat as Dan's fist landed square on his jaw, crunching bone. The man was knocked out cold, but Dan grabbed his shirt even as his two mates rushed him from either side.

Holding the unconscious leader like a shield, Dan turned left and cannoned into his attacker.

Three of them went down in a heap, with the last gangster behind them. Dan rolled off and was on his feet in the same movement.

The gangster on his feet kicked hard and caught Dan in the midriff, winding him. It was a heavy blow, but Dan did not let go of his leg. He lifted till the man came off his feet and landed on his back. Dan straddled his chest instantly and double-punched him. The man's eyes rolled back as Dan lifted him up by the collar and head-butted him with savage force, spraying bone and cartilage from his nose.

Dan was on his feet just as the last gangster got to his.

One-on-one. Dan wanted to glance at his watch. He was dangerously short of time now.

The drivers could be getting back to the truck any minute now, and Dan couldn't let them drive off without him.

The thick, heavy-set face of the gangster curled up in hate as he lifted his fists and approached Dan.

The man feinted with his left and punched hard with his right. It caught Dan on the shoulder as he ducked. But the blow was good. It turned Dan around, and he stumbled backwards.

Dan swayed out of the way as another punch came for his face. The man had put too much into the blow, and it was his turn to stumble in the follow-through.

Dan hit him hard in the midriff just below the sternum. The man doubled up as the breath left his chest. Dan grabbed his head and brought his right knee up, smashing the face down. The neck loosened. The limp body sagged uselessly to the floor.

Dan glanced at the parking lot. The trucks were still there. He ignored the four bodies lying on the floor. They would be out cold for a while.

He went back inside the container and began dragging out the steel cages that held the explosives, missiles and rifles. He took the missiles out of their shelves and put them on the floor. Anyone who came up here would see the container had been tampered with and should raise the alarm.

And they sure as hell would not miss the four bodies.

He picked up the suitcase of C-4 explosive and jumped on the forklift transporter. The machine had an ignition and a steering wheel. He turned the ignition key and the engine purred smoothly to life. With the suitcase at his feet, Dan drove around the *Living Aid* container and headed out to the hauler park.

He flicked the light switches of the transporter on. It was 2100 hours now, and the sun had set, leaving the sky in deepening shades of black. The hauler park was dark. Lights farther away lit up the road.

The Volvo was still there. Three of the other trucks had left. The Volvo's cabin was still empty. Dan got closer. The truck was loaded with the deep blue container full of mountain bikes.

Lashings had secured it tightly to the truck bed. Lights in the cabin were off and Dan figured the men were having dinner.

He worked quickly. He put the C4 suitcase on the ground and used the steel claws of the transporter to grab it and lift the suitcase to the roof of the Volvo's container. He drove away and parked the transporter back near the stack of containers.

Dan returned to the Volvo, grabbed the lashings at the back of the container and pulled himself up. Using the bolts and camshafts as leverage, he climbed upwards, and heaved himself onto the roof of the container. He could see the suitcase. He crawled towards it, pushed the suitcase out to the middle, and pulled two lashings till they covered the suitcase like a strap holder. Then he lay down spreadeagled.

He didn't have to wait long. The drivers came back, smoking and cracking jokes. They got into the cabin and flicked on the light switches. The ignition fired, gears clashed and with a deep rumble the leviathan pulled out of the park.

CHAPTER 36

The Volvo moved slowly out of Felixstowe Port. Once it hit the dual lanes of the A12, the road heading back to London, it picked up speed. Traffic was lighter now, but the twelve-wheel machine wasn't built for speed. It rumbled along at 40mph, Dan estimated.

He was holding onto the lashings on either side of him. The steel surface was recessed and cut into his stomach and legs. Dan did a quick calculation. When they joined the M25, the truck would pick up speed. When it came off the M25 at the other end, there would be traffic on London's roads. There always was. He looked behind him. One car, lights blazing, overtook the slower Volvo. Then it left the road in darkness, lit up only by the truck's headlights. He wouldn't get a better chance than this.

Dan let go of the lashing with one hand, and pulled out the Sig. The suppressor was still screwed on. Then he slid forward on his belly, using the recesses on the steel. He got close to the side of the container.

Black asphalt flashed below him. Wind whipped at the lashings. The blurry white line on the road ran along the side of the huge tires.

He steadied himself, transferring his weight back. He looked behind briefly. The road was still empty. Dan leaned his gun arm over the side, extended his elbow and aimed for the side-view mirrors. The rattling of the container wasn't helping. Neither was the wind. He held the gun butt tighter. Then he fired. The round went into the road, picking up a puff of dust. Dan swore and refocused his arm. This time the shot cracked into the mirror, destroying it.

He had been prepared for the swerve, but when it came it still surprised him. He almost went over the side as the truck moved sharply to the left, but he managed to hold onto the lashings and pull himself in.

He knew how important side-view mirrors were for a truck driver. They did the job of rear-view mirrors. The driver was now blind on the right side.

As Dan expected, the truck moved onto the hard shoulder, decelerating. He glanced at the suitcase, it was secure. As the truck came to a stop, Dan was already at the back. His feet were on the camshaft bolts, and he slid down lower, holding onto the lashings. As the truck belched out a final puff of exhaust and shuddered to a stop, Dan dropped down to the road. The headlights went off and it was very dark all of a sudden.

He crouched behind the rear wheel. The driver's cabin door opened, but the man didn't come down. Instead, Dan could just about make out the muzzle of a rifle. The rifle poked out further, and Dan could see the man turned around inside the cabin, twisting his body so he could use his weapon. Dan heard the passenger side open and the other man jump down. He would have a weapon as well, and would come around Dan's back.

He couldn't allow that to happen. He had to maintain the element of surprise.

There was no wind now and he was rock-still. He could see half of the driver leaning out with the rifle. That was enough. He fired, and the sound of the strike was like the squashing of a watermelon under a hammer. The driver screamed and fell out the cabin, breaking his fall against the door. The rifle clattered uselessly to the ground. Dan ran forward, firing again. The bullet made contact, somewhere in the upper body. It was hard to tell in the dark. The body collapsed on the ground and was still.

Dan heard a sound behind him and threw himself on the ground. The first bullet whined over his head. Dan rolled to the front of the truck as another bullet kicked up dirt on the asphalt. He could hear the man running. Dan ran around the side of the vehicle and threw himself under it. The man's legs appeared on the other side. Dan squeezed off two rounds and heard the dull smack of impact. The man screamed as the rounds tore into his calf muscles. He went down and Dan fired twice more, aiming for the head. Both bullets found their mark. The body slammed on the road, jerked once, then was still.

The motorway was still empty. Dan grabbed both bodies by the collar and pulled them over to the grass verge. He shone the flashlight on them. The driver was hit in the chest and neck. He was close to being finished. The second guy had met a 5.56mm NATO round with his head, and the result wasn't pretty. Dan looked behind him. The grass verge rose up four feet, then a steel fence appeared. He checked the men's pockets, and found their RAF identity cards and cellphones. Then he picked up the bodies and dumped them over the fence.

He went around the back of the truck and climbed back up to the roof. He got the suitcase and brought it down. It wasn't easy. He dangled with one hand on the camshaft bolt of the container door, while the other held the heavy case. He jumped to the ground and fell over, bruising his shoulder. He put the suitcase in the cabin and got into the driver's seat.

CHAPTER 37

The nurse tapped the keyboard. She spoke without taking her eyes off the screen.

"BIBA yesterday, you said? Gunshot wound?"

Chloe was standing in Chelsea and Westminster Hospital's Accident and Emergency Department, a long queue of disgruntled people behind her. It was 8 am, but the queues had already started. She had tied her hair up in a bun, and was wearing a baseball cap.

"Was he brought in by ambulance?" the nurse asked Chloe impatiently. BIBA. Chloe twigged.

"Yes," she said hastily. "Name is Simon Renwick."

"And you are?"

"Close friend."

"Wait here." The nurse got up and left. Chloe looked around. On either side were receptionists and nurses manning the desks. Behind her, a large space was lined with seats, filled with the muffled coughs and occasional groans of the sick and needy. The nurse came back and this time she had a doctor with her.

"Come to this side, please," the nurse said. The doctor opened a door, and Chloe walked through.

The doctor was Asian, in his early thirties, with closely cut black hair. He regarded Chloe with interest.

"How can I help you?"

Chloe repeated herself, and this time she described Renwick as well. The doctor frowned.

"Someone matching that description was brought in yesterday. One hell of a trauma. Heavy bleeding, but we managed to stabilize him with four liters of blood. They took him to theater. He was very lucky. The two bullets missed the major arteries. Part of his liver had to be removed, its blood supply had died."

"Where is he now?"

"In ITU. Intensive therapy unit, I mean. He is still in a critical state. I must ask you again, what is your relation to this man?"

Something in the doctor's voice bothered Chloe. She kept her face passive and met his gaze. "I met him in the course of my job, we had an important professional connection. He knew my father well. I'm concerned about him."

The doctor sighed. "Look, I don't mean to cause offense. But there was a big police presence when this guy turned up. His condition was critical, but we were also told not to allow any visitors, or *anyone* for that matter, near him. Don't ask me why."

Chloe nodded. "I see. So, you don't think I'll be allowed to see him?"

"I very much doubt it."

Chloe took the elevator to the first floor and followed directions to the ITU. It was at the end of a long concourse, lined by wide windows that looked down onto a leafy Japanese garden below with a fountain and stream. Two RMP-uniformed men with machine guns stood on either side of the doors. They stared at Chloe as she approached. One of them put a hand out.

"Can we help you?"

"I'm here to see a patient. Simon Renwick."

"Wait here."

One of the guards went inside and came out with a nurse.

"Mr Renwick is not allowed any visitors," the nurse said, looking a little flustered. Chloe didn't miss the glance the two guards exchanged, and how they tightened the grip on their weapons.

"Is there a reason why not?"

"His condition is still critical. Touch and go. Next of kin have been informed. We can inform you, too, if you leave us your details."

Chloe shook her head. "No, thank you. I'll contact the next of kin myself and come back at a suitable time."

"As you wish," the nurse said.

Chloe went back down the concourse, thinking to herself. The Royal Military Police were guarding Simon Renwick. Someone high up was protecting him. Well, they must have realized now that he was at risk. After he almost died. If it hadn't been for Dan…

Chloe felt Renwick knew what this was all about. Her father dying, Dan getting framed. What Dan had seen in that compound. The weapons. She thought hard about her meeting with Renwick. The DSO was promoting new military hardware like fighter jets and satellites. There was an air show in Farnborough, which was the UK's largest trade—which meant weapons and associated technology—and public air show.

Billions of dollars' worth of sales were made each year. She had seen the advertisement on the wall while she was waiting for Renwick.

And today was the first day of the air show.

She had intended to cover it for *London Herald.* Several MoD officials would be there, most of them in senior positions. Last year, even the Secretary of Defence had been there. But the trade fair was held on separate days, when members of the public weren't allowed. Chloe came out of the hospital and called her office. Her name was already down on the press list. All she had to do was get her ID badge from the hotel room and head down to Farnborough.

*****

The sun was shining as Chloe approached the Press Exhibitor's counter of the Farnborough International Airshow. Her ID was checked, and she was given a new ID necklace, which she had to wear at all times. At the final check-in counter her handbag was searched and Chloe was patted down by a female guard inside a room.

Outside, she gaped at the massive spectacle in front of her. Chloe was facing the Outdoor Exhibition Area, a huge, three-square-kilometer enclave which included a runway. Several commercial jet airplanes were parked on the grass verge, their massive bodies glinting in the sun. People milled around them like ants. She saw Boeing and Airbus jets of various sizes. After the commercial passenger planes, the line of military airships started. The first stall was so big she mistook it for a new section of the show.

It was the area dedicated to BAE Systems, the largest weapon manufacturer in Europe, and the third-largest in the world. Headquartered in London, BAE Systems were the builders of everything from all-terrain vehicles to the latest warplanes. Chloe walked slowly around the new Solaris drone, its twenty-meter body so slim and streamlined it seemed almost impossible such a thing could fly at thirty thousand feet.

That was until she saw the range of missiles attached to the underbelly of its wings. A man in a suit, standing in front of the machine, was explaining the drone's abilities enthusiastically to a group of foreigners, including an Arab dressed in a white *dishdasha* and the traditional *keffiyeh*.

She came to the Cyclone jets, the next generation of traditional fighter jets. The relatively small size of the cockpit, and the enormous wingspan attracted her attention most. Machine guns were mounted on the wings, built in so that only the muzzles protruded. Beneath the wings, she saw a stunning array of missiles. The man explaining was pointing to the missiles, and indicated inside the plane's belly where more bombs lay hidden. The jet seemed like an airborne weapons depot, designed to fly anywhere in the world, ready to drop its seeds of destruction.

After a while, Chloe was feeling dizzy. She stopped at a drinks counter and sipped on a Diet Coke. She decided to head inside to the Indoor Exhibition Area. An enormous, dome-shaped tent had been created to house it. The cool hum of the air-conditioners was a welcome relief after the heat and bustle outside.

She headed for the toilets. She followed the signs, and went inside. It was empty. Chloe stood in front of the mirror, and took out her make-up bag. She took out her lipstick and froze.

In the mirror, behind her, she could see a large man. He had a grin on his face. Chloe opened her mouth to scream, but she was too late.

In one swift movement, the man stepped forward and wrapped his hand around her mouth, pulling her into his chest. Chloe fought back. She managed to lift her upper lip above the hand clamping down on her mouth. It smelled of cigarettes.

She bit down hard on the hand, feeling the bone crunch.

"Bitch!" the man screamed. He let go of his hand and spun Chloe around. A fist smacked against her face, and Chloe fell backwards, her eyes going black.

CHAPTER 38

Dan was parked in a street opposite the Intercept HQ.

He had found a café nearby for breakfast. He had barely slept, and the tiredness was giving him a headache.

He flipped open the cellphone that Burns had given him, connecting the battery to the phone.

Burns did not answer. Dan got off and went to a nearby store to buy himself a drink.

As he was walking to the truck, his cellphone beeped. He took it out and stared at it. Chloe's number. He pressed answer.

"Chloe?"

There was a pause, then Dan heard a man's voice. A voice he knew.

It was Burns. "Hey, Dan, it's me."

Dan frowned, then felt his heart suddenly hammer against his chest. He had difficulty speaking. "Burns."

"Yes, buddy, it's me." Burns' voice was light, relaxed.

"What are you doing with Chloe's phone?" A dreaded chill was spreading through Dan's body. He tried to fight it off. But it kept coming back. His rational mind kept trying to find a reason why Burns would have Chloe's phone. It couldn't find one.

Burns said, "You got the truck, Dan?"

Dan opened his mouth and forced himself to breathe. Words were frozen in his mouth.

"How do you know about the truck?"

"I know everything, Dan."

Dan leaned against the truck, feeling the ground opening up beneath his feet.

The cellphone. The GPS beacon. The truck had a satellite feed. They could track him, and Burns had given him every single item.

"Where's Chloe?"

"Oh my, wouldn't you like to see her?"

"You're bluffing. She's not there. You just found her phone."

There was a scuffle, and some muffled voices. Dan could hear his heart pumping.

"Dan? Dan, is that you?"

He closed his eyes. It was Chloe. She sounded scared. He spoke quickly.

"Yes, it's me. Don't worry. I'm on my way. They won't do anything to you."

"Go straight to the police, Dan…" Another scuffle as the phone was ripped off her hand.

The same voice came down the phone. "Believe me now?"

"Felix."

There was a pause at the other end. Burns' voice hardened. "We need to meet up, Dan. Tonight. After dark, at 10 pm. I'm giving you an address. Don't even think of going anywhere else. The truck has a tracker, and I can see it on my screen as we speak."

"Let her go first."

"Negative. You bring the truck into the address. Leave the truck here and take the girl."

"And let you kill us both?"

"I guess that is a chance you will have to take, Dan. Unless you want the girl to die a slow and horrible death. After my boys have had some fun, of course." He laughed, a derisive, high-pitched snort, and Dan could hear other voices laughing in the background.

"You are a dead man, Burns," Dan said softly.

"Spare me the hero talk. I will call you at 9 pm to give you the address. If you're not here, we start playing with the girl. I can see on my screen where the truck is. If you start moving around, or if you tamper with the truck's GPS tracker, the girl dies. Do you understand?"

"Got it."

"I know what you are trying to do. If you go inside Intercept, or go to the cops, or the US Embassy, if you speak to anyone at all, you know what's going to happen."

Dan didn't say anything. He could hear Burns breathing on the other side. "Wait for my call." Burns hung up.

Dan gripped the phone tightly in his hand. He had no options. He hopped out of the truck cabin. He locked it, and took the tube back to Clapham Common. Inside his hotel room, he assembled his weapons and checked them. He sat down to wait.

As darkness claimed the skies over London, Dan left to get back in the truck. He had packed all his weapons on him, with extra ammo. He was sitting inside the truck at 2100 hours when his cellphone rang. Caller ID withheld. Dan put the phone to his ear on the second ring.

"It's me," he said.

"Dan, how nice to hear your voice again." Burns said.

"I want to speak to her."

There was a delay, then Chloe's voice came on the line. "Dan."

"I'm coming. Hang on."

"Dan, I…" Chloe could not complete her sentence. Dan heard a faint scream. He closed his eyes and hardened his jaw.

Burns came back on the line. "Hope you are satisfied now, Dan. Here is the address: number 345, Bickersteth Road, E14 3ST." The line went dead.

Dan flicked through his phone. He knew the address. It was one of the three addresses on the sat nav of Guptill's car. He sat for a moment, collecting his thoughts.

He looked at Google Maps and checked the satellite image of the address. It was a warehouse. He would have to go inside with the truck, there was no space to unload it in the courtyard. Dan glanced at the seats in the truck cabin.

He bent down and had a look at the side of the seat. There was a catch, and if he released it, the seat lifted up. He found another gun in the hollow inside, an M4 carbine rifle. He took it out and emptied the contents of the suitcase. He sliced the top of the wire casing with his kukri and fitted the detonator. He put the C-4 explosive next to it and shut the seat.

He picked up the empty suitcase, went to the back of the truck and opened the container doors.

*****

It was close to 2230 hours when Dan approached East Central London. It was the area around Canary Wharf, the heart of the city's financial district. The bright lights in the skyscrapers sparkled, turning night into day. Dan nosed the truck past the State Street and J.P.Morgan buildings, heading south towards the Isle of Dogs, where the Thames formed a tight noose of land, hanging over a thin line of its muddy waters.

He got closer to the river. A sharp turn led him into the flat, drab expanse of an industrial estate. Warehouses lined both sides of the road. Number 345 lay smack bang in the middle, next to a waste recycling center. It seemed as if the plot opposite also belonged to the waste center—it was lined with waste disposal trucks. Dan peered at the structure in front of him. A triangular, aluminum-frame roof enclosed the warehouse.

There was a small courtyard in the front. Three black Lada's were parked there with diplomatic number plates. As Dan watched, two men in black suits came out the front door, illuminated by the headlights. One of them gestured to Dan to cut the lights, and he obeyed.

In the dim street light he could make out the men pushing the front gates. There was a loud whirring noise, and the entire front of the warehouse opened up to reveal a hangar-like structure inside. The men pointed to Dan, and he slowly eased the Volvo into the yawning darkness.

"Turn the lights on!" one of the men shouted. Blinding lights came on instantly. The place seemed smaller with the truck in there. Pallets of goods were placed around the warehouse. In the far corner, and near the gates, he saw two offices. Two more cars were parked inside, both black Range Rovers. Four men, all in suits, leaned against them.

Burns stood a few steps in front of the Range Rovers. Dan couldn't see Chloe. He wound the window down. He took his time to light a cigarette that belonged to the dead driver. He took a drag, then turned back to them, blowing out smoke.

"Where is she?" he asked.

Burns smiled. He lifted his hand. One of the four men behind him opened the back door of a Range Rover and pulled Chloe out. Dan's heart jumped when he saw her. She looked calm and unhurt. Her hair was crumpled over her face, and black stains lined her eyes and cheeks. She stared at Dan. He glanced at her briefly, nodded, then looked around. In the far-right corner, he could see the back door. It had a bolt on it. The front door had been shut after he came in. There was no other way out.

Burns said, "I know what you're thinking. But let me save you the trouble. There's no way out. Now, why don't you throw your guns out the window and come down very slowly, with your hands in the air?"

Dan threw the two guns belonging to the dead men. They dropped with a clatter on the ground.

"And *your* weapon," Burns said.

He threw the Sig down, too.

"Can I keep my cigarette?"

"No, throw that down as well." Dan did as he was told.

He opened the cabin door. Four men were circling him. Each one had an MP7 sub-machine gun pointed at him. Dan jumped down onto the floor and raised his arms. One of the men came forward, went around to his back and searched till he found the kukri. He chucked it at his boss's feet. He picked it up.

"Interesting," Burns said, looking at the knife. "A kukri, I believe." He threw the knife casually behind his back. Dan noticed there was now one man with Chloe. Another had come to stand next to his boss. Four were surrounding him. Seven men, including Burns. All with MP7s, apart from Burns, who certainly had a weapon. And Dan didn't even have his kukri. He didn't like the odds.

"My name is Robert Cranmer." Burns said.

Dan said, "You sure that's your real name?"

"Hey, you got to have a couple, right?" Burns smiled. Dan didn't like it. Burns looked relaxed, easy, like he had done the hard work.

Dan said, "Or is your name Felix?"

"Ah. A nickname I never knew I had. Rather fetching, don't you think?"

Dan said, "You were in Afghanistan waiting for me when the mission started. You pulled strings to make sure the terrorist wouldn't be there."

"That's right."

"Guptill gave the mission the green light. You wanted to stop it, but you couldn't. I found out all about it, and took the photos. You destroyed the camera, didn't you?"

"Correct again, Dan."

"You kept me alive all this time to see what I could find out about Guptill's investigation. Who was he working for? CIA? With Renwick?"

"Well, Dan, you're gonna be dead soon, so you might as well know. Yes, Guptill had become an undercover CIA agent. Renwick was a CIA agent as well. Both were making life difficult for me. Of course, they didn't know who I really was."

A rage was building inside Dan. But he kept his voice even. Losing it now would not help him. He said, "You put the bomb in that pub, didn't you? Where Lucy worked."

Burns smiled thinly. "I enjoyed that," he said. "Got everyone shook up, but also showed my clients what I could do for them."

"You're a traitor. Selling weapons to the enemy."

Burns smiled. "But also getting closer to the enemy, Dan. Who do you think provides the intel on their whereabouts? All these drone strikes. I sell them weapons, they tell me where the big dogs are hiding. Just a little give and take."

"Selling our weapons for heroin, that's what you call give and take?"

"It's how you win a war, Dan. Divide the enemy. Make them fight against each other."

Dan snorted. "You only live for yourself. You use the Russian Mafia to sell your drugs on the streets." Dan indicated the Russians around him. "And the cash you get, you keep for yourself."

A voice spoke up from behind Cranmer. "These men are Spetsnaz. Not the Mafia."

Cranmer said, "Meet my business partner, Yevgeny Lutyenov."

"Everyone knows about the Kremlin's links with the Russian Mafia. Spetsnaz doing your dirty work does not exactly surprise me," Dan said.

Dan came a step closer. The four machine gun bearers shuffled forward with him.

Dan was now standing within an arm's length of Burns, who hadn't moved. There was silence for a second, punctuated by their heavy breathing.

"You're a clever man, Dan," Burns said softly. "You should be working for me. Shame you have to die tonight."

Dan looked past him at Chloe. She was staring at him with wide eyes.

Dan said. "You are insane."

Burns laughed. Two men dug their rifles into Dan's chest and pushed him back.

Burns said, "Goodbye, Dan. Believe me, I have more important things to attend to. It was nice knowing you."

"How much you making, Burns? A few million a year?"

Burns said, "You really think this weapon selling is my main thing? This is just a sideline."

Burns looked at Dan, and Dan felt someone squeeze his heart in a vice-like grip. What Burns had told him a minute ago flashed across his mind like a meteor.

Got everyone shook up, but also showed my clients what I could do for them.

Burns stepped forward. His eyes blazed. "I will make billions, Dan. 2.5 billion dollars to be exact. When this shit goes down, the whole world will come down with it."

Dan's heart was hammering in his chest. He remembered the CL-20 explosives he had seen in the compound. Burns had access to the latest in military-grade explosives.

He said, "What are you talking about?" He needed to keep Burns talking, stall for time.

"When it happens Dan, you will know. Trust me. Fingers will point everywhere, and nuclear weapons will be flying around. It will be the end of the world."

"You're gonna use the CL-20 in some public place," Dan said. "Somewhere prominent. In London."

Burns smiled again. A hard, calculating smile. "My, my, haven't we got our thinking hats on today."

An ice-cold fear gripped Dan. He felt his legs buckle as the realization hit him like a sledgehammer.

He looked at Burns with wide eyes. "No," Dan whispered.

Burns cocked his head to one side. "Excuse me?"

Dan said, "The US Embassy. You can get in there, right? I bet you have the right creds."

Dan was talking faster now, the words tumbling out of him. "We will blame the Middle East, and your Russian friend here will leave a trail that leads to the Kremlin."

"Aha," Burns said.

"We retaliate against Russia…. and…"

Burns clapped his hands together. "Bang," he said. "So, you finally figured it out. Well, it's too little and too late," Burns sneered. "Goodbye, Dan."

Dan asked again, "How can you do this?"

Burns said, "Because I look after myself, Dan. This has been planned for a long time. Tonight is the big show."

Burns indicated to Yevgeny. A forklift truck whined and lifted a pallet onto the back of a waiting truck. It repeated the process four times. Dan watched with a sick feeling in his heart.

He knew what was in those pallets. Burns gave Dan a last look of contempt, then turned and left the warehouse.

Five men were left inside. One of them held Chloe by the open car door.

A tall, wide guy approached Dan. Two men held Dan's arms. The man hit Dan hard in the face. A broken tooth and some blood spurted out of Dan's lips. A raw, blistering pain lashed across his face.

Dan straightened himself. He looked at Chloe and nodded to her.

The man in front of him smiled. "Say goodbye to your girlfriend." He pulled out a handgun. A Colt M1911. He pointed it straight at Dan's head.

"It's time for you to die," he said.

"No," said Dan, raising his voice so Chloe could hear him.

"It's time for *you* to die."

CHAPTER 39

Before anyone could move, Dan pulled his arms around together as hard as he could. He heaved using every ounce of strength in his colossal shoulders. The two men holding him turned and smacked together in the middle.

As they collided, the fuse that Dan had lit while lighting the cigarette sparked the detonator. It exploded instantly, firing the one hundred pounds of C-4 explosive hidden inside the front seat of the truck.

The shattering explosion blasted Dan off his feet.

He flew in the air, dimly aware of an orange fireball erupting in waves around him. Debris cascaded in the air, and a heavy object hit him in the head, knocking him down. He smashed against the side of the car where Chloe had been standing and crumpled to the floor.

A charred, burning smell was in his nose and mouth. He felt dizzy. He tried to open his eyes, but his head swam. He forced his eyes open. Apart from the black fumes and a fireball where the truck's front cabin had been, he couldn't see anything else. The pallets of goods had been blown apart. They were used weapons. Components of old Kalashnikovs and heavier Russian guns lay strewn on the floor.

One of the Spetsnaz guys lay face-up on the floor. He wasn't moving. Dan rolled over and removed the KEDR from his hands.

Dan saw movement to his extreme right. An arm raised itself, and pointed the muzzle of a gun at him. Dan fired a long burst from the KEDR, the gun's recoil surprisingly light. The figure went down. Dan crept along the floor, past the dead bodies, until he saw another man lift his head. He fired another burst into that body. The man shook as the rounds pumped into him, then he was still.

Dan felt an arm reach over his neck and pull him back. One of the men on the floor had sneaked up on him. Dan leaned forward, and the man tightened his grip. Dan saw double. The room swam before his eyes. His breath came in gasps, and the man was now leaning forward. Dan wanted that. He was holding the KEDR with both hands, but the sub-machine gun was light. He pointed it backwards past his own midriff. At point-blank range, he fired. The bullets tore into the man, sending him spiraling backwards. Dan fell forward, retching and coughing. He looked around, trying to catch his breath, ready to fire again. The bodies remained still.

He needed to find Chloe, but all he saw was inert bodies.

His heart stopped when he looked beneath the car and saw wisps of blond hair. It was Chloe. Dan removed another body in the way and reached for her. He grabbed her soot-blackened finger, then pulled her arm, but she didn't stir. Dan dragged her out of the car. She was breathing and her mouth was open. He moved the hair from around her face. Dan slapped her cheek lightly. After what seemed an eternity, her eyes fluttered open.

"Chloe. Can you hear me?"

"D…Dan?"

He held her with one hand and lifted the KEDR to point at the destruction in front of him. None of the bodies on the floor moved. Flames were licking the truck and starting to move back towards the fuselage. With an effort, he stood, picking Chloe up.

"We need to get out of here. Now."

He lifted Chloe with a fireman's lift onto his shoulder. When he tried to walk, he realized he was dragging his left leg. Blood trailed on the floor, seeping from a lower leg wound. The leg felt numb. He grit his teeth and picked up his pace. He went past the dead bodies, the burning truck, and into the open. He reached the gates, pushed them open and walked out. He wanted to run, but couldn't. Somehow, he kept putting one foot in front of another.

He'd gone a hundred meters when the Volvo's fuselage ignited. The explosion lifted up the roof of the warehouse, sending a mushroom of gray cloud rising into the night air. The sonic wave made the ground shake under his feet and he sank to his knees. Chloe came off his shoulders, and she pulled him into the perimeter wall of a vacant warehouse opposite. Shards of aluminum and other debris clattered on the road in the distance. They crouched as the rumbles faded.

Chloe was on her knees, facing him. She wiped a hand across his face. It came away red with blood.

"Dan," she said weakly. "Your head's bleeding."

He looked at her and managed a smile. "I've been through worse," he said.

Dan grabbed the wall and pulled himself upright. He looked around him wildly. Then he stumbled out to the middle of the road. Fire crackled in a yellow blaze where the warehouse stood.

Dan fished inside his pocket and smiled. He pulled out a black, cylindrical object.

It was the GPS beacon that Burns had given him. Dan pointed it upwards and pressed the buzzer.

"What is that?" Chloe asked.

"Something Burns will regret giving me." Dan ran towards the wreck. He could feel Chloe coming after him. He stopped.

He said, "No, you stay here when the helicopter comes. I need to get myself a weapon."

Dan gave her the beacon. "Here, hold this. If you point it up, it sends up an infrared beam which the pilot will be able to see."

Chloe did as she was told. Dan stumbled inside the wreck. The heat hit him like a wall. His left leg was hurting like mad, making him limp. He fought the flames, looking around for a weapon.

He also kept an eye out for a stray bullet. Just in case they were not all dead. He rummaged around in the hellish carnage, till he found an MP5 sub-machine gun that still worked. He slid the mag out and slapped it back in. He fired a shot. For good measure, he picked up a handgun as well. It looked like a Colt, and it still fired.

As he was heading back to the road, he heard the sound of the rotor blades above. They grew louder, and he was suddenly bathed in a brilliant glow of yellow light. Dan pointed to a vacant spot, moving his hands till the bird shifted. It was an MH-17. The bird landed on the road, and the pilot kept the engine running. The sound was deafening, making the warehouses shake.

A technician dropped down from the cabin and hurried towards them. Dan cupped his hands over the man's ear.

"The US Embassy is under attack!" He shouted the words twice till the man understood.

They got on the bird, and Dan waited till they hooked him up to the comms system.

Dan said, "Terrorist attack on US Embassy London, Grosvenor Square, Mayfair. Head there, now. Pilot, do you copy?"

The pilot nodded and gave Dan a thumbs-up. The rotor blades whined louder and the bird lifted up in the sky.

The technician in the cabin with Dan was getting flares and rockets ready to be fired if they were engaged. Dan went over to the 0.50-caliber mounted machine gun at the doorway. He checked the weapon was ready.

London's lights glittered brightly under them like a blanket of jewelry. At any other time, the sight would have been beautiful. Now it was ignored.

Dan stared ahead. He nodded to Chloe, who was curled up at the back. She nodded back.

The pilot's voice came in Dan's ear. "Embassy approaching. Instructions to land?"

"Damn right," Dan said. "Hurry up. They are in there already. We are losing time."

Dan listened as the pilot got in touch with air control. They hovered over the Embassy's helipad.

"Alpha Two Zero requesting permission to land, over."

The pilot repeated his message twice before he was answered by the Embassy's air control.

"Identify yourself, Alpha Two Zero."

Dan was on the radio, and he broke in. "My name is Dan Roy. Ex-Delta Force. The Embassy is under attack. I repeat, under attack. A terrorist is inside. His name is Michael Burns, but he could have an alias of Robert Cranmer. He has credentials. Let us land. Repeat, let us land."

The controller was not getting the urgency. He said, "Negative, Alpha Two Zero. What is your authority?"

Dan could have screamed in frustration. But shouting would only make it worse.

"This is an emergency…." Dan continued. The bird did rounds in the air above the Embassy, wasting precious time. Dan groaned inside as the pilot argued for landing with the controller. Below him, he could see a flurry of movement as security guards ran out with their weapons.

That gave him an idea. He told the pilot, "Get me Colonel McBride. Fort Bragg, NC."

Dan chewed his lips as the pilot searched the number. It would be afternoon in Fort Bragg. With any luck, McBride would be in.

An eternity seemed to pass, and sweat poured down Dan's face. He was starting to hate this wait. Then his earphone crackled into life.

"This is Jim McBride. Who the hell is this?"

"Sir, this is Dan Roy. Intercept. We met in Afghanistan, sir."

"Yes, I remember. What's going on, Dan?"

Dan told him as fast as he could. He heard McBride's voice change.

"My God. And you know he is in there?"

"He has to be. The basement would be the best place to plant the CL-20. He'll have it on a timer, and explode it later tonight. He will be far away by then."

"Ok, give me five," McBride said. He hung up.

Another age seemed to pass, while the pilot engaged his radio again. Dan sat there, fists clenched, shaking his head.

Eventually, the controller got back to the pilot. Slowly, the bird began to descend. Dan felt the blood surge in his veins as the *H* sign of the helipad rushed up to meet them. He checked his weapons. Then he waved to Chloe, who nodded at him.

In a flash, Dan realized what was happening.

He was on the most important mission of his life. Failure was not an option.

When the bird was inches from the ground, Dan jumped on the roof of the Embassy.

CHAPTER 40

Dan ran as fast as he could to the rooftop entrance. The door was locked. He pulled out the Colt and fired twice, making the lock snap. He kicked the door open and rushed down the stairwell.

All of a sudden it was quiet. Lights buzzed into life around him. Motion sensors. He was in a sterile, white stairwell, with stairs going straight down. Dan took three at a time.

He was on the tenth floor. On the third floor the doors burst open and Dan raised the MP5, ready to fire. But it was one of the security guards, and another appeared behind him. They pointed their rifles at Dan and screamed. Dan put his rifle down and raised his hands up.

"I came from the bird!" Dan shouted. "The Embassy is under attack." The guards shuffled closer and lowered their weapons when they realized Dan was telling the truth.

"Did you see a black Range Rover come in, say, 30 minutes ago?" Dan demanded. One of the guards spoke on the radio and nodded.

He said, "We are checking the car as we speak."

Dan said, "The guy who came in the car could blow this place sky-high any minute. How many men have you got?"

"We got a team of twenty guarding the property."

Dan said, "Get a team onto the rooftop to guard the bird. They could try to fly it out. You two, come with me to the basement."

They descended rapidly. Apart from the occasional chatter on the radio, the silence around them was getting deeper. As they got to the doors of the basement, Dan motioned to the guards to turn their radios off.

Dan put himself at the front. He motioned with his fingers. He would go first, and the guards would take either side. Dan looked in through the glass panel on the door.

The space outside was a corridor, and it went around in a circle. Dan was first out, heading for the room directly opposite.

This, the guards had told him, was the plant engine room. It housed the boiler machines that plumbed the heating system to the entire property. Next to it they had the room that stored the main electric circuit boards.

Dan nudged the door open with his rifle. It was dark inside, but there was a light source deep inside the room that cast a hazy glow. Dan could see shadows of pipes crossing the ceiling. Large machines hissed steam. Water dripped somewhere, the sound loud in the silence.

He listened, then crept in. Stealthily, he advanced, rifle raised, butt on his shoulder.

The cages of machinery made a maze inside. Behind him, in the distance, he heard muffled shouts, then the unmistakable sound of gun fire. Dan ignored it.

A sixth sense kept moving him forward.

A sudden metallic sound. Like a spanner hitting a metal surface. Dan froze. It was silent again. The sound had come from his right, behind the hump of several dark machines. Light did not reach there.

Dan dropped to the ground. He crawled as fast as he could, to the right, then to the left, dodging the big metal cages. Then he saw it. A black shadow, scurrying behind a corner. Dan got to his feet. Before he could move any further, the darkness was shattered by the ear-splitting sound of automatic gun fire. Bullets whined above his head and kicked up dust around him.

Dan dived backwards and crawled against a cage. The heavy gun fire continued, the rounds falling to his left. He waited for a while, making sure he had the angle of fire correct. Then he got up, and ran to his right, then straight ahead. He would have to box them, and sneak up from behind.

The gun fire was less, and then stopped. Dan came upon a water tank. It was big, and he had to circle around it. He stopped and looked upwards. Electric wires. He looked to the ground around him. He saw cans of oil used to grease the machines. He picked one up and sniffed. Kerosene. Dan felt in his pockets. His Zippo lighter was still with him. He picked up the smaller of the kerosene cans.

Then he continued to box around. Another burst of gunfire. They were worried that Dan was creeping up on them. Their friends were being engaged by the security guards outside.

By firing that weapon, they had given their position away again. Dan surged to the left. He knew exactly where they were, and what he would have to do.

"Dan!"

The loud shout stopped him in his tracks. It was Burns' voice.

"Dan, I know it's you. Answer me."

Dan stayed silent, and moved towards the sound. The light was slightly better now. A bulb glowed in the far corner.

Burns shouted again. "I want to tell you this. This place is going up tonight. You will die, and so will your girlfriend on the roof. Is that what you want, Dan?"

Dan found a machine with ladders by its side. He tested a rung. It took his weight. He climbed up carefully till he could see them. Four of them were crouched next to one of the wooden pallets. He guessed the pallet was full of CL-20, enough explosive to send this building into orbit.

To bring the world to an end.

"I have the trigger in my hand, Dan. Show yourself, unless you want to die."

More sound of muffled gunfire. Dan guessed they had put more of the pallets elsewhere in the basement. The guards had found them.

Dan aimed at the body farthest away from him. At an angle against the wall. If they moved, that would be his first miss.

This MP5 rifle did not have a suppressor. It made a loud bang as the round left the barrel, the sound exploding in the darkness. Dan saw the body slump, and he fired rapidly. The advantage of surprise was gone. He got two of them, but the other two returned fire. Dan ducked his head, but he still had a view and fired back. The third body went down.

One left. He was doing most of the firing. Before Dan could take even partial aim, a bullet streaked close to him, and he flinched. The round slammed into his left shoulder. He felt the sharp, hot burn of metal in his flesh. He cried out, and the gun fell from his hands. He lost his balance on the ladder, and fell backwards heavily.

He landed on his back. Air exploded out of his lungs, and he couldn't breathe all of a sudden. The pain in his left shoulder was excruciating. Black shapes swam before his eyes. Waves of nausea hit him. He put his right hand to the shoulder wound and it came away sticky.

He tried to get up. His left leg gave way, and he fell again. With a superhuman effort, gritting his teeth, he raised himself. Bullets whined above his head. He had lost his rifle in the dark. But he still had the Colt in his back belt.

A round pinged off the metal cage next to him. He crouched down, hand over his head. He needed cover. As he stumbled away, he heard a skittering sound. Something sliding towards him.

He looked down towards his feet, and his worst fears were confirmed.

A flashbang grenade. The cylindrical object was about ten feet away from him.

Adrenaline pulsed into every fiber of his body. His eyes opened wide. From a deep corner inside his soul, the strength of survival ripped apart the darkness and pain.

He *was* a survivor. A warrior.

A shout emanated from his lungs as his legs found purchase on the ground. He was moving, running, flying across. Arms outstretched, he was airborne.

The flashbang lit up the space in an orange and red glow. The sound was cataclysmic, and the explosion caught Dan in its grip, hurling him further away. His shoulder smashed against the corner of a metal grid and he collapsed against the corner.

He couldn't see anything. His ears were ringing. The pain in his head and shoulders was back. He shook his head and tried to crawl. It was useless. His body felt heavy like lead. He lay there, panting.

His fingers touched something wet on the ground. He sniffed his hand. Water had spilled from the water tank.

"Dan." It was Burns. "Don't try to hide, I'm right behind you."

Through a mist of pain and dizziness, Dan craned his neck upwards. He shook his head repeatedly. He could just make out, in the hazy smoke, the thick, electric cables above. He lifted up his gun, and fired. Electric sparks flew in the air. He fired again, and again, till the cables gave away.

The cables swung like sparkling fireworks as they fell to the ground. Dan crawled away.

"Oh, Dan," Burns' voice was playful. "I can see you." Dan wondered how he could see.

Dan felt a kick in his ribs, a blow that sent shards of pain through his body. He grunted and tried to move, but this time the kick came to the side of his head.

Dan fell back, his eyes suddenly black again. There was a roaring sound in his ears, replacing the ringing. He blinked his eyes open. A few feet away, there was a dark shape. A man. He was pointing a gun straight at Dan.

"I have the detonator in my hand, Dan. You might as well know, I'm going to set this thing up for tonight. Sure, I need to give myself some time to get out of here. Then it's time for fireworks."

Dan lifted himself on one elbow. He could not see well; the smoke was still stinging his eyes. But through the haze, he could make out that Burns was wearing a gas mask. Which meant he had perfect vision, and he didn't have to breathe the noxious fumes of the flashbang.

Burns wrenched the gas mask off his face. He said, "I have to give it to you Dan, you are tenacious. As soon as my men told me a helicopter was hovering overhead, I knew it had to be you. Giving you that beacon was a mistake. Hey, I can correct it now."

Burns smiled. He raised his gun. Sweat was pouring off Dan's head.

He panted, "How could you do this, Burns? How could you become a traitor?"

"Oh please, Dan. You don't think our country plays games? You have no idea."

Dan tried to sit up. "When war breaks out over this, and we die, what about your family, Burns? You don't care about them either?"

Something changed in Burns' face. He came a few steps closer. Dan watched him carefully.

"My family were wiped out in a terrorist attack, Dan. No one did anything. Why the hell should I care?"

Dan needed to keep him talking. "How did they die?"

Burns' face wasn't visible, but the bitterness in his voice radiated across to Dan. "They were in a convoy of SUVs, heading out of Baghdad. Their car got hit by a drone. Wrong intel and wrong target."

"I'm sorry about what happened. I know nothing will bring them back. But think about what you are doing now. You're going to kill us all."

"Sorry?" Burns gave a cold, maniacal laugh that chilled Dan to the bone. "All they said was sorry. No one really cared. No one did anything."

Dan shouted at him, "How can you say no one did anything? Nothing hits the media, no one gets to know. That doesn't mean it's not happening. You of all people should know better."

"I do know better. That's why I've got more money than I will ever need. You will die in this hell hole, while I live like a king. So, fuck you, and everyone else."

"You know what your problem is, Burns?"

Dan shifted back, and Burns stepped forward again, following him with the gun. Dan's right arm was in darkness, but he was gripping something. Something Burns couldn't see.

Burns was right where Dan wanted him. Five feet away from him.

Burns took aim with the gun. He held the detonator in his other hand. He said, "Enough talk, asshole. Time to die. So will your bitch, up on the roof."

"You never knew the importance of your position," Dan said.

Burns frowned. "What did you say?"

"I said, you never knew the importance of your position."

Burns threw his head back and laughed. "What position?"

Dan smiled at him. "Your position now, motherfucker."

CHAPTER 41

Burns was standing over a puddle of water next to the water tank. The water stopped two feet away from Dan. In the shadows, Dan's right hand was gripping one of the electric cables that he had shot down from the ceiling.

In a flash of movement, Dan threw the live electric cable into the puddle of water. The move was unexpected.

Burns did not have time to react.

240 volts of live blue electricity streaked through the water and ignited into Burns' body.

There was a sudden flash of white and blue lightning, then Burns shook like a rag doll. He screamed but the sound died in his throat. His body glowed, bolts of blue flashing through his legs, arms, eventually lighting up his face.

But he had already fired his gun. It was a reflex shot when he saw Dan move. Dan had recoiled as soon as he threw the wire, but the bullet still hit him. It was a wild shot, and it grazed his lower leg. He felt the hot burn of metal again, and he rolled away as fast as he could.

He looked up at the ghastly scene before him. The last blue sparks were still flying off the top of Burns' head. His hair was charred and sticking up straight. The smell of burned flesh floated into Dan's nose. Burns stood standing for a few seconds more, a look of utter incomprehension on his destroyed and burned face.

Then he dropped to his knees and fell forward, face down in the puddle of water. His body jerked as flashes of electricity still pulsed through him.

There was a sound at the doorway. Dan looked up. He pointed his gun, and lifted himself on one knee, then the other. He managed to stand up. The last wound was a minor graze injury. He gripped the gun in his right hand, wincing at the pain in his left shoulder.

A loud voice shouted, "Who's in there?"

A terrorist would not announce his arrival. Dan shouted back, "It's Dan Roy. I came in the bird."

Running feet, and one of the security guards came into view, rifle raised at his shoulder. He stopped when he saw the scene in front of him.

"Jesus Christ," he said.

Dan said, "Turn off the electric mains. You know where they are?"

The man nodded and ran off. Dan heard the electricity wind down with a hum. The shooting blue sparks from the wire faded, then died completely.

Dan stood in the darkness with the gun in his hand, listening hard to the sound of silence.

Strobes of flashlight danced in the air. It was the security guards again.

Dan directed them away from the scene, and towards where he had seen the wooden pallet. They found the explosives and secured them.

Dan walked around the rest of the basement with the guards, looking at all the other pallets. They were stacked full of CL-20 explosives. He shuddered inside when he thought of the mayhem this would have created.

It would have resulted in World War III.

The pain was surging through his body and his headache had returned. His shoulder and leg were bleeding. He rode the elevator up to the roof. The bird had powered down, its rotors still in the night air.

Chloe jumped down and ran towards him. She put an arm under his shoulder and helped him up into the cabin. The technician put a bandage on his wounds while Chloe fed him some painkillers.

Dan hooked himself onto the comms channel. McBride's voice crackled in his ears.

"SitRep, Dan."

"Threat neutralized. Evacuation in process. Over and out."

Dan took the headphones off his ears. The pilot fired up the engine. The rotors whined into a deafening sound and dust flew up around them. The bird's nose dipped as it gathered speed, then it rose vertically up in the air, flying over the night lights of London once again.

*****

Sun streamed in through the huge windows of Heathrow Airport. The massive, black nose of a Boeing 777-300 Jumbo jet gleamed in the sun outside the window, several feet away from where Chloe and Dan were sitting.

Chloe's hands were in Dan's. They all but disappeared inside his large palm. She stroked the rough surface of his knuckles. Dan lifted up her hand and kissed it gently. Dan's left arm was in a sling, supporting his shoulder.

Chloe said, "What about your job?"

Dan shook his head. "I retired already. This was always going to be a one-off, and now it's over."

"What will you do?"

"Just get on the road. See where it takes me."

Chloe looked down at their entwined hands. Dan put his right arm around her shoulders.

"Hey," he said. They had talked about this. Dan needed to get out of London, and sort out his affairs back home in Bethesda, West Virginia.

Intercept had agreed to let him go. He had his last meeting with McBride and another man he did not recognize, but whose aura of real power put McBride in the pale. They had listened to him, looked at the evidence, and absolved him of any wrongdoing.

Now, he was free. Free from the life he had led for so many years. Free from the relentless cycles of combat and training. He longed to be on the road.

Chloe could not come. She had her own life in London. But they would always be friends. Chloe had been the best thing that had happened to him in a long time. She had made him feel human again. He would never be able to express what that meant to him. She knew regardless, and that was all he cared about.

The last call for the flight to Dulles Airport came on the PA. Dan stood, and picked up his backpack. The only piece of luggage he possessed.

They embraced. He saw tears in her eyes, and he wiped them with his fingers. Then he kissed her on the forehead, feeling a lump in his throat.

He walked to the end of the line, limping on his left leg. Then looked back. Chloe was standing there.

He waved, and she waved back.

Dan ducked into the passage that took him into the plane. He sat down and closed his eyes, feeling a pain behind them. Eventually the plane took off.

He stared at England, the green isle spread out below him. Then he looked ahead. The plane was streaking through the clouds.

Somewhere out there, far away from all the madness, lay his freedom. He did not know if he was going to find it, but at least he was free to try.

THE END

ALSO BY MICK BOSE

DARK WATER (Dan Roy Series 2)
THE TONKIN PROTOCOL (Dan Roy Series 3)
SHANGHAI TANG (Dan Roy Series 4)
SCOPRION RISING (Dan Roy Series 5)
DEEP DECEPTION (Dan Roy Series 6)

STANDALONE THRILLERS

ENEMY WITHIN – A thrilling manhunt set in USA during WW1.
LIE FOR ME – A complex psychological thriller.
DON'T SAY IT – A stunning suspense thriller.

Made in the USA
Middletown, DE
04 March 2020